THE
NIGHT
OF THE
PARTY

BOOKS BY ANNA-LOU WEATHERLEY

The Woman Inside

The Stranger's Wife

The Couple on Cedar Close

Pleasure Island

Black Heart

Vengeful Wives

Wicked Wives

ANNA-LOU WEATHERLEY

THE
NIGHT
OF THE
PARTY

Bookouture

Published by Bookouture in 2022

An imprint of Storyfire Ltd.
Carmelite House
50 Victoria Embankment
London EC4Y oDZ

www.bookouture.com

ISBN: 978-1-80314-108-4
eBook ISBN: 978-1-80314-107-7

For Louie

In the long run, the most unpleasant truth is a far safer companion than a pleasant falsehood.

THEODORE ROOSEVELT

ONE

'Please, darling, just before you go... Una and Jim would *so* love it if you did.' Evie Drayton looks at her daughter imploringly. 'Her music teacher says she has such ability, a natural talent.' She turns to her guests at the dining table, almost visibly expanding with pride. '*Please?*'

Libby Drayton leans against the kitchen door. 'Oh, but, *Muuuum*, I only came down to say goodbye.' She sighs heavily, twisting a lock of her long hair around her fingers and inspecting the ends. 'I'm supposed to be meeting Katie now and I'll be late. There's a band on at St Saviour's hall tonight that we want to see.'

'Ooh, a band! How exciting.' Una clasps her hands together and squeals. 'I remember those days. Your mum and I were regulars at all our uni gigs back in the day, weren't we, Evie? Proper little groupies!'

'Una!' Evie shoots her friend a look across the table and tuts. 'We were *never* groupies!'

'You off out to meet some boys? Aww.' Una cocks her head. 'She looks so lovely, doesn't she? Doesn't she look lovely, Jim? ...

Jim!' She turns to her husband. He's staring off into space, his mind somewhere else completely. She nudges him.

'Yes...' He reacts swiftly to the jab. 'Yes... lovely.'

'"A real gift" – that's what her teacher says anyway.' Evie knows she's boasting but she can't help it. Her daughter really does play piano beautifully.

'Cocktails.' Tom Drayton slaps his knees with his hands and stands. 'While we're listening to our little Mozart in the making. Come on, darling.' He ushers his daughter from the kitchen diner. 'Five minutes – do it for the old man, eh?'

Libby rolls her eyes. 'Oh, all right then, just quickly,' she acquiesces. 'I don't want to miss the start of the band.'

Tom triumphantly winks at Jim as they all begin to make their way into the living room next door.

'Espresso martinis all round, I think,' he announces as Libby takes a seat at the piano, the centrepiece of the room, a lavish – not to mention expensive – tribute to their daughter's burgeoning talents.

'And one for me too, yeah, Pops?' a voice calls from the doorway and everyone turns in the direction of it.

'Ah, Brandon!' Tom beckons his son into the room. 'You're just in time to hear your sister play.'

'*Half*-sister,' he whispers underneath his breath as he walks into the room, but Evie hears him and inwardly stiffens.

'Brandon! Darling! I didn't know you were down for the weekend!' Una casts Evie something of an accusatory backward glance as she rushes to greet him. 'Goodness me, what's it been? Six months... no, more.' She grips his upper arms and steps back to inspect him like a rare sculpture. '*So* handsome, and even taller than when I last saw you.' Her throaty laugh is amplified by the acoustics in the room. 'A cocktail for Brandon too! C'mon, Tom, he is legal after all.'

Evie glances at her husband. She really wishes Una wouldn't encourage him. Legal or not, Brandon and booze don't mix well. But she says nothing. She doesn't want to live up to her role as the wicked stepmother, one she feels she's been cast as unfairly.

'Mozart,' she says, bringing the attention back round to her daughter. 'Concerto number 23... you know the one, sweetheart, the one your father and I love...' She presses her hands together and brings the tips of her fingers up to her lips. 'Wait until you hear this! I honestly don't know where she gets it from – not me, I tell you, no one musical on my side. Must be from Tom's.'

Tom starts fixing the drinks as his daughter begins to play, filling the room with a sweet, melodic sound, eliciting a collective sigh of 'oohs' and 'ahhs'.

Evie snatches a clandestine glance at Una. 'See – I told you,' she says, hoping she doesn't sound as smug as she feels. 'Incredible, isn't she?'

Una accepts an espresso martini from Tom with an over-exaggerated lick of her red lips and a whisper of appreciation.

'Incredible.' She shakes her head in awe. 'Oh, to be so young and beautiful *and* talented!' She sighs into her cocktail. 'I only ever managed the first, and that was some time ago now!'

Evie's eyes try not to wander towards Brandon but she can't help herself. He appears to be smirking, but then again, perhaps she's just looking for it.

'I bet the boys are like bees to a honey pot, aren't they?' Una remarks as she gazes at Libby. 'She's so naturally pretty, not like a lot of the girls I see today, faces all caked in make-up and flashing their clout all over Instagram and what-not.' She sighs deeply again, swallowing a mouthful of her drink.

'And OnlyFans, don't forget OnlyFans,' Brandon mutters under his breath.

Evie decides that it's probably a derogatory comment, even though she hasn't a clue what OnlyFans is. She takes a sip of her cocktail and audibly catches her breath. *Jesus*. Tom's made it far too strong. She doesn't want them all drunk before she even serves the starter; she's gone to a lot of effort with the menu tonight.

'Yes, well, there's plenty of time for all of that,' Evie says without taking her eyes from her daughter. 'She wants to concentrate on her music and education first – doesn't want that kind of distraction.'

'Ha! Not like me then?' Una chuckles. 'Falling in love on Friday, heartbroken by Monday. Mascara forever running down my cheeks – and that was only last week!' She throws her head back and releases another trademark husky laugh.

'I suppose we're lucky really,' Evie concedes, her eyes still firmly fixed on her daughter. 'We've never had that kind of bother with her. At least not yet, have we, Tom?'

'What, darling?' He's too engrossed in the rendition to hear what she's said.

Bringing the concerto to a pleasing crescendo, Libby stands and, smoothing her hands down her skinny jeans, she takes a coy little curtsey. 'I've really got to go now. Katie will be waiting for me. We're walking to the gig together. I'll be back by 10.30 p.m. latest.'

'Shall I pick you up, sweetheart?' Evie asks once they've all finished clapping and whooping their applause. 'It's cold tonight and I don't want you walking home through the path in the dark – it's not safe.'

'No need,' she sings back. 'Katie's mum is giving us a lift home.' She slings her handbag across her body and makes for the door.

'Right. OK, well, that's nice of Susan. Are you sure? And you have your phone, yes, fully charged?'

'Yes, Mum.'

'And you'll text...'

'Text when I get there, yes,' she finishes her mother's sentence for her with another eye roll. 'Don't I always?'

Evie smiles warmly. She doesn't have to worry – Libby's a sensible girl.

'Have a lovely evening, poppet!' Una shrieks enthusiastically. 'Enjoy the band!'

'Thanks. You too. Goodbye, Uncle Jim.' Libby stoops to kiss him on both cheeks. 'Lovely to see you again.'

'Yes... you too, Libby.' He throws back the rest of his espresso martini as he watches her leave the room, the soles of her trainers squeaking against the shiny parquet flooring.

'Right, I'm off out now too,' Brandon says, draining the dregs of his glass and placing it down on top of the pristine piano, something Evie is sure he's done on purpose to irritate her. *It's not a bloody coffee table.* 'Bit of business to attend to.'

'Yes, well, make sure you've got your key,' Tom reminds him. 'And try not to wake the whole bloody house up if you intend staying out until the early hours, hmm?'

'I won't be long.' He turns to Una. 'You'll still be here by the time I'm back, I'm sure.' He kisses her on the cheek before following his sister from the room.

Evie is brushing away some chives from the chopping board when Jim suddenly curses loudly, causing Una to spin round.

'What? What is it, Jim?' Una enquires. Jim is looking down at his phone again.

'I'm sorry, guys.' He shakes his head. 'The alarm down at the practice has gone off and I'm the key holder on duty tonight.' He rolls his eyes and exhales heavily. 'I'm really sorry. I'll have to pop down there, check all's OK. It's probably nothing, just a false alarm. Damn thing is so temperamental, always going off. I won't be long.'

Una pulls a face. 'Oh, Jim... but we're about to start dinner!'

He drops his shoulders. 'What can I do, Une? It's my responsibility, and I've got to be seen to be doing my bit especially since... well, now that I've been made a partner and everything.'

Evie stops what she's doing at the work surface and turns round to face him. 'They made you a partner! Oh my goodness, Jim! Una!' She looks at each of her friends respectively. 'That's *wonderful* news!'

Una starts to laugh, clasps a hand over her mouth and does a little celebratory jig on the spot.

'We were going to announce it over dinner, but now Jim's ruined my big moment and gone and let the cat out of the bag!'

Ruined her *big moment? Typical Una.*

'Congratulations, mate!' Tom comes round the table and shakes Jim's hand enthusiastically. 'That's fantastic news! Absolutely fantastic!'

'Thanks... thank you.' Jim flushes a little as he pulls his coat on.

'It's been a long time coming, hasn't it, darling?' Una remarks. 'But *finally* they got round to it. And more importantly, now it means I might actually get to go on that cruise I've had my eye on!'

Evie and Jim exchange a knowing wide-eyed glance.

'I'll be as quick as I can,' he says, zipping up his coat and grabbing his car keys from the table.

'You can't drive, Jim, you've had a drink!' Una's eyes shoot towards the empty glass on the table.

'Oh, don't fuss, Une.' He dismisses her a little sharply, which Evie thinks isn't like him. 'I've only had one... and it's only up the road. I'll be twenty minutes, tops. And please, guys' – he turns to Evie and Tom apologetically – 'don't wait – start without me, yes?'

He's walking from the kitchen diner before anyone can object.

'We'll crack open a bottle of fizz when you get back then,' Evie calls out to him down the hallway, 'to celebrate your good news. Stick a bottle on ice will you, Tom?' she instructs her husband. 'The Veuve Clicquot.' Her eyes wander towards the clock on the wall. *Tick tock... tick tock... 8.02 p.m.*

'About bloody time as well,' Tom says to Una once Jim has left. 'If anyone deserves to be made a partner in that practice, it's Jim. He's a dedicated doctor, one of the best GPs there is. You must be so proud of him.'

'Oh God, I am, I am.' Una swoons. 'Now let's have that starter and get stuck into some wine to celebrate. I'm gasping to try that Chablis.'

An hour later and two more bottles in, Evie can't concentrate, can't fully participate in the merriment and banter that's flowing as freely as the wine between her friend and husband. There's been no word from Libby; no reply to the text she sent half an hour ago, asking her if she arrived OK. This really isn't like her. She tries not to think it but the question pushes its way through to her consciousness, breaking the surface. *Is something wrong?*

She swallows heavily, tries to ignore the nagging sensation that's gaining momentum in her chest cavity. She opens her mouth to say something to Tom and Una, but the doorbell rings and she hears Jim calling through the letterbox. Tom goes to answer it. Libby's just forgotten to text when she got there then probably hasn't heard her phone beep over the music. That'll be it, she tries to reassure herself. But embers of an internal struggle between reason and fear have already begun to smoulder inside of her. She sips at the Chablis in a bid to extinguish them.

'Bloody hell, Jim, where have you been?' Una snaps as he follows Tom into the room; her voice is a little softer round the edges now, thanks to the wine. 'I was about to send out a search party – twenty minutes tops you said!' She glares at him, but something in his demeanour isn't right. 'Gosh, are you OK?'

'Yes... yes, I'm fine.' He clears his throat. 'Just need a glass of water.' He hurries over to the kitchen sink and runs the tap, audibly gulps back a few mouthfuls. 'I'm sorry, God, I'm so sorry.' He looks at his watch and apologises, a little breathless, his hair damp and messy from the cold late November drizzle outside. 'I had a bit of a nightmare down at the practice. Couldn't turn the damn alarm off. Had to call the police station in the end, wait for them to turn up and give me a hand. Felt a right twit.'

Una pouts at him.

'Well, you're back now. Sit down and have a glass of wine,' Evie says, pouring him some white from an opened bottle on the table and topping herself up while she's at it. She hears her daughter's voice resonate inside her head.

'Text when I get there, yes. Don't I always?'

'Yes, have a drink, twit.' Una turns to her husband affectionately. 'You've got a bit of catching up to do.' She nods at the empty wine bottles on the table as he sits next to her. 'You sure you're OK, darling? You look a bit stressed.' She begins to run her hand through his damp, thinning hair in a bid to smooth it out. 'Oh! There's a scratch! There on your temple.'

Jim's hand shoots up to his face. 'Oh, it's nothing. Must've caught it on something when I was trying to sort the alarm out.'

The next hour and a quarter passes agonisingly slowly for Evie as they work their way through the main course of pan fried sea bass and baked Alaska dessert, neither of which she could fully enjoy. Finally, she can take it no more and rises from the table, her chair scraping against the wooden floor. She doesn't want to articulate her concerns about Libby to the rest of them. Tom will only say she's being neurotic. *'Let the girl breathe, for goodness' sake, Eve... she's seventeen; she's not a baby anymore!'* Besides, she attempts to convince herself, it's not as if she's even late home yet. But it is out of character for Libby not to respond to her. In fact, she can't recall a previous occasion when she hasn't.

Tick tock... tick tock... Evie has never been consciously aware of how loud the kitchen clock sounds until now. Suddenly the nasty little ticking noise it makes is all she can focus on. She grabs her phone again while she pretends to search the bits and bobs drawer for something, her fingers lightly shaking as she sends another text.

Libs, PLEASE txt and let me know U R OK! I'm worried.
M xx

Scrolling up, she checks for the 'message read' notification from her previous text. But there isn't one. Evie takes a breath and places her phone on the worktop. *Stay calm. Don't fuss. Nothing bad has happened.*

She instantly picks it up again. She'll call Susan, Katie's mum; she'll put her mind at rest.

'Hello? Hello, Susan?' Yes... Hi... it's Evie, yes... yes, I'm fine thanks and you? Oh, good, good... yes, um, is Libby there with you? I know she and Katie were out together tonight... and... what? Sorry... *what?*' Evie slowly turns to look at Tom, her eyes widening. There's a moment's pause as she listens, her mouth gently falling open. 'But... but she said you were picking her up, picking them both up from the gig at St Saviour's hall tonight... that you were bringing her back... I... I don't understand.'

There's another pause on the line. Evie gasps suddenly and it causes Una to instinctively follow suit. 'But that *can't* be right... no... no. Oh God... *Oh God... then where is she?*'

Evie stoops forward as though she's been winded by a blunt object and grips the chair for support. Fear violently spikes through her, shooting off in all directions like faulty fireworks. She looks up at the three pairs of eyes in the room staring back at her.

'What is it, Evie? What's she saying?' Tom's voice is still soft but stoic in the background. *Tick tock... Tick tock...*

'...Yes... yes please, Susan. Oh God, I'd be so grateful if you would... yes, yes, I'm sure she will... yes... yes, I will, of course... thank you... thank you.'

She hangs up and for a moment she is unable to speak. Suddenly the room feels darker, like a black cloud has descended upon them.

'Evie...' Tom prompts her. 'What did Susan say? Is Libby with them? Are they on their way back?'

Her head is shaking involuntarily, and she feels unsteady on her feet, like the ground is disappearing beneath her.

'She... she isn't there.' Her voice isn't her own, like someone else is speaking on her behalf. 'Susan said that Katie's staying at her grandparents' in Chester this weekend. She didn't have a clue what I was even talking about... about picking them up. She knows nothing about it.'

'Oh, well, so she's just gone and told you a little lie then.' Una raises her hands. 'She'll have gone with a boy to watch the band. She'll not have wanted to say anything in front of us, probably felt embarrassed. That's what it'll be. She's a teenager, for Christ's sake. It's practically mandatory to lie to your parents.'

Evie is looking at her husband now as if he's the only person in the room.

'Tom.' Her voice sounds low but surprisingly calm, in direct contrast to how she feels inside. 'Susan said that St Saviour's hall is closed, has been for over a week for essential maintenance works or something. There is no band on tonight.'

Tick tock... tick tock... They both turn to look at the clock. It's 10.29 p.m. and they stare at it simultaneously as the big hand makes a final nasty click to 10.30 p.m.

TWO

DAN

I'm just about to sit down with a cold beer and a ham sandwich to watch a documentary I've recorded when my phone rings.

'Really?' I say aloud just as my backside is about to connect with the sofa. I check my watch. It's just gone midnight and I'm the only one still up. Pip is tucked up in bed with Fiona. She's not sleeping well at the moment – Pip, not Fiona, although as a result of that, she's not sleeping well either. Fiona reckons it's down to 'attachment issues' or something and has taken to letting our eighteen-month-old daughter sleep between us in bed, which pretty much guarantees that none of us gets any decent kip whatsoever. Juno, or Pip as I call her, is as active in her sleep as she is when she's awake, like sleeping with an octopus in a string bag. As a result, I've retreated to the sofa for now. It's safer if nothing else.

'Riley.'

'Hey, boss, did I wake you?'

Ah, it's my dearest trusted colleague, DS Lucy Davis.

'Yes, Davis, you did,' I lie to make her feel bad. 'I was having a particularly pleasant dream that I'd just scored a hat trick for England in the World Cup final.'

'I didn't think you were a football fan, gov.'

'I'm not,' I reply. 'But that's beside the point.'

'I know it's your night off,' she says slowly, 'but something's come in and Archer wants you on it.'

'Of course she does. Go on,' I say, taking a bite of my sandwich. Something tells me I'm going to have to eat it while I still have the chance.

'Missing teenager. Libby Drayton, seventeen, lives down by Windmill Woods. She was due home by 10.30.' I check my watch again instinctively. 'Her mother called us. Said she was going to watch a band at St Saviour's hall with a friend...' She pauses. 'But it turns out that the friend is actually in Chester with her grandparents and St Saviour's hall is closed for refurbishment.'

'So she lied to her parents about where she was going?'

'Looks that way, boss. And now she hasn't come home. The mother, um... Evie Drayton insists that she's never lied to her before and that she always keeps in contact whenever she goes out, texts her to let her know she's safe. Tonight she didn't, and she hasn't replied to any of her mum's texts, phone calls, nothing...'

'But her phone is on? Any tracker?'

'Mum says it was ringing out earlier this evening but now it's going straight to voicemail. And no, I don't think so.'

I feel the first flushes of adrenalin begin to bubble inside my guts, or perhaps it's the sandwich – the ham was only three days out of date. I discard it on the plate, half eaten.

'Has Mum done a ring round her friends, checked with family?'

'Yes, boss. Nothing. No one has seen her or knows where she is.'

'Boyfriend?'

'The mum insists she doesn't have one. Says they're very close, no secrets between them.'

'Everyone has secrets, Davis.'

'Even you, gov?'

'Especially me,' I quip.

'Really? Like what?'

'Well, they wouldn't be secrets if I told you, would they? Any falling-out with the family, an argument?'

'Doesn't sound like it, gov. The mother is in pieces. Says it's completely out of character. Says she's a good girl, sensible. Says she's never gone missing before, never not contacted her.'

Out of character. This is the phrase that causes my heartbeat to accelerate slightly. People are generally creatures of habit. When they do act or say something out of the norm, it tends to set off alarm bells.

'Right you are then,' I sigh. 'Run all the necessary checks.'

'I'm sending you the address now – Millbank House. It backs onto Windmill Woods.'

'I'll meet you there,' I say, my antenna twitching. Instinctively, I don't like the sound of this. And my instincts are, regrettably, rarely wrong. Fifteen years on the job has made sure of that.

'Boss.'

'Oh, and Davis, bring Parker with you.'

'Parker?' Her tone falls somewhere between surprise and outrage. I smile, though obviously she can't see this.

'Yes. I'd like you to bring him in on this. He showed real potential on the Rose Petal Ripper case, so I want to see what else he's got. You can show him the ropes.'

'Me, gov?'

'Yes, you, Lucy.'

I can almost hear her eyes rolling in their sockets.

'Great, I get put on babysitting duties.'

'Now, now, don't be like that. You were a fledging once too, remember? The boy has to start somewhere.' I say 'boy' but Parker is probably of a similar age to Davis.

'What's so special about Parker anyway?' She sounds a bit sniffy.

'Do I detect a touch of the green-eyed monster?' I can almost hear her stiffen up.

'Don't be ridiculous, boss.'

'Aw, Lucy, I'm touched. You know you'll always be my number one – or number two to be exact.' I can tell she's smiling now. 'Besides, look at it this way. At least there'll be someone else to make the tea.'

'Every cloud, eh?' she says before hanging up.

It's dark and there's freezing drizzle in the air as I pull up outside Millbank House. Even having the car heater on full whack the entire journey has done little to combat the bitter arctic cold that seems to have penetrated through to my bones. I try not to think about a young woman potentially missing in such conditions as I wrap my coat around me and make my way up towards the house.

It's set back, almost invisible from the road, which is more of a lane, I suppose, and is tucked away behind a wall of hedgerow that's starting to glint with the lightest dusting of morning frost. If you didn't know it existed, you wouldn't know it was there. I glance over at the woodland behind it, black shadows of trees that stretch far back, shrouding the house almost ominously. I shiver a little and wonder if it's due to the cold or something else.

'Evening, gov.' Davis's presence startles me a little.

'Morning, you mean,' I correct her, my breath visible in the low orange streetlight. 'Where's Parker?'

On cue he appears from the darkness behind her. 'Morning, sir,' he says.

'No,' I say, 'not sir, please not sir. Boss, gov or even Dan if you must, anything but sir. I'm not a bloody schoolteacher.'

'Yes, si— Sorry, boss.'

'Right. Lucy, I want you to be the calming influence here. We need to be as sensitive as we can and get as much information as we can and we won't be able to do that if the mum's a hysterical wreck. So let's take things very gently, OK?'

'Gov.' Davis nods. She knows the drill.

'And Parker, I want you to listen to Davis, watch and learn. Don't speak unless you're spoken to – let Lucy and I do the talking, ask the questions, OK?'

'Yes, boss.'

'You just keep your eyes open and observe. Look for any odd behaviour, body language, get a sense of what might be going on in the family. Teenagers go missing for many reasons, almost always usually due to some kind of domestic issue, so be astute.' I wrap my arms around myself. 'It's one hell of an evening to go AWOL, so we want to get this young lady home and safe in the warm as soon as possible, OK?'

'Yes, boss, absolutely.'

'How are you at making tea?'

He shrugs. 'Haven't had any complaints so far.'

'Good, because mine's milk and one sugar.'

He nods. 'Yes, boss: milk, one sugar.'

'Right, let's do this,' I say and ring the doorbell.

THREE

DAN

A small woman with bobbed jet-black hair answers it quickly.

'Thanks for coming,' she says, ushering us through the hallway out of the cold. 'Everyone's in there, in the kitchen.'

I'm unsure what hits me first, the heat or the oppressive atmosphere as she opens the door.

'Oh, thank God! Thank God you're here!' A small slender woman with long honey-coloured hair stands up. Immediately I ascertain that this must be Evie Drayton, Libby's mum. Her eyes are rimmed red where she's obviously been crying. 'You have to help us... our daughter... she's gone, she's missing, she hasn't come home and I can't get her on the phone and...' She begins to gabble, the words tumbling out from panicked lips.

'Mrs Drayton... Mrs Drayton...' I speak slowly, keeping my voice at an even tone. 'Please, let's sit down, shall we? Let's sit down and relax a little and then we can start from the beginning.'

She does what I ask without complaint and takes a seat. I notice the empty wine bottles and dirty plates on the large table, remnants of what looks like a dinner party.

'I'm Detective Inspector Daniel Riley; please call me Dan. This is DS Lucy Davis and this is DC...'

'Alistair. DC Alistair Parker,' he says softly.

'I'm Tom Drayton.'

The man stands and shakes my hand sturdily – always a good sign. A sturdy handshake is the mark of a man. That's what the old man always says anyway and I make him right.

'I'm Libby's father, and this is my wife Evie, Libby's mum,' he says, squeezing her arm. 'My son, Brandon.' He points to a young man sitting across the table from him. He looks up and nods. 'And these are our close friends, Jim and Una Hemmings.'

'I'm Una.' The woman who answered the door stands to shake my hand. 'Pleased to meet you. This is my husband Jim – Dr Jim Hemmings.'

Parker has started to take notes.

'Can we sit down?' Davis asks, pulling up a chair and placing it next to Evie Drayton, whose elbows are resting on the table. She buries her head in her hands, sporadically dragging them down her cheeks.

'We're here to help, OK?' Davis says gently. 'We're here to help you get Libby home safely. But to do that we need to ask a few questions, find out as much as we can about why or how she's gone missing, or if she's even missing at all. I don't want you to be upset by any of the questions OK, Evie? We ask them for a reason, and the reason we ask them is so that it can help us to locate her as soon as possible.'

'Yes,' she says. 'Yes, of course. That's all I want.' She wipes her nose with the back of her hand. 'I just want her home, where she should be, with us, where she belongs.'

'Tissue, Parker,' I say, and he jumps up, pulling one from the inside pocket of his coat. Parker carries tissues with him. He's come prepared – gold star for Parker.

'We had a dinner party tonight, as you can probably tell,' Evie says, gesturing at the mess on the table almost apologetically as she blows her nose. 'Una and Jim came over. Libby was here – she played piano for us...'

'Beautifully too,' Una interjects. 'Wasn't it, Jim?'

She nudges her husband.

'Yes,' he says quickly, nodding.

'What time did she go out?' I ask.

'It was about – oh, I don't know, 7.45 p.m., something like that. She was worried about being late to meet her friend.'

'Katie?'

'Yes. Katie Parsons. They're best friends.'

'So she said she was going to meet Katie...' I lead her on.

'Yes. She told us that they were going to watch a band at St Saviour's hall – they sometimes have live acts play there, local usually, no big names or anything. She said she was meeting Katie and they were walking to the gig together.' She exhales loudly and I can see she's struggling to hold it together.

'What is the distance from here to St Saviour's hall?' I enquire.

'Fifteen, twenty minutes tops on foot, not far at all,' Tom says. 'There's a pathway next to the lane through the woods that leads you almost straight there. It's fairly well lit. She's done it before, many, many times. We didn't have any concerns about it, like I say – it's well lit, and she was supposed to be walking with her friend, with Katie.'

'But she wasn't with Katie... and Katie doesn't know where she is, hasn't heard from her?'

'She said she would text me to let me know she'd arrived safely.' Evie's voice crackles like the embers of a fire. 'That's our thing, you see,' she explains. 'She always, *always* texts or calls me to say she's safe.'

'I see. How old is Libby exactly?'

'Seventeen,' she sniffs. 'She'll be eighteen next April.'

'What time did she say she would be back home?'

'Ten thirty,' Evie replies quickly. 'She said she'd be back by

"10.30 p.m. latest" – those were her exact words. When I hadn't heard from her I began to worry. I... I just had this horrible feeling, oh God... a terrible feeling that something had happened, that something *has* happened.' She clutches her chest with a slim hand and her husband puts his arm around her and makes reassuring noises.

'I understand completely,' I say. 'But as yet we don't know if anything has happened at all.' Though I doubt this is of any consolation to the poor woman whatsoever.

'I rang her, kept calling her phone, but it just rang out... and then when I tried again later, it clicked straight onto voicemail, which, when I thought about it, was strange. It is strange, isn't it?'

She looks up at me but I don't respond. At this point I recognise it's better neither to confirm nor deny. I need to keep an open mind.

'Libby has never told me a lie before in her life. I had absolutely no reason to question it. I realise now that I should've done, I should've called Susan and checked with her... Oh God.' She buries her head in her hands again. 'This is my fault... I just want her home... Oh, where is she?' Her voice slips into a desperate heart-wrenching whine. 'Where could she be?'

'Come on, Evie,' Davis says, putting an arm around her shoulder. 'There's nothing at this point to even suggest that anything bad has happened to her. We've got to stay positive, OK?'

She nods, but of course that's what she's thinking. She's thinking what every parent thinks when their child goes missing. I'd probably think the same. In fact, knowing what I know about human beings and what they're capable of, I'd probably think far worse. Missing person cases involving minors are always distressing for both the families and the officers investigating them. I've worked on a few and they leave an indelible print on your memory, even the ones with happy endings.

The predominant and overriding emotion in these cases is fear. Fear that it could happen to you, to your family. The fear of not knowing; of your own imagination conjuring up your worst nightmares and playing them over and over inside your head, sending you mad. In past MP cases involving minors, I'd experienced that fear by proxy, was able to imagine the horror and panic the parents felt, the raw anguish of not knowing where your child is, or what's happened to them. But now that I'm a father myself, it's different. I don't just imagine those feelings; I *feel* them like they're my own, like they're happening to me and that it's my Juno, my Pip, who hasn't come home.

'Take Libby's number, Parker.' I beckon him over. 'Keep calling her phone, OK.'

'Yes, boss. Can I make anyone a cup of tea?'

'Yes, tea's a good idea,' I say as he makes his way over to the kettle.

'The cups are in the left-hand cupboard,' Una says.

'Right,' I continue. 'So Susan didn't collect them?'

She shakes her head. 'When I called her, she told me that Katie was away for the weekend, visiting her grandparents. She knew absolutely nothing about it. She asked Katie to call round some of their mutual friends but none of them has seen or heard from her or knows where she is... I mean, she's got to be *somewhere*, hasn't she? She can't have just disappeared, for God's sake.'

'Does Libby have a boyfriend?' Davis asks.

I look at the young man sitting opposite her, Brandon. He shifts in his chair and drops his head slightly.

'No, she doesn't, and before anyone says it' – Evie looks directly at Una – 'I would know because she'd tell me if she did. She'd have no reason to keep it a secret from me. Tom and I would be happy for her, wouldn't we?'

'Of course, yes,' he agrees.

'Does she have any ex-boyfriends?'

She shakes her head vehemently. 'She's never had a boyfriend. Never. I mean, I know she has boys who are friends, from school—'

'Like who?' Davis interjects.

'Like... oh, I don't know... I can't think of anyone specific off the top of my head – my mind's scrambled.'

'St Saviour's School – that's right, isn't it?'

'Yes,' Tom says. 'She's studying for her A levels, wants to do some kind of arts degree at university, or possibly languages – she can speak fluent French and she plays the piano.'

'Very beautifully too,' the lady with the black bob says again.

'So there's no other family she could've gone to visit? No one else she could've met up with that you can think of? Aunties, cousins... old neighbours?'

'No...' Evie's voice is a whisper. 'No, there's no one. No one at all we can think of.'

'And everything was OK at home?' This is always the question that I dread asking the most but also usually the most telling too.

'Absolutely!' Evie says quickly. 'She's an incredibly loving and happy girl. We all get on well, don't we?' She looks at her husband and then at Brandon, but he doesn't look up. 'We're more like sisters than mother and daughter. She's a sensible girl, isn't she, Tom? She's never given us a moment's worry, not up until now anyway. She's always been such a good girl, a good daughter.'

Brandon suddenly stands. 'Excuse me,' he says. 'I need to use the bathroom.'

I sense stiffness in his body movements as he brushes past me.

'And she seemed OK in herself, no issues with friends, anything that could've upset her?'

Evie shakes her head. 'No, nothing I can think of. I mean, a boy in her class, Harry... Harry Mendes committed suicide a few weeks back... and Libby was naturally upset about it, but they weren't particularly close or anything.'

'Terrible business that,' Una says, shaking her head and tutting. 'Such a young boy as well. I saw the mother the other day – she looked absolutely haunted, poor thing, what with losing her husband recently as well and...'

Tom stands abruptly. 'So what's next?' he says, beginning to pace the room.

'OK, well, that's given us a good picture. Speaking of pictures, we'll need one of Libby, to give to the team and to put out on social media.'

I'd checked her Facebook page out on the way here. Nothing had jumped out at me from a quick scroll through, just the average teenager's page really – a few pictures, comments and tags from friends, emojis and various YouTube links, nothing remarkable, no immediate red flags. It'll all need to be gone through carefully though, which is what the team back at the nick is hopefully doing as I sit here now. Her last post, dated at 6.05 p.m. yesterday, did, however, strike me as a little odd, a little cryptic perhaps.

'Her latest post, yesterday, early evening, said something about a chapel. "The chapel isn't a place of rest" or words to that effect. Have you any idea what she could've meant by that?'

Evie starts to cry again, shakes her head.

'What was Libby wearing when she went out? Can you remember?'

'Jeans. Skinny black jeans and a pink hoodie with a black Nike logo on the front. She had a black fleece jacket on and trainers, her new ones, Balenciaga, and a small bag. One of those cross-body ones all the girls wear now. It's Gucci. She bought it herself.'

'Ah, so she works then? A part-time job?'

'No,' Evie replies. 'We give her an allowance each month. We want her to put all her efforts into her schoolwork for now. Maybe find something part-time during the next summer break if she wants to.'

Gucci, Balenciaga – big-name designer brands. Must be some allowance for a seventeen-year-old.

'Any jewellery, tattoos, distinguishing markings?'

'Gosh, no, no tattoos – she's far too young. Jewellery, yes, a Pandora charm bracelet. She's had it forever and it's practically full with charms. We get her one every Christmas and birthday, on special occasions, don't we, Tom?' She turns to him tearfully. 'Little hearts, presents, teddy bears, butterflies, a little mother-and-daughter charm...' I can see she's upsetting herself.

'How tall is she?'

Brandon walks back into the room and takes his seat silently.

'Does anyone mind if I smoke?' Una says. 'I'm a bag of bloody nerves.'

Her husband, the one she had been at pains to tell me is a doctor, silently sips on a glass of wine. His face is ashen.

I shake my head. 'Not at all.'

Evie is sobbing now and I look over at Parker again.

'No answer, boss,' he says, bringing mugs of tea to the table. 'Straight to voicemail.'

'Small, about five foot three. No more than 110 pounds.' Tom takes up the question while trying to comfort his wife. 'Her hair is brown, long and wavy, although it's naturally straight – she tongs it. Brandon.' He turns to his son suddenly. 'Libby put a message on Facebook last night, something about a chapel not being a place of rest. Have you any idea what she could've been talking about, what she might've been referring to? Brandon's almost twenty,' he explains. 'They're a similar age, only a couple of years in it. He might know all the jargon these kids use today. Different bloody language, half of it.'

My eyes fix upon Brandon.

'No idea,' he shrugs.

'Boss.' Parker edges towards me. He's broken the rule I gave him earlier of only speaking when spoken to. I hold my hand up.

'Just a moment, Parker.'

'So, you were all here together the whole evening, yes?'

'Yes.' Jim Hemmings speaks for what I think might be the first time since we arrived. 'Except when we went out looking for Libby. Myself, Tom and Brandon drove down to St Saviour's hall and then into town, to see if we couldn't see her milling around, hanging around outside a bar or something.'

'Why did you think she might be in town? Did she often go there, her and this... Katie?'

'No,' Evie says. 'She doesn't go to bars. She's too young. She sometimes goes shopping there with Katie – we go together on the odd Saturday too – but not of a night-time, unless it's to the pictures at the Odeon on the corner.'

'Boss.' Parker tries to catch my attention again but I ignore him.

'She doesn't even drink,' Evie says. 'Doesn't like the taste of it, she says.'

She sounds bereft. Something doesn't feel right and I think she's right to feel it too. A mother knows her own child – her instincts are telling her that something's wrong and it's not something I could or should ignore.

'Hang on, you went out earlier, didn't you, Brandon?' Evie says suddenly as though it's just come to her. 'Just after Libby left. You followed her not more than a few minutes later. Said you had a bit of business to attend to...' She looks at him intently. 'Where did you go?'

He shifts awkwardly in his seat again. Sits up a little. 'I... I went for a walk, to make a phone call.'

'A phone call?' Evie is sitting forward now, almost leaning

across the table at him. 'Why would you need to go out to make a phone call? You said you had some business to sort out.'

Davis glances at me. It's a silent exchange but it speaks volumes.

'I did,' he says. 'I had to speak with someone privately.'

'Did you see her? Did you go after her?' She's glaring now, accusation loaded in her voice.

'No!' He raises his tone to match hers. 'Why would I have done that? Look, I just wanted to have a breath of fresh air and speak to a girl in private – that's all.'

'Fresh air... but it's freezing out tonight!'

'Eve, darling... come on, this isn't helping.' Tom attempts to soothe his wife. 'If Brandon says he didn't see Libby, then he didn't see her. It's his sister, for goodness' sake. Let's not let our imaginations run wild, yes? Focus on Libby.'

Evie stands now. 'I am focusing on Libby, Tom. I'm the one who called the bloody police while you all stood there umming and ahhing, wasting precious time while our baby could be out there, catching hypothermia, dead on the side of the road... anything.'

Una sighs and extinguishes her cigarette.

I leave it for a moment before I speak. Allow everyone to settle down.

'The team will be contacting the hospitals,' I say, adding, 'It's just a precautionary measure, standard stuff. We have to rule everything out.'

Evie makes a sound in her throat almost like a wounded animal.

'My colleague, DC Parker is going to stay with you,' I say. 'Anything you need, you ask him, OK. He's here for you and to support you.'

Parker nods and smiles.

'And he also makes a half-decent cup of tea.'

Tom smiles gently when I say this, acknowledges my

attempt at trying to throw a little light onto the shade, but Evie's face remains cracked with anguish.

'I'm so sorry and I know this is hard; I know how difficult this must be for you, all of you, but we have to wait, have to stay here and be patient for now.'

'But shouldn't you be out looking for her?' Evie asks. 'Helicopters, dogs, search parties... that's what I've seen on TV before... what about all of that?' She looks at me, her eyes imploring. 'Please, Detective... Dan. That's right, isn't it? Your name's Dan?'

I turn to her. 'Yes,' I say, sitting down next to her. I look her in her bloodshot eyes and see such terror in them that I have a job to prevent my own from filling up.

'I'm a father myself,' I tell her. 'I have a daughter, a very young daughter, and please believe me, Evie, when I say that my – our – priority is finding Libby and bringing her home safe and well – you can be absolutely sure of that. You have my word that I will do everything in my power to make sure that happens, OK?'

She nods, a small smile of gratitude juxtaposed against the tears that are streaking her skin.

'We'll check with local cab firms and Uber to see if anyone has picked her up in town. The team will start house-to-house enquiries for any sightings, witnesses et cetera, and we'll speak to her friends again, see if maybe they know more than they might be letting on as to her whereabouts. We'll start with that.'

'But we can't sit here the whole night not knowing where she is. I won't... I can't... Oh God, help me. My daughter is out there. She's missing and it's freezing cold. We need people out there looking for her, actively trying to find her, searching for her. What if she's had an accident and is hurt or injured? She might not last the night and—'

'Evie, sweetheart.' Her friend begins to comfort her. 'Look, you're working yourself up into hysterics. Let the policeman do his job. He's the expert on this stuff. He's right. They'll not be able to search for her in the dark. Come on now, my darling.'

Evie brushes her friend's hand off her shoulder and starts to pace the kitchen instead, gnawing on a thumbnail, my reassuring words evaporating in the ether.

'The best thing you can do now is try and get some rest,' I say, watching her, knowing how futile this statement is, knowing that these poor people won't get a wink of it until their daughter is safely back home. But I say it anyway. Protocol insists.

'We'll stay here tonight, stay with you, OK?' Una says gently. 'We can't leave you like this. We can't go home and leave them like this, can we, Jim?'

'No!' Evie raises her voice again. 'No,' she says, lower this time. 'It's fine, Una, honestly. You and Jim should go. There's nothing you can do here. Really, go home and get some sleep.'

I detect a slightly hurt expression on Una's face.

'Well, perhaps Jim can prescribe you something – a Valium... It might help if you take—'

'I don't want a bloody Valium. I want Libby to come home,' Evie snaps.

I leave the room for a moment, beckoning Davis and Parker to follow me. I close the door so we're out of earshot.

'Well, gov. What do you think?' Davis searches my face for clues to my thoughts.

'I've got a bad feeling.' I look at her and she mirrors my thoughts with her own expression. 'Something's off.'

'I get the impression there's tension between the mum and the son, Brandon,' Davis says.

'Yes, so do I. And she says he went out a few moments after Libby left...'

'Wasn't convinced by his explanation.'

I nod again. 'Me neither.'

I pause for a moment. 'We'll need to question him again.

Find out who he called and the duration of the call, see if he can back his story up.'

Davis dips her head, and I sense that she senses exactly what I'm sensing. Neither of us wants to say what we know the other is thinking, although both of us know that we'll have to the longer Libby remains missing.

'It's a freezing cold night.' I instinctively wrap my coat tighter across my chest. 'No one wants to be out in this weather longer than they have to be. It's possible she's with someone, a boyfriend, someone she might've even met tonight, and it's also possible, given what we've heard about Libby's character, that something's happened to her and that she's come to harm.'

'Kidnapping?' Davis suggests. 'They've obviously got money; I mean, you've only got to look at the house.'

'Possible,' I reply, though I'm not convinced. Davis is right about the Draytons clearly being well off, but my intuition isn't leading me down that path. I consider my next steps. Regrettably, my gut is telling me that something has happened to Libby Drayton and that she hasn't simply gone off with someone and lost track of time. You get a feel for these things after time; can call them even without yet being in possession of all the facts. I can only hope I'm wrong on this occasion. I'd be ecstatic with wrong.

'Get uniform out here doing the house-to-house; get the posters printed up and get the team onto social media. The whole house needs to be checked over, her bedroom searched for anything that might give any indication to where she could be or who she's with, a diary, letters, anything. We'll need the laptop if she has one. We'll get her on the missing persons database and we'll start intel... Check phone records, where her phone last pinged, any CCTV from the route she was supposed to have taken, and if there's still no sign of her, we'll start a search at first light and—'

'Boss,' Parker interrupts me again, his voice inching towards urgency.

'What *is* it, Parker?' I'm short with him. Time is of the essence. In my experience, there's only a small window in which we'll have the chance to find her and bring her home unharmed. These first few hours are absolutely crucial. A missing teenager on my watch is unsettling enough; a dead one doesn't bear thinking about.

'The Facebook post.'

'What about it?'

'I think she might've been talking about the new place in town, a bar – The Chapel. It's in the basement of a crypt.'

Davis looks at me, eyes wide with a half-smile across her lips.

'Well, Parker,' I say turning to him, 'you might've said something earlier.'

FOUR

DAN

'Sod off, mate. We're closed!'

This is the response that comes as Davis raps on the doors of The Chapel bar, which is situated a little way back from the high street, to the north of a small green, underneath a disused church. I say disused, the graveyard is still here, and there's a small smattering of unkempt headstones pushing up through the grounds surrounding it. I attempt to read the weather-worn inscriptions that are barely visible through the grime and moss, words that have been eroded and faded over time, like the memories of the loved ones underneath them.

'Not my first choice for a nightcap,' Davis observes. 'Bit creepy, isn't it?'

I nod, unable to take my eyes from the headstones. It's strange to think that just a few metres below us lie the bones of strangers. Stranger still, as Davis has pointed out, that people would want to make such a location a place of entertainment. But then again, I'm not a seventeen-year-old teenager.

Suddenly I think of my dearly departed Rachel – the girl I never got to marry – and how glad I am that I scattered her ashes at sea. I don't think I'd like the feeling of people stomping over her every day.

'Police,' I say sternly. 'Can you open the door please? We need to speak to you.'

I hear a muttering sound and the rattling of a chain and bolt.

'What do you want?' A stockily built man with a bushy ginger beard that obscures most of his face peers from behind the door.

Nice to see you too, Sunshine.

'Detective Inspector Riley.' I flip him my ID.

'DS Davis.' My partner follows suit. 'Can we come in?'

He slopes away from the door without speaking, leaving it open. We follow him inside.

'Don't tell me, this is about complaints from the locals again, isn't it, about the noise?' he says. 'Seriously, we've only been open a few months and they haven't let up, the miserable bastards. Listen, we're fully licensed till 1 a.m. you know – the council approved it and everything. I can show you all the paperwork if you want, like I did to your lot who came before. What the punters do when they leave ain't our problem, you get me? Actually, it's more *your* problem.' He's ranting a little. 'You'd think, what with everything else going on in the world today, you lot would have much better things to do than harass people like me – ordinary businessmen just trying to make a living. Police fucking harassment, that's what this is.' His tone has quickly migrated into hostility.

'Are you the owner of this establishment, Mr...?'

He shifts his bulk behind the bar and begins to load some glasses into the dishwasher behind him. The Chapel isn't a particularly large establishment. Darkly lit with low ceilings, it has a claustrophobic feel to it. Gothic memorabilia is dotted about the place – I suppose in keeping with the whole crypt vibe – there are skulls on the walls and silver candelabras with dripping candles in them on the small wooden tables, and there's a raised platform to the left with what looks like a coffin on it. I assume it's empty.

'It's the DJ stand,' he explains, catching me looking. 'Custom made. That was my idea.'

'Nice touch,' I remark. 'Mr...?'

'Barrett. Richard Barrett. But I'm known as Dick.'

I can't say that surprises me.

'And yes,' he says. 'I'm the manager, part owner. Are you going to tell me why you're here, or did you just fancy a nightcap? Because if you don't mind, I was just about to leave and go home to bed to get some beauty sleep.'

I resist the urge to tell him it'll be a long night then. Instead, I take my phone from the inside pocket of my coat.

'This girl,' I show him Libby's image on my phone. 'Was she here tonight?'

He leans forward awkwardly, as though it's a big effort. He looks at the picture, shakes his head. 'Nope.'

'You're sure?' Davis says.

'Yep.' He turns away, starts rearranging stuff behind the bar again.

'You were here all night tonight, behind the bar?' I ask.

'I was here, yes, serving and DJing. That's me on the flyer there. I'm also known as Dickie B – it's my stage name.'

Davis raises an eyebrow. 'Do you have CCTV?' she enquires.

He sighs heavily. 'Yessss, we have CCTV. We're a professional establishment.'

'Good. Because we'd like to see it,' Davis says.

'Do you know the girl in the picture, Mr Barrett? Has she been here before?'

'Yes,' he says with his back to us. 'She's been here a few times.'

'Do you know who she is?'

'Don't know her by name. Just seen her in here.'

'When did you last see her?'

He audibly exhales, gives up pretending to do whatever he's doing and leans across the bar again and looks at the photograph once more. 'Night before last.'

'Wednesday night? This Wednesday night?'

'Yeah. It falls between Tuesday and Thursday. *Wednesday* night.' He looks at us with mild contempt. 'Why? What's she done? Not returned a library book or something?' He sniggers.

'No actually,' I correct him. 'She's missing. She left her house at around 7.45 p.m. and hasn't come home, hasn't contacted her parents.'

'Ha!' He snorts.

My dislike of 'Dickie B' is rapidly gaining momentum. 'Well, you might find the idea of a seventeen-year-old female going missing on a night like this amusing, Mr Barrett, but we certainly don't, and neither do her parents.'

He looks at me with piggy little eyes that seem incongruous to the rest of his imposing features.

'Seventeen? I... I... wasn't laughing... I don't think it's... I just meant it's not unusual for kids not to tell their parents where they're going, is it?'

'Kids?' I say, noting his choice of words. 'You said "kids".'

'Yeah... but... what I meant was... you know, young people.'

'It's against the law to serve alcohol to minors, isn't it?' I turn to Davis.

'Yes, gov. It is.'

'Criminal offence that,' I add. 'Could lose that licence of yours.'

'I had no idea she was seventeen,' he replies quickly, less cocksure now. 'She looks a lot older than seventeen in the flesh than she does in that picture, trust me.' He stares at both Davis and me simultaneously. 'Look, I don't serve alcohol to kids, OK? We always request ID if we think someone's underage. That girl... she's always done up, you know, make-up, miniskirts, high boots and all of that, looks over twenty-one easily.'

'That's what she was wearing when she came here last?' Davis asks.

'Yeah,' he replies defensively. 'I remember her because she was, you know, a pretty girl, a *very* pretty girl... a head turner. Caught your eye. And she's gone missing, you say?'

I nod.

He throws a tea cloth down onto the bar almost in surrender.

'Do you remember who she was with?'

He strokes his beard, maybe looks a touch on the nervous side.

'Look, she's been in here a lot, OK. Pretty much a regular since we opened. I've seen her in here with a few different people.'

'Was she here with someone on Wednesday?'

He pauses, as though he's thinking how to answer carefully. 'No. I think she was on her own. I dunno. Maybe. I saw her talking to people.'

'What people?'

'I dunno!' he says again. 'Just a few of the regulars, you know, chatting at the bar.'

'Men?'

He shrugs. 'Yeah. It's not a crime to talk to men now, is it?'

'Depends what men you're talking to,' Davis says. 'Anyone in particular?'

'She's been here before with another girl, I think, yeah, maybe a couple of times.'

'Would you recognise this other girl?'

He shrugs again. 'Probably. Dunno. Maybe.'

'But she never came here with a boyfriend, or someone who you thought was a boyfriend?'

'Don't think so. Look, it's a bar, right? Loads of different people come here and chat to each other. I don't keep tabs on who's talking to who. I just serve the drinks and take the money.'

'And DJ, don't forget that,' Davis adds, reminding me why I love working with her so much.

'You still got the CCTV from Wednesday night?'

'Yeah. We keep it for a month then erase it. That's not a crime now as well, is it?'

'Can we see it?' I ask. 'If it's not too much trouble.'

I suspect that it is too much trouble, but I think Dickie B is just about intelligent enough to recognise that while it may be disguised as such, it's more of an instruction than a polite request.

He exhales heavily, wearily, his bushy beard appearing to grow longer by the second. 'I was about to go home, you know. I have to be up in four hours. Can't this wait until—'

'No,' I interrupt him. 'It can't wait, Mr Barrett. A young woman is missing and something may have happened to her. She mentioned this place on her social media and you say she was here the day before yesterday so we need to try and retrace her steps.'

He rolls his eyes. 'Yeah, but she went missing tonight you said, not Wednesday.'

I sense he's reluctant for us to go through the CCTV, which instantly gets my antenna twitching.

'You can give it to us if you like, Mr Barrett. We won't hold you up any longer, then you can get home to your... beauty sleep.'

'It's through here,' he says resignedly, leading us into a small back room. There's a screen on a desk, a chair and some other office paraphernalia scattered around. He takes a seat and begins to fiddle around with the computer in front of him, lights a discarded roll-up from an ashtray and sucks on it.

'Yeah... it's here,' he says, standing from the chair and

allowing me to sit down. 'I've rewound it to opening time, 7 p.m.'

Davis and I watch the tape: images of people coming through the front door, young men and women, groups, couples – there's a doorman just visible to the left of the screen. We watch for ten minutes or so. I'm conscious of time. Uniform should have arrived at the Draytons' by now and I need to get back there, try and contain the area before the press gets wind and the whole area becomes contaminated by hacks and camera crews. I think about Evie and Tom Drayton sitting in the kitchen of their impressive home, their guts churning over, wondering where the hell their daughter is and when or if they'll see her again. The idea of 'if' is something I cannot – *mustn't* – entertain. As far as I'm concerned, Libby Drayton is alive and well until there's any evidence to the contrary – and it's my job to find her and make sure she stays that way.

'Fast forward it a little please.'

Dickie B does as I ask, and Davis and I automatically lean in closer towards the screen.

'It's good and clear at least,' Davis says, remarking on the quality of the footage.

'State of the art that,' he says proudly. 'I told you we was a professional outfit.'

He rolls the tape forward slightly and...

'Stop!' I say. 'Roll it back a little... there!'

Libby's image comes into frame. She looks different, older, just like he'd said, but immediately I recognise her from her photograph, the long wavy hair, 'tonged' as Tom Drayton had said. She's small, though she's wearing high-heeled boots, and she's not exactly dressed for the cold in a miniskirt and leather jacket.

Davis and I don't take our eyes from the screen as she confidently walks past the doorman through to the bar area. She orders a drink – a bottle of beer by the looks of it – and turns her back to the bar, resting her elbows against it. I note the time on the CCTV: 8.13 p.m. It's relatively early but the bar looks busy, not least for a Wednesday night, or perhaps it just appears that way because it's a small place.

'Roll it on a little,' I say, my pulse increasing. I can feel it throbbing against the cuffs of my shirt as I lean forward. 'Stop it there.'

'Someone's joined her,' I say as the figure of a man comes into frame. He appears to greet her at the bar, but they don't kiss. They're talking. He buys a beer. He looks older than her – twenties or early thirties maybe. He's tall, around six feet at a guess, and he's dressed in dark clothing, jeans and trainers, a leather jacket with a hood. He has tattoos on his hands that I suspect go up his arms.

'Do you know who this man is, Mr Barrett? Do you recognise him?'

He sniffs, shifts in his seat, stubs his roll-up out in the ashtray and shakes his head.

'No,' he says. 'Never seen him before.'

His body language suggests he might be lying.

'You sure?'

He stands. 'Yeah. I'm sure.'

Davis glances at me.

'OK. Well, if it's OK with you, we'll be taking this footage with us, and please, don't erase anything from the past four weeks as we may well need to go through the lot.'

His piggy eyes widen slightly. 'What?'

'We may need it as evidence.'

'Don't you need a warrant or something?' He looks at me shiftily. 'You can't just take it, can you?'

'Yes, Mr Barrett,' Davis interjects. 'We can. And I'm sure, given that this is a "professional" outfit and a young girl is missing, you'd be delighted to help in any way you can.'

He looks away. 'Fine. Take it. You lot do whatever you want

anyway.' He mutters something else under his breath but I don't catch it.

'Yes, well, thank you for your concern.'

'Can I lock up and go home now?' he asks, looking at Davis. 'Or maybe you'd like to come with me, eh, sweetheart? Read me a bedtime story perhaps?' He smiles lasciviously at her, bearing a set of surprisingly neat and white teeth.

'We'll be in touch,' I say as Davis and I take our leave.

He walks us to the door. 'Don't leave it too soon,' he replies, smirking.

'We'll do our best.' We step outside into the freezing cold.

'You've been immensely helpful, thank you,' Davis says as he makes to shut the door behind us, '*Dick*.'

FIVE

DAN

'Any news, PC—?'

A young-looking uniform greets me as Davis and I hastily pull up outside the Draytons' house. There's a palpable sense of urgency in the air mixed in with the freezing fog, and it makes for an unsettling combination.

'Singh, sir. PC Singh. And no, sir,' he informs me, shuffling from foot to foot in a bid to keep his circulation going. It's minus two tonight, the coldest night of the year so far, the coldest November on record for decades. 'We're just waiting on your instruction, sir, to do the torchlight search. It's pretty dark out there tonight, not much visibility.'

I turn to Davis; she's talking on the phone and I can see the condensation from the warmth of her breath as it meets with the icy air, like cigarette smoke.

'Right, well, Davis and I will be joining you.'

Davis cancels her call and swings round. 'Us, gov?'

'Yes, Davis, you and I.'

'But shouldn't we get back to the nick, boss? The team have been put together and will be waiting to be briefed... Archer says she wants us back right away.'

'And we will be,' I say, 'just as soon as we've searched the pathway.'

A young girl is missing and I've promised her parents I will do everything I can to find her and bring her home safely. If that means scrabbling through woodland in sub-zero temperatures on my hands and knees in pitch bloody darkness in the early hours of the morning then so be it.

Davis doesn't challenge it. She knows me well enough to know that would be counterintuitive and a waste of precious time. It reminds me of something the old man says sometimes – 'You can replace anything you lose in life, Danny Boy, except time.'

I address the small group of uniformed officers. 'Right, I want four of you to take the left side of the pathway, and the rest of us will take the right. PC Singh, you'll come with DS Davis and me.'

He nods, looking pleased, like it's a privilege to be asked.

'We're looking for anything that might suggest Libby Drayton walked along this path around 7.45-ish last night. A phone, handbag, items of clothing, anything... Visibility isn't good, but let's see what we find, and if we draw a blank then we'll organise a wider blanket search of the whole area first light, bring out the dogs.'

'So we're looking for a body then, sir?' PC Singh says.

He's straight to the point, I'll give him that. Simply by being here he knows that I'm already thinking this must be a possibility. Yet I'm reluctant to answer him.

'Anything from door-to-door yet? How about CCTV?' I look up at the house; notice the security camera above the front door. 'Has anyone checked if the Draytons have CCTV?'

'I'm not sure, sir. We're approaching the neighbours now. Nearest one is a couple of minutes away on foot, just along the road.'

I glance left, looking out at the woods that shroud the Draytons' residence; imposing, almost like they're somehow closing in on the house, swallowing it up in dark jaws. I imagine that the Draytons initially chose this property for its idyllic position and the privacy that such a location would afford its owners. But now I'm wondering if such seclusion might work against them. If you didn't know where you were, you could safely assume you were in the thick of the countryside somewhere. London can be quite deceiving that way sometimes, its hidden little pockets of tranquil beauty and nature juxtaposed with a sprawling concrete high-rise. Either way, their privacy and peace is soon going to be shattered. Once the press get wind of this, their little slice of heaven will look like something from a Hollywood movie set.

'See if any of the neighbours have CCTV. Someone might've picked her up as she made her way past.'

This is, of course, presuming Libby took the route through the woods towards the town centre at all. As Davis pointed out earlier, someone could've picked her up in a car along the adjacent lane, but my feeling is that she went on foot along the path through the woods and, effectively, it's the only direction she could've taken. The opposite direction leads through to the back of the woods where there's no footpath, just dense trees and foliage which would be difficult for anyone to navigate, not least in darkness.

I glance into the woods again and try to extinguish the fear that has ignited in my guts and is now dancing and flickering like fire. Something about those woods is instinctively drawing me to them, almost whispering to me, calling my name. *Please, God; please don't let her be in there.*

The Draytons were right – the pathway is lit, though I wouldn't go as far as saying particularly well. There's a small streetlamp every hundred metres or so emitting a low orange glow, but visibility on the whole, especially given the time of day, is poor, just a couple of metres in front of you. It would've been lighter, though only marginally, when Libby had made her way down the path, which, if Evie is correct, was around 7.45 p.m. last night. It would've been dark by then but perhaps not blind dark like it is now, and I wonder if the streetlamps are set on a timer.

Still, I understand now why Evie feels guilty. I don't think I'd want my seventeen-year-old daughter to walk such a path in the dark, but then again, the Draytons believed she was with a friend, and it was a route she'd taken many times before. Plus it's the only real route out of the area on foot. I assume all the local residents must use it to walk into town. People become complacent through habit; statistically, they say you're most likely to have an accident on a road that you are most familiar with, one you travel on every day. The Draytons shouldn't reproach themselves for it – they thought it was safe because it's always been safe, and maybe it still is safe and absolutely nothing sinister has happened.

I shine my torch in front of me, scanning the immediate area. The pathway is narrow, and frozen leaves and twigs crunch and crackle underfoot with each tentative step I take. I hear the small team of officers behind me to my left – can see the beams from their torches shining in different directions like lasers. The icy cold air stings my cheeks and I pull the zip on my coat all the way up. If Libby has had an accident and is lying unconscious somewhere then it's fair to say that she wouldn't last the night in these temperatures. A sense of urgency pushes me forward, keeps me mentally sharp.

'What did you think, gov,' Davis says as she walks adjacent to me, shining her torch on the opposite side of the path in a bid to cover as much area as we can, 'about the bloke down at The Chapel, *Dick?*'

'I thought his name suited him.' I reply.

She laughs. 'Yeah, but did you think he was kosher?'

'No, not entirely,' I say. 'I suspect he wasn't telling us everything.'

'You mean about when he last saw Libby?'

'Possibly. Almost definitely about the bloke she was seen with on CCTV.'

'You think he knew him.'

'Yes.'

'Maybe she went to meet him last night. Maybe she's with him now.'

'I hope she is,' I say. 'Assuming he's safe to be around.'

'She didn't exactly look uncomfortable with him, did she? The body language between them... a secret lover perhaps?'

'Perhaps.' I'm concentrating on every inch of woodland in front of me, taking slow, painstaking steps, turning to my right and shining my torch into the shadowy woodland that runs alongside the pathway.

'You know she might not have come this way at all, boss,' Davis says. 'She could've caught a bus down the lane into town, the fifty-one. Why walk on such a cold night when you can get the bus?'

'If she did get the bus then she'll be on camera,' I say. 'The team can check that.' But my intuition is telling me that Libby didn't take the bus. She walked; she walked down this path, I feel sure of it.

We continue in silence for a while. The air is still and cold, so cold that it stings my eyes. PC Singh, who is a little way ahead of us up front, stops abruptly. He's shining his torch into the woodland, stepping into it.

'Sir!'

'You got something?' I call out to him.

'Sir, you need to come—'

He drops his torch and begins to back away from the verge. I quicken my pace to reach him, Davis close behind me. The expression on the young PC's face sends my adrenalin into fifth gear. *Oh no. No, no, no, no, no.*

He lowers himself onto his knees and starts to cough and choke, an amplified sound that echoes through the stillness, alerting his fellow officers up ahead.

It's sticking out of the wooded area, to the side of the path. In this light – or lack of it – it looks almost blue in colour, a pale translucent blue, like it's bathed in moonlight. A sickening sensation drops down into my guts, the reserves of hope that I've been desperately holding on to evaporating like icy morning mist at sunrise. I recognise it instantly: it's a human hand.

SIX

DAN

It's her. I know it's her. Yet still there's part of me, as I pull back the brambles and brush that are loosely covering her body, that hopes that somehow it's a dreadful mistake and it's not Libby Drayton but some other poor unfortunate soul. Hope – it's the last thing ever lost. And now, as my eyes force me to accept the truth of what they're seeing, it vanishes before me like a magic trick.

'Oh, Dan...'

I hear Davis's voice from behind me; can hear the team of uniforms approaching. I can barely breathe, and when I do, the icy air burns my lungs like fire. Emotion rises within me, swells and expands until it feels like it's crushing my internal organs.

Her hand is blue, mottled pale in the darkness as I brush more of the brambles aside, my breathing heavy and visible in the cold. She's naked – no, not naked, but her skirt or dress – it's difficult to tell which it is in the darkness – has been pulled up above her waist and her tights ripped and torn, hanging in shreds, like cobwebs around her legs. Her torso is tilted back slightly, covered by more brush and brambles, shrouding her upper body and her face.

I shine my torch closer, move further into the woodland, branches snapping underfoot as I tread carefully, dread shadowing me with each tentative step. Davis is talking in the background; she's calling SOCO, calling for backup. And so the process begins...

I exhale, my hands shaking uncontrollably as I scrape back the thorny brambles in a bid to try and see her face, identify her, still the tiniest grains of hope dancing inside my twisting guts. Instinctively, I jump back as horror ripples through me in hot waves and gasp; place my hand over my mouth, nausea rising up through my diaphragm. I suppose I'm what people would call a 'seasoned' homicide detective, and as such, I'm used to witnessing horror and devastation, blood and gore that conjures scenes from the worst grizzly movies only the most vivid, disturbed imaginations could muster up. But nothing, no amount of years on the force, has prepared me for this.

'It's her, isn't it, gov?' Davis is a little behind me now and I gesture for her to stay back. I want to spare her from the image in front of me.

I stare at the girl – for that's what she is, just a girl. In place of where her features should be is a mass of tissue and blood and bone, indefinable, unidentifiable lumps of raw red flesh. It is, without exception, the most brutal and shocking thing I have witnessed; something I can never un-see and something so inhumane that it's difficult to process, to comprehend.

At first, I think that maybe she's been the victim of an animal attack, but somehow I know that this is not the work of a starving fox or badger. Even a brown bear would struggle to make such a mess of her face. No. This is man's work. And whoever did this wanted to cause the victim extreme damage. We call it 'overkill' on homicide, when a perpetrator inflicts wounds or violence that goes above and beyond what would be sufficient to end someone's life. Whoever did this didn't just want Libby Drayton dead; they wanted her completely *annihilated.*

And it hits me then: Evie and Tom, her parents, will never be able to identify their daughter, to kiss her face one heartbreaking last time and say goodbye to their beloved child. They will not be granted this small modicum of comfort.

Duty bound, I look down at the desecrated body once more and see Juno's face, my Pip's baby face where their poor girl's once was. And I start to cry silently, grateful for the darkness around me for the first time tonight.

SEVEN

EVIE

She knows. She knows as soon as she opens the front door to them – it's there in the briefest flicker of an eye, the slightest drop in the detective's shoulders, the tiniest downturn of the female officer's chin. *Oh God, please no.* In that split second, a thousand emotions flash through Evie, a sensory overload that causes a crushing sensation to explode inside her chest as if she's just been shot. Her breathing instantly increases, a surge of adrenalin making her feel weightless. She's scared to move for fear she will float away, like a balloon, up to the sky.

She's experienced this feeling once before, something similar anyhow, the time Libby fell down those steps when they were on holiday in Tenerife with the Hemmings and fractured her skull. She'd been just a few months shy of her fifth birthday. They'd taken her up to the esplanade to get her an ice cream – a welcome distraction – and she'd just turned her back for a second... She can still hear the screams to this day – sickening, terrifying, blood-curdling screams – and the sudden flurry of activity at the bottom of the steps. She recalls the sense of panic inside of her as she saw Tom and Jim running, arms flailing, shouting indecipherably, melted ice cream mixed with blood on the pavement below...

'Can we come in, Evie?'

She hears the detective's words but they sound distant, as if she's recalling a dream. She's not sure but she thinks that maybe she gasps and says something like, 'No. NO,' as her hand flies to cover her mouth, to contain the screams she can feel rising upwards within her. There are footsteps behind her. Tom is coming up the hallway from the kitchen; it seems to take him forever to reach her.

'Detective Riley, DS Davis,' he says. His tone is upbeat, like he's greeting friends, just as he'd done a few hours earlier when Una and Jim arrived and they'd all been smiling in anticipation of a great evening ahead. It feels like a lifetime ago now, the dinner party, and she's suddenly conscious of an irrevocable shift inside of her, a definable moment between the distinction of the Evie she was just a few hours ago and the Evie she knows she's about to become.

'Tom,' the detective says. 'Evie...'

She doesn't want him to speak, has to fight back the urge not to lunge at him and physically cover his mouth with her hands to stop the words from coming out. 'I'm so very sorry...'

She fractures then, like she's a windscreen that has been hit by a piece of flying grit at ninety miles an hour.

'Oh no... no, no, nooooooo! Please, PLEASE... PLEASE... PLEASE... Not my Libby, NOT MY DAUGHTER...'

DC Parker is standing next to her suddenly; she sees him in her peripheral vision as she drops to her knees. And she hears Brandon bang his fist on the kitchen table. He says something but it doesn't register with her.

Explosions of agony burst through her chest as Tom tries to help her up from the floor but instead falls down onto her; covering her like a blanket over a rock. Anguish sends her onto her side; she's curling herself up into a protective ball. The detective crouches down next to her and he's speaking gently, holding her in his arms.

'We've found a body, and... and we believe in all likelihood that it is Libby. I'm so sorry, Evie... I'm so sorry.'

Tom is speaking now. 'So... so, it might not be her? There's a chance it might not be Libby?'

The detective is silent for a few seconds longer than she would like him to be.

'We will need her to be officially identified, but I'm so sorry... we think that there's every chance that it's Libby. The body fits her description, and the location... I'm sorry, I'm just so, so sorry.'

The word 'chance' is another reason for her to clutch on to hope. Chance is not fact. Chance can move in either direction, even with the odds stacked against you.

'It's not her.' Evie's voice sounds detached from her body. 'It's not Libby. She's not dead. Libby isn't dead.'

'We found her up along the pathway, partially concealed by the outskirts of Windmill Woods,' the female detective says.

Evie can't remember her name now though she remembers it begins with an 'L' – she's usually so good with names.

'A young female, mid-to-late teens we believe.'

'Oh Jesus... oh dear God help us...' Tom is gripping her tightly, rocking her back and forth as he looks all around the kitchen and the respective faces in it. 'What happened to her? What has happened to her? Jesus Christ, this can't be... it's got to be a mistake.'

He gets up and begins pacing the kitchen back and forth, just as she'd done for most of the night, only now she can't move – now she's paralysed, like she's turned to stone.

'I mean, she was here, just a few hours ago, larger than life! She was playing piano for us, for God's sake... she was only on her way to see a band... she... she...'

'She was found partially clothed,' the female detective gently interjects. 'And there were severe injuries to her head.'

Nausea. It hits Evie like food poisoning, violent and swift. *Partially clothed... severe head injuries.* Her imagination immediately begins to process these images, images of a stranger tearing at her child's underwear, forcing himself into her before bashing her skull in. She throws up, the contents of her carefully prepared dinner party spilling out onto the floor, putrid liquid running into the grooves of the slate tiles.

Hands are reaching for her now, arms pulling her upwards, supporting her over to the sink.

'I want to see her,' she says as she retches into it. She can't catch her breath, the offensive smell of vomit hitting her nostrils. 'I won't believe it until I see her.'

The detective is looking over at his colleague and dips his head. 'Evie...' His voice is calm and gentle. 'I'm going to see if we can organise a press blackout, for now at least, just while we initiate our immediate enquiries and secure any evidence, OK. Because, Evie... listen to me' – he has hold of her by the shoulders – 'please know that we *will* find whoever did this. We will find them, and they will be brought to justice. I promise you, Evie. I won't rest until I do, even if it takes me a lifetime.'

Why is he still talking as though this body is definitely Libby's? Why is he doing that when it could be anybody, couldn't it? It could be some other poor soul's child who's been violated and murdered. Every chance he said, only every *chance.*

'I want to SEE her! Tom!' She looks at her husband but doesn't really see him. Now she understands what the term 'blind panic' means. 'I have to see her... until I see her, I can't believe it; I *won't* believe it's her.'

'Evie, listen...' The female's voice is almost a whisper as she comes closer towards her, runs the tap at the sink and fills a glass with water, hands it to her. 'We really don't advise that you see the body as it is. It would be too upsetting for you. We're so sorry, so very sorry.'

Low moans emanate from her diaphragm – animalistic, primeval noises that sound inhuman as it dawns upon her that there must be a reason they won't let her make a positive – or negative – identification.

'I'm afraid the injuries she's suffered... you don't want to see her like that, to remember her that way.'

'Oh God, what's he done to her?' She begins to sob hysterically. 'Somebody tell me... *what has he done to my daughter?*'

The detective has hold of her again and she doesn't want him to let go for fear she will crash to the floor.

'There's other ways of identifying her body, Evie. DNA... there's other ways... Please, you can't put yourself through that.'

Multiple questions rush her at once but she can't gain purchase on a single one.

The sound of the doorbell startles her, and the female detective leaves the room. She re-enters with a uniformed officer a few seconds later and he's holding something with a blue-gloved hand. She recognises it. It's Libby's rucksack, one she sometimes takes to school when she has a lot of books to carry. She feels dizzy as she stands, oxygen rushing to her head.

'It's Libby's bag!' she cries. 'It's her rucksack.'

Tom stands too now. Clothes... Libby's clothes... her pink Nike hoodie and skinny jeans, her trainers... the clothes she was wearing when she left the house last night.

'Uniform found it, gov,' Parker says. 'Not far from the body, hanging from a tree, and they found this too.'

He hands the detective something silver. It's her daughter's bracelet, her Pandora bracelet with all the charms they'd bought her over the years, Christmases, birthdays, when she'd obtained all her gymnastics badges and passed her eleven-plus exam... every one of them a meaning, a milestone. And as she looks at it all the 'likelihoods' and the 'chances' evaporate like morning mist over the ocean.

'Has SOCO arrived yet?'

'On their way, boss. We're sealing the area off now.'

Evie has no idea who they're talking about; she can only focus on the bracelet and the clothes... Libby's bag. She wants to pick them up and smell them, breathe in the scent of her daughter. But she can't move. All strength, like hope, has finally abandoned her.

'Do you recognise these? Is this Libby's bag, her bracelet?'

'Yes,' Tom says, though his voice sounds strange. 'It's the clothes she was wearing when she left the house last night – and the bracelet... it's Libby's charm bracelet, her Pandora one.' There's resignation in his voice now – he has given up.

She tries to scream, to shout and cry, release some of the raw anguish that's tearing her up from the inside, but nothing comes. She feels numb, her heart frozen solid, turning into an iron fist inside her chest. She looks around the room, at the ashen faces of the police, of her stepson and her husband, and suddenly she notices something – the kitchen clock. Throughout the last agonising eight hours since her daughter has been missing, it was all she could hear, that irritating and offensive *tick, tock* sound that had only served to highlight each painful, passing second. Now, however, it has stopped.

EIGHT

DAN

'Who *was* Libby Drayton?' I rub my gritty eyes as I address the sombre-looking team in the incident room. I point to her picture up on the board, one of Libby as she once was – beautiful, young, happy and smiling for the camera; a picture that seems all the more incongruous next to the scene-of-crime photos, a horrific, unimaginable juxtaposition. 'What do we know about her? What was she like? Who were her friends? What were her interests? Where did she hang out? We need to build a picture of who she was.'

I pause for an intake of breath.

'You've all got eyes so I don't need to tell you – you can see for yourself – Libby's injuries are some of the worst I've ever seen as a homicide detective, the result of the fullest expression of human fury – but why? Who would want to do that to a young woman? What caused them to flip? What happened to make them commit such a brutal act of violence?'

I pause again.

'The answers to these questions will be what leads us to the perpetrator, so let's dig deeply and thoroughly, people. Let's look to those closest to her first – family, friends, boyfriends, teachers... because my instincts, not to mention the manner in which she was killed, suggest this was an intimate crime – someone she knew – although at this stage we can't rule anything or anyone out. Right now, everyone is a potential POI, so let's eliminate as many people as we can, OK?'

I nod at Davis to continue.

'Our guess is that someone knew Libby would be making that journey along the path adjacent to Windmill Woods. It's unlikely that this was a random stranger attack so we need to find out who knew she would be there at that time,' Davis says.

'Has she been formally identified yet?' DC Mitchell says.

Davis goes to speak but I interject. 'She's with the pathologist now so we should have official confirmation any moment. But it's her. She matches the description, age, build, height – and the parents have identified the clothes and an item of jewellery found near the body, so right now we're working on the assumption that it's definitely Libby.'

'We know that Libby left her home at approximately 7.45 p.m. on the evening of the twenty-first,' Davis continues. 'And that she told her parents she was meeting her friend, Katie Parsons, and that they were going to St Saviour's church hall to watch a band. We've interviewed Katie already and she confirmed that they never met – or had ever made any plans to, as Katie was away visiting her grandparents – and there was no band anyway as St Saviour's is currently closed for refurbishment. So she lied, and we need to know why. Who was she going to meet and where was she headed?'

'So how about the friend?' DC Mitchell says, looking down at her notes. 'Katie... Parsons? Did she shed any light... a secret boyfriend perhaps?'

Davis shrugs. 'She says she had no idea who she could've been meeting and doesn't know of any secret boyfriend... seems genuine enough. Obviously she's shocked and upset, and I'm pretty sure if there was anything to tell us, she would've done.'

'We need to follow every line of enquiry,' I put in. 'Get intel on her phone records – it hasn't been recovered yet, by the way – PC and social media. Let's find out who she was texting, calling and when her phone last pinged and where. Her clothes, both the ones she was found in and the ones in the rucksack, and her bracelet are all with forensics now.'

'Any sign of the weapon yet, gov?' DC Mark Harding says.

'No. SOCO are still down there now and we've organised a fingertip search. If it's there, we'll find it.'

'Any idea what was used?' Mitchell asks.

'Blunt object, I suspect – no visible stab or gunshot wounds.'

'We're going to pull the brother in – the half-brother, Brandon Drayton,' Davis says. 'Dan and I sensed some animosity there, between Evie, Libby's mum, and potentially with Libby too. Plus Evie Drayton told us that Brandon left the family home moments after Libby and returned home, inebriated, a couple of hours later. He later claimed he'd gone to make a phone call.'

'A two-hour phone call?' DS Sarah Baylis raises an eyebrow.

'I sensed it too,' Parker says. 'Some sort of animosity... plus he's got previous. Nothing serious, possession of a class B, some years back.'

'Possession of class B? In that case, we're all bloody murderers then,' Harding snorts. 'I hated my sister growing up and once smoked a joint at a party.'

There's a low titter across the room but no one picks up the banter baton and runs with it like they might usually. These are the golden hours and every single member of my dedicated teams knows it. Statistically, if we haven't got someone in custody within twenty-four hours, then our chances of finding our killer are slashed by half. It's like the old man says to me sometimes – 'What a difference a day makes!' And he's right, because yesterday Libby Drayton was alive and well with her whole life ahead of her, and today she is dead, her body stiffening in the mortuary, waiting for a post-mortem to take place. These next twenty-four hours feel like the most crucial of my whole career so far. And every single one of them counts.

Davis flips open her laptop. 'On Wednesday the nineteenth, Libby was captured on CCTV at The Chapel bar on St Saviour's Lane.' She begins to play the footage. 'We see her here, arriving at 8.13 p.m., alone.' She taps the screen with her pen. 'Fast forward around twenty-five minutes and she's joined by a man... this man here...' She taps the screen again. 'The body language between them suggests they knew each other, were friendly, maybe intimate. They drink a beer together and then they leave... We need to identify him fast. The manager of The Chapel claims he doesn't know who he is, but Dan and I think he's holding something back.'

'Mitchell, I want you to go through the past three weeks' footage with a fine-tooth comb. Dick, the manager – apt name by the way,' I add, 'said Libby was something of a regular. So let's see if we can pick her out on other occasions, see who she was with, who she was talking to and, most importantly, who was there on the night she went missing. My guess is that she was supposed to be meeting someone there but never made it and—'

Gwendoline Archer, my boss, pokes her head around the door. 'Dan... a quick word please. In my office,' she says, which immediately doesn't sound good.

'Ma'am?' I say as I close the door behind me.

'Sit down, Dan.'

I do as I'm told. To be honest, I could do with the rest.

'You look like shit.'

'No, please, ma'am,' I reply, 'tell me what you *really* think.'

She sighs, though I'm unsure if it's in sympathy.

'This CCTV footage of her in the bar – I think we should

release it to the media ASAP, see if we can get a positive ID on the man she was with. As soon as she's been formally identified, I'll give a statement to the press. We'll let the Draytons know so that they can be prepared.'

I'm silent for a moment.

'Is there a problem, Dan?'

'My worry is if we release that footage too soon, ma'am, then he may go into hiding, do a runner, if he's guilty of something.'

She straightens up in her seat, tucks a lock of hair behind her ears. 'It's a risk I'm willing to take, Riley.' She's dropped the 'Dan' all of a sudden.

'We're pulling the son in, the half-brother, Brandon Drayton,' I say. 'We sensed some bad feeling and think he may have a couple of hours unaccountable for on the night.'

'I see,' she says. 'Well, be thorough. Get the forensics and intel...'

'Of course.' I can feel my shoulders sagging with fatigue. I don't want to get up out of the chair, but then I think of Libby Drayton's face – or lack of it – and I stand.

'We're speaking to the parents again, and we'll need to interview the Hemmings.'

She looks up. 'Hemmings?'

'The couple who were at the house the night she went missing. The Draytons were hosting a dinner party. They're old friends apparently, from university, go way back together. And they're Libby's godparents.'

She fidgets with her laptop, manoeuvring it until it's precisely straight and parallel with the edge of the desk.

'Well, you know what you have to do,' she says, adding, 'So go do it.'

'Ma'am.'

'We need this bastard in custody as soon as possible, Dan. I don't want a public outcry. I know you think this is a domestic, someone who knew her, but we can't have people thinking there could be a murderer on the loose and panicking.'

'Ma'am.' I want to add that my own motives for wanting to make sure we secure our perpetrator as soon as possible slightly deviate from her own, but I haven't got the energy. I've got a killer to catch, and a brutal one at that.

NINE

'We really shouldn't be here, you know.' Katie's eyes dart nervously around the crowded bar. 'If my parents find out...'

Libby rolls her eyes. 'And how will they find out exactly? Jesus, chill out, why don't you? Have a beer, relax.'

'Can you even get served in here?' Katie says. 'Don't they ask for ID or something?'

Libby smiles wryly. 'Watch this,' she says, strutting over to the bar. She promptly returns a few moments later, clutching two bottles of Budweiser. 'See? You're such a stress head, do you know that?' She takes a swig of her beer and hands Katie the other. 'The barman didn't even give me a second glance, at least not to guess my age.'

'Bit creepy in here though, isn't it?' Katie says, observing the decor in the bar. 'All these skulls and coffins and that, gives me the willies... I thought Halloween was months off yet.'

'It's a crypt, Katie,' Libby says, 'hence the name, *The Chapel*. That's the whole vibe.'

'Yeah, well, it's creeping me out.' She tentatively sips on her bottle of beer and pulls a face. 'And I don't even like beer.'

Libby rolls her eyes again. Sometimes she wonders why

she's friends with Katie, although she supposes she's nothing if not loyal.

'You know, Katie, you really do need to lighten up a bit, hun. Start living a little. This place is supposed to really get going as the night goes on. Maybe we can score some coke or Es or something, get the party started.'

'Drugs!' Katie's eyes widen in horror. 'No way am I touching any drugs. And neither should you, Libby.' She looks at her earnestly.

'What, not even a *leedle spleef*?' Libby brings her thumb and forefinger together in a pinching motion and laughs.

'You're off your head, do you know that?' Katie says, but she's smiling a little now.

'Not yet,' Libby says, 'but I intend to be!'

Libby's phone beeps and she takes it from her handbag. It's her mother asking her how the studying's going with Katie. She's told her they're revising together tonight, said she'd be back around ten, ten thirty latest. Her mother starts to get a little stressed if she's home any later than that, especially on a school night.

Libby sighs as she fires off a brief response, complete with mandatory kisses. She'll be home by ten thirty as usual and then sneak out again around midnight when her mother has gone to bed. Anyway, all the time she's getting good grades at school and keeps up with her piano lessons, her mother suspects nothing. God, she hates piano, really fucking loathes it. And her teacher, Mr Longhope (or Mr No Hope as she prefers), is a pervert who's always staring at her tits. Thankfully, though, as with most things, she doesn't really have to try too hard at being good at it.

'Can't believe your mum let you out dressed like that?' Katie's eyes scan Libby's attire – a shiny low-cut vinyl catsuit that sticks to her figure and highlights her breasts.

'She didn't. I changed into it down the lane, on the way here.'

'Are you actually serious?' Katie blinks at her. 'You stripped off in the woods and changed your clothes?'

'I do it all the time. I left the house in jeans and a hoodie and kicks, took this with me and left my other clothes in a bag hanging from a tree. I'll change back into them before I get home.'

'You're insane.'

'Insanely clever,' Libby corrects her. 'And my mum is an insanely stupid bitch. This way, I get to wear whatever the fuck I like, no aggro. Simple. You should try it.'

Katie sips on her beer, glances at her. 'Why do you say horrible things about your mum? I really like Evie – she's always been so nice to me.'

She rolls her eyes again. 'Yeah, well, mums are like packed-lunch sandwiches.'

Katie throws her a puzzled expression. 'Packed-lunch sandwiches?'

'Yeah... everyone else's always look so much better than your own.'

She rubs the scar on her temple, can feel a slight headache coming on. She suffers from them from time to time, piercing and sharp, although thankfully they pass quickly. *The smell of her perfume in the air, that sweet and cloying scent... hands on her small shoulders... the force of them... falling... the sound of bone impacting on those hard concrete steps... the searing pain shooting through her small body... her head exploding... the scent of blood... her own blood.*

She glances at Katie's outfit, a fluffy jumper and boring 'mom' jeans, those grubby Converse trainers that she always wears. 'You know you'll never get a boyfriend wearing that,' she remarks, eyeing her up and down.

'Good, 'cause I don't want one,' Katie says, quickly adding,

'Although, I suppose I wouldn't exactly mind if Harry Mendes threw me a second glance. Do you think he'd ever come somewhere like this? I'm not sure it's his kind of scene.'

'What, somewhere fun, you mean?'

Katie frowns at her. 'I'm being serious. He's been pretty quiet at school these past few weeks since he's been back. I'm worried about him; I hope he's OK.'

Libby inwardly smiles. She knows *exactly* why Harry Mendes has been a little secretive recently. 'Well, his dad committed suicide a few weeks ago, so I'm guessing he's probably *not* OK.'

'Yeah, well, I guessed that too obviously.' Katie rolls her eyes. 'Maybe I should try and talk to him?'

'Wow. You've really got it bad for him, haven't you?' Libby grins, swigs her beer. She knows Katie has it bad for him; she's known it forever. 'You should talk to him and—'

Suddenly, someone at the bar catches her eye and immediately she tunes Katie out, her full attention focused on him. He's tall and covered in tattoos, a sleeve of ink on each of his exposed, well-defined arms, his white vest, she thinks, an obvious bid to showcase them. His jeans are tight on his slim frame, and his hair is pulled back into a small ponytail – a man bun – she can see it tucked up on the back of his head, more ink running down his neck and, she assumes, his back.

A rush of cortisol hits her bloodstream and ignites her senses, placing them on high alert. She stares, waiting for him to turn around so that she can see his face. He's talking to a girl, two girls actually, a blonde and brunette. They look older, older than her anyway. They're laughing at him, gazing at him in adoration. She watches him carefully as he surreptitiously hands the blonde something, which she places in her pocket without making eye contact. It's clearly a clandestine exchange. Adrenalin fizzes through her like an effervescent tablet.

He shifts to his left slightly, finally affording her a profile of his face. He has a goatee beard that obscures his features like a disguise – and she wonders if this is his intention. There's something about him, something she senses in her subconscious, a magnetic pull in her chest. Intrigued, she decides she must talk to him.

Katie is droning on in the background, a low hum like a washing machine, as she continues to watch, waiting for the two girls to leave so she can go over on the pretext of ordering another beer and starting up a conversation. A few minutes pass before the opportunity presents itself.

'I'll be back in a bit,' she says, cutting Katie dead midsentence, leaving her standing alone in the crowded bar.

'Wait... what?'

His aftershave smells strong as she approaches him, woody and masculine. She imagines it's something expensive, like Tom Ford or Dior. He likes to be noticed. She squeezes in next to him and places her elbows on the bar.

'Jesus, who ordered the stripper?' he says after a moment, giving her the once-over and laughing to himself. Far from offended, this is just the kind of opener to the conversation she was hoping for – and expected. He hasn't disappointed.

He turns back to face the bar, ignores her.

'I want to buy some drugs,' she says.

He stares straight ahead. She notices a small scar above his right eyebrow, not far from where her own is, a knife injury perhaps? Excitement ripples through her.

He turns sideways and looks at her from the corner of his eye, sips his beer slowly, audibly swallowing. 'And what makes you think I've got drugs to sell?'

She cocks her head to one side, lets her eyes run the length of his body, up and down.

'The fake Gucci,' she says, letting them rest on his belt.

He starts to laugh into his bottle, shakes his head a little. 'And how do you know it's a fake, huh?'

'I know the real thing when I see it,' she says.

He stops then, turns to face her fully, slight perplexity registering on his features. 'Do I know you? Have we met before?'

'No, I don't think so. I think you'd remember if we had.'

He smirks, raises a thick eyebrow. 'Oh, you do, do you?' He stares at her, more intensely now. She has his full attention. It hadn't taken long. 'Jesus, you're not undercover Old Bill, are you?'

She fixes him with a stare. 'I just saw you handing drugs to a female. You're under arrest. You don't have to say anything, but anything you do say may be taken down in evidence and...'

She holds his gaze for a moment longer, enjoys the slightest flicker of uncertainty as it registers on his face.

'Wait, you're not being for real, right?'

She pauses for a long moment then starts to laugh.

'Jesus,' he exhales.

'I had you there for a second, didn't I?' She raises a pencilled eyebrow.

He shakes his head. 'You're fucking crazy.'

'Ah, but I did though, didn't I? For a second there, you really weren't sure, were you? You need to work on your poker face. I sense you'd fold under questioning.'

He laughs a little incredulously.

'So.' He takes another swig on his bottle. 'And who exactly might *you* be?'

'Buy me a beer and I'll tell you,' she says, but then the two girls he'd been talking to earlier suddenly return to the bar and come and stand next to him, flanking him either side.

'Who's this then?' the blonde says, eyeing her cautiously. 'Didn't realise you were babysitting tonight.'

The brunette laughs.

Libby looks at them. They're older, twenties, maybe even thirties perhaps. The brunette has lines around her eyes, which are heavy with cheap make-up. The blonde is softer in the face but a little overweight. She needs to get rid of them so that she can talk to him.

'So.' She leans in towards him, whispers in his ear. 'About those drugs... I've got money, *lots* of money,' she says, patting her Gucci bag. He looks down at it. 'And for the record, this is not a fake.' She leans back.

The two women begin whispering to each other and she knows they're talking about her, pair of old skanks.

'Meet me outside in five minutes,' he says quietly with a nod. 'Not in here.'

She knows he's watching her as she walks back to where she'd left Katie standing, can feel his eyes upon her. Only Katie isn't alone anymore – she's talking to someone, a girl, and oh no... what's *she* doing here?

Her bubble bursts instantly; it's Gabriella Langford, from one of their sixth-form classes, another loser she can't stomach. She's with her equally as pathetic boyfriend, Lewis Wright (or Lewis *Wrong* as she prefers to call him), who thinks he's someone special because he drives his dad's knackered old Audi and owns a pair of last season's YEEZYs. Now she's going to have to pretend to be nice to them, at least for five minutes.

Noticing Katie's grim expression as she approaches, she greets them with a breezy, 'Hiiiii! Oh my God! It's you two! What are you guys doing here?'

Katie glares at her, eyes aflame. She can tell her face is red, even in the dark and that she might even be crying as there's mascara underneath her eyes. What has this stupid bitch gone and said to her?

'Hey, Libby,' Gabriella says.

Lewis mumbles a perfunctory 'Hi' from behind her.

'You look' – she gives her the once-over – '*nice.*'

Sarcastic bitch, Libby thinks as she returns a fake smile. But she's more interested in Katie and whatever it is that Gobby Gabby has said that's clearly gripped her shit.

'I'm leaving now,' Katie says, slamming her beer bottle down onto a nearby table.

'Katie!' Libby turns to Gabriella in confusion. 'Hang on, wait!' She watches as Katie stalks out of the bar, pushing through the crowd with purpose.

'What the...?' She turns back to Gabriella again. 'What have you said to her?'

Gabriella's eyes widen and she shrugs, glancing shiftily at her lapdog beside her. He stares ahead, like a waxwork dummy.

'Nothing... I... I didn't say anything to her.'

She doesn't believe her, but before she can enquire further, she feels *him* brush past her, making his way towards the door, the scent of his aftershave hanging in a heavy trail behind him. Abandoning Gabriella and Lewis immediately – those pair of saddos can wait – she follows him, her heartbeat increasing with each step.

TEN

DAN

Vic Leyton, my favourite pathologist due to her no-nonsense approach, impeccable credentials and attention to detail, greets me with an efficient smile.

'Ah, Dan!' she says breezily. 'I've been expecting you.'

'Aren't you always?' I reply.

She smiles again, more knowingly this time. 'Yes, well, I suppose we'd both be out of a job if I wasn't.'

'True,' I say, though not without a hint of regret.

I watch her as she vigorously washes her hands in the sink, dressed in full green scrubs and rubber boots, and it strikes me that I have never once seen her in her civvies in all the years I've known her. For some reason I imagine she prefers the 'country lady' look – jeans and sensible tweed jumpers, floral scarves and a Barbour jacket – though I could be completely wrong. I'm hardly a sartorial expert when it comes to women, but suddenly I'm intrigued to know.

'So, what have you got for me?'

'Blunt force trauma,' she says, pulling back the sheet covering Libby's body like a magician revealing a trick. I suck air from behind my mask as I look down at it. 'And to clarify, it's definitely Liberty Drayton. DNA and blood samples match.'

The confirmation brings me no modicum of satisfaction at all.

'Timing of injuries coincide with the same time as death, which was between approximately 8 and 9 p.m. on the night of the twenty-first. So effectively, and mercifully, she died pretty quickly. Which is unsurprising, given the extent of her injuries – and the brutality of them.'

'Weapon used?'

'Hmm, well, this is interesting,' she says.

'Go on.' I like the sound of 'interesting'.

'Well, there's cranial vault injury, which suggests she was hit with something hard, but the impact wounds, notably the one to the back right of her skull, left a slightly jagged imprint...' She turns Libby's desecrated head to the right, turning my stomach with it. I'm grateful that it's currently empty.

'A hammer? A claw hammer perhaps?'

'No,' she says. 'I'd say not. A claw hammer tends to leave a different imprint in the skull...'

She pauses, cocks her head to one side as she examines the abhorrent sight in front of her with a clinical lack of compassion. That's not to say she doesn't have any – compassion, that is – but it's her job to be objective.

'I'd say, though not one hundred per cent conclusively, that it was a rock of some sort, a broken piece of concrete perhaps. Forensics will be more accurate from the residue collected. Anyway, the initial impact wasn't enough to finish the job; it incapacitated her and perhaps rendered her unconscious or semi-unconscious at least. She was struck to the back of the right side of her head, splintering the skull; it was enough to cause a small fracture but not to kill her outright. Interestingly, there's an old injury to the skull, a fracture across the temporal lobe, one I would say she sustained when she was much, much younger – under five years old.'

I write down, 'Old head injury from a child, fractured skull' and make a mental note to ask the Draytons about it.

'Anyway,' Vic continues, 'I suspect she fell forward from the impact, as I found soil and debris on the surface of her wounds and on the front of her hair, where there are also linear fractures, see...' She points, encouraging me to come closer to the body to take a look, but I can't. My feet feel like they're glued to the floor. 'There... just along the hairline.'

'When I found her, she was lying on her back. So the killer turned the body over?'

Vic tilts her head. 'I suspect so. And that's when they went to work on the face. This is where the serious damage was done.'

I inwardly grimace. 'No shit.'

She casts me a thin almost disapproving smile, like a schoolteacher chastising a favourite pupil. 'After an impact on the face, the palate may become separated from the maxilla, a blowout fracture of the orbital wall. In this case, there were multiple blows, one after the other. As many as maybe forty or fifty.'

I shake my head. 'Jesus.'

'Her lungs filled up with blood as a result of the blows, particularly those to the nose – which was obliterated – obstructing her airways. So, Dan' – she looks at me intensely – 'to simplify it for you' – she sighs a little – 'she choked to death on her own blood.'

I close my eyes momentarily. 'Lord have mercy,' I say.

'Indeed,' Vic replies. 'Only sadly it seems the killer possessed none of that. The attack was frenzied, the blows coming in very quick succession. Many more after she was already dead – overkill to the extreme. Whoever did this certainly wanted to make sure she never got up again.'

'No *shit*,' I say again.

'There are almost no other marks on her body at all. A few abrasions and bruising that I suspect she obtained when she fell, but no defence wounds or injuries, nothing on her hands or arms, which is where you would expect to find them.'

I draw breath. 'So you think the killer surprised her...?'

'Yes, and possibly themselves! This doesn't smack me as especially premeditated – more of an opportunistic killing, though one can never truly rule anything out. What I can say is that I'm pretty sure whoever did this was full of anger and hatred.'

'What about sexual assault? Her skirt was pulled up and her tights ripped.'

Vic shakes her head. 'No evidence of sexual assault.'

'Really?' Now I *am* surprised. 'You're sure?'

She gives me a sideways glance. 'Yes, Dan,' she says measuredly. 'I'm *sure*. There are no traces of semen or sexual activity, no bruising to the vaginal walls or anus, nothing to indicate any recent sexual activity. Though as I'm sure you know more than anyone, that doesn't rule out a sexual motive entirely. The interference of her clothes could've taken place when the perpetrator moved the body.'

My mind begins to wander. Why then, if the motive wasn't predominantly sexual, would someone do this to her?

'She was a very healthy young woman,' Vic says, 'lungs, heart, liver... all as you would expect for someone of her age. No signs of any damage. Not a smoker, and no alcohol present. Though we did find traces of barbiturates in her blood.'

'Barbiturates?'

'Yes. Xanax. It's a member of the benzodiazepine family, usually prescribed to treat anxiety and panic disorders. They act on the brain and central nervous system, producing a calming effect on the user.'

I write the name down in my notebook – I'll need to check

with Libby's GP to see if she was being prescribed it legit-
imately.

'Barbs aren't your average street drugs really, are they?' I say
aloud. 'I mean, ecstasy, cocaine, speed, crystal meth...'

'More common, especially among teenagers,' Vic agrees.

'Anything else? Prints, hair... anything?'

She nods. 'Particles of skin and minute traces of blood
found underneath her fingernails. We should be able to get a
profile from them.'

'That's great.'

'Fibres too. Woollen, I'd say, possibly from a pair of gloves or
a coat perhaps – it was a very cold night, which incidentally was
a good thing – it's helped preserve some of the evidence.'

'Well, forensics are down at the scene now, doing a fingertip
search, so with a bit of luck they'll find the murder weapon
and—'

My phone rings.

'Boss.' It's Davis. 'Anything from path?'

I suck air into my lungs, turn away from the body on the
slab.

'Possibly some DNA from underneath her fingernails... but
no prints, no fluids – and no sexual attack according to Vic.'

'Oh?' Davis sounds as surprised as I am. Though admittedly
part of me is relieved. The idea that there's a sadistic rapist on
the loose is not one I relish, not on my patch.

'Traces of drugs though, barbiturates... Xanax, prescription
drugs. We need to get in touch with her GP. Do we know who
it is?'

'Yes, gov. Hemmings. Dr Jim Hemmings. He was one of the
Draytons' dinner-party guests – a family friend.'

'Ah yes. Great. Let's get round there for a chat. We need to
re-interview everyone at the Draytons' last night anyway.'

'Yes, well, you'll be pleased to know that SOCO has lifted a
partial tyre print.'

She's right – I am extremely pleased to hear this. 'And... moreover, boss, we found something else at the Draytons'.'

'Go on?' I can feel my heart rate beginning to accelerate.

'Libby's underwear, a pair of knickers... used... they were found in her brother's room, stuffed at the back of a drawer.'

'The son, Brandon?'

'Yes, boss.'

'Christ...' I pause, attempt to gather my thoughts and decide upon my next move.

'Let's get him in pronto,' I say. 'And let's get an ID on the bloke from The Chapel's CCTV as soon as possible. If forensics get a full DNA profile then it'll be a process of elimination I feel sure.'

'Parker's down at The Chapel now, gov, putting pressure on *Dick*, if you'll excuse the pun.'

I stifle a snigger; it doesn't seem appropriate to laugh aloud given my current location.

'Bring Brandon in,' I add. 'But let's be gentle, Davis,' I warn her. 'The family are going through enough right now. The idea that the son could've done this to his own sister, half or otherwise, is enough to tip them over the edge... and let's get as much from CCTV as we can.'

'Boss.'

I hang up and turn my attention back towards Vic Leyton.

'Positive news?' she asks.

'Depends from whose perspective you're looking at it,' I reply, and she gives me a ghost of a smile.

'Well, thank you, Ms Leyton. As ever, you have been—'

'I haven't quite finished yet,' she interjects. 'There's something else, something quite important.'

'Oh?' I check my watch, mindful of time, my mind filling up with tyre marks and underwear in drawers...

'Did Libby have a boyfriend?'

I shake my head. 'Not according to her parents she didn't.

Apparently, she was more of the studious type... why do you ask?'

'Well,' Vic says in her breezy, matter-of-fact manner that could be misconstrued as abrupt to the uninitiated ear, but which I have come to appreciate over time, 'I'd have to refute their assumption on that.'

'Really? Why's that?' Vic likes to do this, build up to a crescendo, then the great reveal. I don't mind indulging her this small pleasure her otherwise gruesome profession affords her.

'Because, Dan,' she says, 'Libby Drayton was pregnant.'

ELEVEN
AUGUST. LIBBY

'Shh... you're making too much noise! You'll wake your mum or sister up!' She places her hand over Harry's mouth, giggling as she continues to run her lips down his torso, covering it in scattergun kisses.

'I can't help it,' he whispers. 'You turn me on so much.'

'Well, if you can't keep it down then I'll just have to turn you *off* instead, won't I! If we get caught—'

'Not possible – you could never turn me off. Anyway, I don't care if anyone hears us.'

He stops her for a moment, pulls her up towards him from underneath the bed covers. 'When are we going to tell people about us? All this sneaking about, having to call you on a secret phone and all of that... I want us to be official. Surely your parents won't go as crazy as you say they will – I mean, it's not like we're doing anything wrong, is it?'

She sighs. 'You don't know my parents, Harry...'

'I know you say they're overprotective but... but all this secrecy... Surely it would be better to come clean, let them meet me properly, see that I'm not some monster out to corrupt their daughter or whatever it is you say they'd think.'

Libby inwardly rolls her eyes. *Not this again.*

'It's not you, Harry.' She's sure to keep her tone sweet. 'They'd say our relationship was interfering with my studies; they'd obsess over it – they'd make my life a living hell.'

She can tell by his expression that he's not buying it though – and she can suddenly feel the onset of one of her headaches.

'But *I love you*, Libby, and I want people to know that we're together, that there's an "us".'

Us. She attempts to mimic his adoring expression back to him. He thinks he's in love with her, maybe he is. But what is love anyway? Three words that anyone can say, words that roll off the tongue with such ease yet seem to hold such incredible value, making people act like they've had a full-frontal lobotomy. Love was nothing but a trick of the mind.

She inwardly sighs as she kisses him, on the mouth this time, tries to distract him, stop him from talking. She really doesn't want anyone to hear them. His weird little sister, Emily, is only in the next room and she can hear her stirring. Apparently, she's got Asperger's or autism or learning difficulties – anyway, she's big for her age, huge in fact, and she sleepwalks and it creeps her out. She looks at him gazing down at her adoringly. Why did he have to complicate things by wanting everyone to know they were 'together'?

'You love me?' She giggles softly into his pubic region, thrilled by the very idea that he believes this, knowing that she holds power over him.

'Yes,' he whispers back. 'And I want everyone to know it.'

She strokes his skin with the lightest touch of her fingers. She likes the feeling of him loving her, or believing that he does at least. But love never lasts, if it even exists at all. People couldn't, shouldn't be trusted with something as fragile as the human heart. It was just too tempting to break it.

'You're the only thing that's kept me going these last weeks since Dad... since my dad went...' Harry is still talking. 'I don't know how I'd have got through it without you, Libs. You've saved me from going under. If I didn't have you... well, I don't know what I'd have done, what I'd do.'

She, however, does know – she knows exactly. Harry had wanted to be just like his father in life, and so too, she imagines, in death – a martyr. Since his father's suicide, he's slipped into a deep depression and has been taking strong medication, some kind of antidepressant that Jim Hemmings had seen fit to prescribe him in place of the truth. The fact that he was so unbalanced right now, though, was a potential defence if needed for what she has in mind for him, what she needs him to do for her.

'You really miss him, don't you, your dad?' she says gently as she begins to dress. It's getting late; she needs to leave. Evie will be asleep by now; she can creep in undetected.

He nods, his eyes glassing over. Oh no, he's going to start crying.

'I love you too, Harry,' she says. 'I'll always be here for you – always. If ever you want to talk, to cry, to let it all out... I'm here.'

He looks so happy that for a moment she almost believes it herself.

'You love me too...!' He's going to burst into tears, she feels sure of it.

'I need the bathroom,' she says, pulling her shirt over her head. 'I'll be as quick and quiet as I can.'

She leaves him basking in the warm glow of her words as she tentatively creeps down the landing, tiptoeing as though she's walking a tightrope; her arms gently outstretched to balance her soft steps as she makes her way to the bathroom, trying to remember which floorboards make the loudest creaks and avoiding them.

It's late now but she can hear voices coming from down-stairs, the low bassline of conversation vibrating up the staircase. This is unusual. Sara Mendes doesn't really have visitors at this time of the night – none that she's ever known in all the weeks she's been sneaking in and out of her house anyway. Intrigued, she strains to listen. It's a baritone, a man's voice... oh! A familiar voice and... *No, it can't be!* What the...? Confusion hits her, unsettling her, causing cognitive dissonance to form inside her mind. Yes, *it is him*, but no, *surely it isn't...?* She stops, leans forward over the balustrades on the landing, shuts her eyes in a bid to sharpen her hearing.

'Please, just go,' the female voice says. It belongs to Sara Mendes. 'I told you I didn't want you here... Why are you here? What do you want?'

'Sara, listen... I'm sorry; I had to come. I had to see if you were OK – to know that you're OK.' There's a pause, some more low indecipherable speech. 'I feel bad; bad about everything that's happened. I feel like it's my fault... please, baby, let me hold you.'

Sara is speaking again but her voice is softer, less audible than his.

'... it was a mistake... can't you just accept that please... I want you to leave... you'll wake the kids...'

Libby's heart is racing inside her chest, beating so loudly she's concerned it will alert someone to her presence. *Well, well, well...* She has to *see* this to truly believe it, so she crouches down onto the landing, carefully leaning over the balustrade in a bid to catch a glimpse of them together.

Sara is facing him, her arms folded, her body language defensive. 'I need to look after Harry... he's not been well; he's taken it so badly... hiding away in his room all the time and...'

He comes into view, and instinctively Libby covers her mouth with her hand. He's trying to embrace Sara but she pulls away from him.

'Please, what can I do to help? I feel so helpless... None of this was supposed to happen, Sara. You know that, don't you? I never meant for any of it to happen, for it all to come to this... I never meant for anyone to get hurt... least of all you, or Harry... I...'

Stunned, Libby pulls herself up from the carpet and—

'Jesus!' She jumps back, startled, her heart pounding. Harry's little sister, Emily, is standing opposite her on the landing in her nightdress, like some kind of ghost. 'Jesus, you almost gave me a fucking heart attack!'

Emily stares at her, her expression blank. Is she sleep-walking?

Conscious that she might let out a scream and alert her mother, Libby meets her eyes. 'I was just going to use the bath-room,' she whispers. 'Go back to bed.'

But Emily doesn't move – just stands motionless, staring.

'Go on,' Libby hisses, shooing her away with her hand. 'And you never saw me, OK?' She brings her index finger to her lips and narrows her eyes.

A few more seconds pass before Emily turns and retreats back to her room.

Weird freak, Libby thinks as she sits on the toilet, trying to pee and regulate her breathing at the same time, attempting to wrap her head around what she's just heard and seen. There's a mix of emotions as a rush of pee hits the side of the pan: shock mainly, but also curiosity as to how she might be able to use her new-found knowledge to her advantage.

Smiling to herself, she opts not to flush the chain in case it makes too much noise and begins to wash her hands carefully, quietly in the sink. It's humid tonight, stiflingly so, and instinc-tively she opens the bathroom window. As she does, she sees him leaving. It happens too quickly as he turns and looks up, drawn to the window opening, and their eyes briefly meet. She jumps back, crouches down with her back against the bathroom wall, her chest heaving with adrenalin. She hears the sound of a car engine starting, the crunch of gravel as it pulls away. Once she's sure he's gone, she dries her hands at the sink and smiles at herself in the mirror.

Emily's door is closed as she tiptoes back to Harry's room, avoiding those creaking floorboards – she has memorised them well.

He's almost asleep when she re-enters.

'I love you, baby.' He stirs as she snuggles up next to him, her words like the arms around him he so desperately needs. 'I'll come clean,' she says. 'I promise I'll tell my parents and everyone else about us soon, take an advertisement out in *The Times* if you want.' He stirs some more, awakens. 'But there's just something I need you to do for me first.'

TWELVE

EVIE

'Pregnant? *Pregnant!* No...' Evie shakes her head. 'Libby wasn't pregnant – she couldn't possibly have been.' She looks to her husband for backup but his head is lowered, cupped in his hands, his elbows resting on the kitchen table. She can feel the exhaustion coming off him in waves. Neither of them has slept for what feels like months. She doesn't even know what day of the week it is. Their house has been taken over by police and forensic teams, people dressed in PPE, faceless masked strangers coming in and out of their front door, traipsing up and down the stairs, taking things away in ziplock plastic bags. They've even asked for Tom's laptop and their phones. They've assured her it's all just protocol, but she doesn't know if she believes them – or anyone – anymore. It all feels so invasive, she feels under scrutiny and exposed.

Now the press are camping outside, vans and TV crews having shown up in their droves, like the circus has come to town. She's seen them all from the window, wrapped up in their bobble hats and scarves and big puffer coats to combat the inclement weather. They keep looking up at the house, hoping to catch a glimpse of something, and they've pounded on the door countless times asking to speak to her, to interview her and take her picture – to see what the mother of a murdered child looks like, to capture her grief and devastation and splash it all over their front pages and screens. Misery sells, doesn't it? It makes people grateful, gleeful even, that no matter what a shit-show their own lives may be, *at least we're not her!*

The neighbours have knocked too: Mrs Stephens from next door – who she usually struggles to get a wave from – and the Braithwaites. She'd let Tom deal with them. Flowers and condolence cards have begun to arrive on the doorstep. She can't bear to look at them, to read them. She can't face anyone. Not even herself. She is scared to look in the mirror, frightened of what she'll see. She hasn't washed or even brushed her teeth and hair. Even the thought of attempting to do these mundane tasks seems wrong somehow, as well as too much effort; she doesn't want to feel like she's carrying on regardless.

The police are telling her things constantly, giving her information she simply can't absorb. She watches their mouths as they open and close, but it's all just white noise that bounces off her like a trampoline – none of it retainable. Her daughter is *dead*; do they not understand this? How can she listen to what they're saying when this is all she can hear over and over inside her head? *Your only daughter is dead.* They've advised her to speak to the press when she's ready to, that they can be a 'useful tool' in helping to catch their daughter's killer. *Her daughter's killer*, the man who's taken her little girl away from her forever, a killer who made sure she couldn't even hold her or see her face one last time. He'd denied her even that.

They – the police – want her and Tom to make an appeal on television, to sit in front of a camera crew on one of those long tables, like they've seen people do on TV when a loved one has gone missing or been murdered. She thinks about those people now, the ones she's seen on TV but didn't really see at the same time. Strangers with anguished faces and tearstained cheeks, ghosts of their former selves. They weren't real people. They weren't people like them.

This was too much; it was all too much! How was it possible that Libby was carrying a child? And whose child was it? How can any of this be real? It is out of control, happening to her and around her and there is nothing she can do about it, nothing at all to stop it.

'I'm sorry, Evie,' Dan says. His voice is gentle like his demeanour, yet she hears a resolve in him that makes his presence tolerable if nothing else. 'The pathologist confirmed it today. She was around eight weeks pregnant, very early stages. It's possible she may not even have known herself.'

Evie feels like screaming, opening her mouth and screaming until the walls fall in around them, a broken pile of bricks and rubble.

'But I would've known if she was seeing someone, if she'd been... if she'd been intimate with anyone. We talked about those kind of things – relationships... sex... boyfriends.'

But even as she says it, Evie isn't sure if they ever really had talked about all of that. It wasn't like they had *never* discussed these things – the subject of boys and sex was never intentionally avoided or taboo – it was more that she'd never really *had* to discuss it in any great detail with her daughter because Libby wasn't that kind of girl. Not that Evie would've minded if she had shown more of an interest; she wasn't a prude, and she'd been seventeen too once, although she hadn't been an early starter in that department either.

Libby had never been boy-obsessed like some of the other girls she knew of the same age. Young women were so sexualised today thanks to social media and celebrity influence, splashing themselves and their bodies all over the place, filtering themselves to look older, prettier, sexier... But Libby had seemed to largely eschew all of that – or so she'd always believed, and she had been proud and grateful for it. The idea that she'd been having sex – unprotected sex at that – was almost inconceivable. It wasn't the sex itself that bothered her, but the fact that she'd kept it a secret from her – that's what hurt. Why hadn't she confided in her mother? She had believed there were no secrets between them, which leads her to wonder if she'd been groomed by someone, brainwashed or coerced?

'Evie.' Dan Riley's voice comes back into focus and she slowly turns to him. 'Did Libby ever use drugs?'

'Drugs?' She hasn't the strength to raise her voice in alarm for a second time in such quick succession. 'No. God, no. She didn't even drink alcohol. Why?'

'Traces of barbiturates were found in her blood, at the autopsy. Xanax, it's a—'

'I know what it is, Detective Riley,' she cuts him off. 'I just don't know what it could be doing in my daughter's blood-stream. *Drugs...* Libby had drugs in her system?'

'Yes,' he says. 'It appears so.'

'Then somebody must've drugged her. Tom?' She looks to her husband for support, but his head is still in his hands and he doesn't look up.

'The murderer must've drugged her and raped her and—'

'She wasn't raped, Evie,' Dan says.

His voice is gentle, calming almost, and she can see the pity in his eyes as he looks at her. *Get used to it, Evie, this is going to be your life from now on: – pitiful looks, people crossing the street to avoid you, avoid the mother of the girl who was blud-geoned to death, her seventeen-year-old daughter, her pregnant seventeen-year-old daughter who was on drugs!*

'Oh, thank God...' Tom stands then, goes over to the window and stares out of it at the throng of news reporters outside.

'She... wasn't raped? But... but I assumed... Why would he have pulled her dress up and left her exposed like that?'

'We don't know yet, Evie,' Dan says.

She wishes he'd stop saying her name. It sounds... so earnest... almost patronising, like when she was at school.

'What we do know is that there was no sign of any sexual assault on Libby.'

She wants to feel relief but oddly it's the opposite. Confusion addles her aching brain. Why would he have killed her if the motive wasn't sexual? And drugs? *Drugs?* Libby had suffered from headaches on and off throughout her life – well, since that dreadful accident on holiday when she was little anyway – and loathed even taking a couple of paracetamol, found them hard to swallow. Drink, drugs, sex, pregnancy... this isn't the Libby she knows. It's nothing like her, the antithesis of her happy, sensible, home-loving daughter. Why are they trying to blacken her name, make her out to be someone she isn't? Why are they trying to do that?

'It appears that Libby took a separate bag of clothes with her the night she was attacked.' Dan is speaking again and she has to make a consolidated effort to focus on what he is saying. 'We think she changed into them as she walked through the woods and that she was on her way to meet someone – a man most likely – possibly at The Chapel, a bar in town. We—'

The detective's phone rings and he excuses himself. Someone offers her tea – the younger policeman, Parker. She'd almost forgotten he was still here, but she can't drink anything. It feels wrong somehow; even the smallest of comforts feels wrong while her daughter is lying in the mortuary going colder by the second. She looks over at her husband. He hasn't moved from the window. She wants to reach out to him, to go to him, but instead she just stares, paralysed by a thousand emotions.

'We've found the weapon – a rock that was used to kill Libby, most probably came from the woods itself.' Dan Riley has returned to the room. 'It'll be sent straight to forensics for testing, so hopefully we'll get some results as soon as possible – there's a rush on it. The autopsy uncovered skin underneath

Libby's fingernails, and fibres were also found. I'm really hopeful that with all of this we'll get a full DNA profile...' He pauses. 'The pathologist found an old fracture, to Libby's skull, possibly obtained when she was very young... can you give me any details on that, how she might've got it?'

Evie looks over at Tom.

'She fell down some steps,' he explains, 'when she was around four years old. We were on holiday, in Tenerife. It was just a terrible accident.'

'And she sustained a fracture to her skull?'

'Yes,' Tom says. 'She was in hospital for ten days. Like I say, it was a dreadful accident – ruined the holiday of course. We took our eye off her for one second, and she toddled off and fell down a flight of concrete steps. We were beside ourselves. She made a full recovery though, thank God.'

'I see.'

Evie buries her head in her hands, the guilt of that day still fresh in her mind as if it had happened yesterday. Libby had suffered terrifying seizures for several years following the accident, although thankfully they'd passed by the time she'd reached the age of ten. The debilitating headaches, however, still persisted.

'Listen, Evie... Tom...'

The change of tone in the detective's voice causes her to look up at him.

'Is Brandon here?'

'Brandon?' Tom turns round.

Evie blinks at him, unease suddenly dancing inside her guts.

The detective inhales. 'Yes. We'd like him to come down to the station.'

'Why?' Tom's face is pale, like all the blood has suddenly drained from him.

'We just need to ask him some questions. It's fairly routine at this stage, just helping us with our enquiries.'

'What has he done?' Panic begins to rise up through Evie's diaphragm. 'Has he done something to her? Do you think he's— Have you *found* something?'

Tom turns to face the detective.

'Look, Brandon was here that night. He hasn't... He wouldn't... You can't think he has anything to do with this!'

But Dan's face tells her something different. That flicker in his eyes, the one she'd seen when she'd opened the door to him and he'd told her the news no parent should ever have to hear.

'You *have* found something, haven't you? Tell me! What is it?' She's almost screaming; perhaps she *is* screaming.

'Evie, for God's sake,' Tom barks. 'This is ridiculous. Let the man speak! Detective Riley, are you saying that my son, Libby's brother—'

'Half-brother!' Evie screams again. 'He's her half-brother... and he's always hated her, always been jealous of her!'

Tom gives her a look that instantly silences her.

'We just need to ask him to clarify some answers for us... about who he spoke to that night on the phone, where he went, and we'll need the clothes he was wearing, his trainers...'

Evie's eyes shoot towards Tom. 'Oh God!' She falls back into her seat. 'Was he lying... did he lie about where he went? He went after her, didn't he? I knew it! I felt it!' She thinks of Libby and how she was found, her skirt pulled up, her tights ripped... She feels sick.

'So you're arresting him?' Tom regains his voice. 'Should we get him a solicitor or something?'

Evie looks up at him. Was Tom trying to protect him? Was he trying to protect his son, a son who may have killed her daughter, *their* daughter? How could he? How could he even think of protecting him!

'We'll be bringing him in under caution,' Dan says soberly.

'Well, in that case, I'll get on the phone to Douglas.' Tom is already dialling the number.

Evie is too dumbfounded to speak. The police must know something they don't; they must suspect something. They don't bring you in under caution otherwise. She's watched enough police dramas on TV to know this.

The kitchen door opens and Parker walks through it, with Brandon close behind him.

'What have you done to her?' Evie launches herself at him instinctively, rage and grief and disbelief claiming the last of her rational thoughts as the policemen try to pull her away. 'What have you done to my daughter?'

THIRTEEN
AUGUST. LIBBY

'Are you out of your fucking mind?'

'No, Brandon, I'm deadly serious.' She sits on the edge of his bed facing him. He's lying down with his hands behind his head, propped up on some pillows.

'And what makes you think that I could get hold of any drugs, let alone thousands of pounds' worth of drugs? And that even if I could, why I would ever do *you* any favours.'

She smiles at him sweetly, a look she's perfected. 'Because I'm your sister.'

He laughs some more. 'My *sister*? When have you ever been *my* sister?'

He drops back against the pillow again. This is going to prove harder than she'd bargained for. 'I need your help, please, Brandon.'

'What the hell are you up to, Libby? I know you've been hanging around The Chapel, mixing with all sorts. I've still got friends round here, you know, people who know me and have told me you've been there, whoring yourself about like a little slut.' He gives her a look of disgust.

She swallows back a hateful retort. She needs him onside.

'Exactly! You *know* people. I can get the cash. I'll even cut you in if you like, say ten per cent... twenty even?'

He's shaking his head, incredulous. 'What, so you're a drug dealer now, are you?' He's mocking her, not taking her seriously. 'Don't you remember how Evie reacted when I was nicked for having that bag of weed on me a few years back? A twenty quid bag of skunk! And you revelled in it all, loved every minute of my fall from grace. And where have you even got that sort of money from?'

'Don't worry about the money. I'll have it.'

'Look, is this some kind of trick – get me to buy you drugs and then have me nicked for dealing, get rid of me for good or something?' He leans closer towards her.

'No!' she protests. 'Of course not. I would never do a thing like that!'

He snorts at her derisively.

'I'm just... helping someone out, doing a friend a favour... a friend in need and all of that.'

'Ha! And what's in it for you, Libby? You wouldn't give someone a light if you were on fire if there wasn't something in it for you!'

She stifles a smile. He doesn't realise how close to the truth he really is.

'You think you can pull the wool over everyone's eyes with your innocent-little-girl act, but that's all it is – an act.'

She inwardly rolls her eyes. Desperation is the only reason she's here, asking *him* for a favour. And it's all Harry Mendes' fault. Thanks to that idiot making a total balls-up of robbing the pharmacy for her and getting himself caught, she's now faced with two major problems.

No drugs, and the potential that Moron Mendes may snake on her to the cops. Fuck Harry. He's such a loser – and she made sure she told him so before summarily dumping his useless sorry ass. He'd been devastated of course, inconsolable in fact, but what did he expect? Surely he hadn't actually *believed* her when she'd told him she loved him?

Brandon wasn't biting so it was time to play her ace card.

'If you don't help me then I'll tell Dad that you've dropped out of university – that you haven't even *been* at university for a whole term. He'll stop your allowance.'

He turns to look at her slowly, his brow creasing. 'Have you been spying on me? Have you been stalking me? Jesus, you're a psycho!'

She smiles. 'Everyone needs insurance, Brandon. That's why I make it my business to know your business.'

'I'll kill you first,' he hisses at her. 'I mean it, I'll fucking *kill you.*'

'So that's a yes then?' she says breezily, cocking her head. 'You'll get the drugs...'

He moves right up in her face so that she can feel his breath on her cheek. A rush of adrenalin flushes through her, fear beginning to prickle at her skin, a potent and not altogether unpleasant sensation.

'No, Libby,' he spits. 'I *won't* be getting you, or anyone else, drugs. So go ahead and tell him, tell Dad that I've dropped out of uni. And then I'll tell him that *you* tried to blackmail me into procuring drugs for you. I'll tell him about this conversation, word for word.'

She stands abruptly. They'd never believe him anyway.

'Have it your way.' She smiles sweetly at him. She'll have to come up with something much more final for Brandon. Something so damaging that no one could ever forgive him, something that will make sure he's disowned and cut off from his family for good – he'll be sorry then. First, though, she needs to work out how to get these drugs. She's made a promise and she's determined to keep it.

'Go to hell, Libby,' he says as she turns to leave his room.

And then it comes to her! She almost smacks her own forehead. Why on earth hadn't she thought of it in the first place and saved herself all of this aggro? It had been right under her nose all along!

'Yeah,' she says, her confidence returning, 'I'll see you there – *half*-brother dearest,' she adds, slamming the door behind her.

FOURTEEN

DAN

You get a feeling about suspects. Maybe it's a skill you learn over time or maybe it's something you're born with, or perhaps a bit of both. But the feeling I'm getting now, sitting opposite Brandon Drayton in interview room three, is not the one I'd expected.

Davis kicks things off: 'Here's what we know, Brandon.' She addresses him politely, her tone friendly. He's young after all, only nineteen. 'You were at your parents' house...'

'They're not my parents,' Brandon interjects. 'Well, Evie's not my mother – she's my stepmother.'

'Yes.' Davis nods. 'And how is your relationship with her, with Evie? Would you say it was good? Do you get along?'

He shrugs, looks at his solicitor, an upright, well-dressed man in a smart, expensive-looking suit. His face is expressionless yet still somehow he manages to exude an air of superiority.

'I don't really spend too much time with her, around her. I only come to visit one weekend out of every four, sometimes more during the holidays.'

'And how about Libby – how did you get on with her?'

His solicitor whispers something in his ear. I watch Brandon's expression carefully. 'Were you close?'

He snorts softly, looks away.

I keep watching him for a moment.

'What were you like as kids? I mean, you've got different mothers, I understand, but did you spend a lot of time together?'

He meets my eyes finally. 'I wouldn't say we were close, no.' His tone is flat. 'And I wouldn't say we got on that well either, now or when we were kids. She... Libby was always...' His voice trails off.

'Always what, Brandon?'

He pauses for a moment. 'Always a little bitch,' he says caustically.

'Little sisters can be annoying – I get that.' I smile thinly. 'Tell me about your childhood. Do you have any happy memories – of the two of you together, I mean?'

His face falls. 'She hated me being around when I was a kid, hated the fact I even existed, or that my dad, our dad, might give me the slightest sliver of attention – attention she deemed exclusively hers. Like, if he ever wanted to do something just with me, take me fishing, say, she would have to come along, even though she hated fishing. She couldn't bear the idea of us having any father-and-son time together; she always had to be the centre of attention, the best at everything... the golden girl. Little Miss Perfect.'

'So she resented you? You resented each other?'

His solicitor whispers in Brandon's ear again but I don't catch it.

'She was always trying to stitch me up, get me into trouble and make me out to be the bad guy. And she was really good at it too. She would do things, bad things, and then somehow make it look like I was responsible, make me take the rap.'

'Bad things? Like what bad things, Brandon?'

I want to keep him talking, give me an insight into the

dynamics of their relationship. I'm sensing there was deep-rooted animosity between them and this, of course, could be motive.

'Like the Princess Castle.'

'Princess Castle?'

He shuffles awkwardly on his chair, pauses for a moment and exhales. 'One summer holiday when we were kids – I dunno, maybe seven and nine years old respectively – Evie and Libby built this enormous castle. It was for Libby of course, for her to put her dolls in and play with. They spent weeks making it, I mean, literally almost the whole six weeks of the summer holidays. They built it out of old lolly sticks, painstakingly sticking each one side by side. Sticking, painting, gluing... it was huge, this castle, almost as tall as she was. It had a working drawbridge made out of old cotton reels and string. It had turrets and windows and a wooden door... everything.'

He pauses again. 'I wasn't invited to join in the making of it of course. I had to *ask* to be included,' he says, the resentment dripping from his voice. 'I think Evie eventually agreed that I could help paint and varnish it. But I remember really wishing that I could build a castle like that, that I could have one just like it too. But it wasn't for me.' Sorrow briefly flashes across his young face. 'Anyway, once it was finished, we all admired it and Evie placed it in Libby's bedroom to dry overnight...

'I remember waking up the next morning to the sound of Evie screaming and crying. The sound of my dad shouting as he came up the stairs... and then he ripped back my bed sheets and yanked me up out of bed by my arm. I remember feeling really shocked, scared and confused... I was only nine, no idea what was going on, what had happened. I'd just woken up, disorientated, and he's shouting at me and pulling me out onto the landing and screaming at me to look over the bannisters at the floor below. Our house, well, you've seen it, it's a big house, three storeys, so I look over the bannisters and I see this... this pile of broken bits, wood and lolly sticks, cotton reels rolling...'

'The Princess Castle?'

He nods at me. 'It was in pieces on the wooden floor below, in bits, destroyed...' He exhales. 'Evie was wailing, "Why, Brandon, why did you do this? How *could* you, Brandon? How could you be so spiteful, so cruel? Weeks, it took us, weeks and weeks and you've destroyed it!" And I'm staring at her blankly, mouth open, confused, and I'm saying, "It wasn't me... I didn't break it... it wasn't me..." But she was having none of it.' He shakes his head. 'She just kept on screaming and wailing, and my dad, he smacked me round the backs of my legs really hard. I can still remember the sting of the slap on my calves... And then he sent me home, made me go back to my mum's, which was worse punishment than the slap.'

He sniffs, sits up a little. 'I remember crying, feeling overwhelmed by the sense of frustration, the injustice of no one believing me. I protested, kept saying it must've been Libby who'd done it, taken it out of her bedroom in the night and chucked it over the bannisters to try and get me into trouble, but Evie said that was ridiculous and that I was lying, that I was jealous of the castle they'd made and jealous of Libby...'

He pauses again, tries – and fails – to disguise his distress. 'I remember, as my mum pulled up outside the house to come and collect me and take me away, I turned back to look at them: Evie, my dad and Libby. They were standing in the doorway together with these disappointed looks on their faces. Libby was hiding behind Evie's dressing gown, peering out at me from behind it, and I remember I looked right at her and... and she smiled at me, gave me this evil little self-satisfied, triumphant smile... and I knew... I knew in that moment exactly what she'd done.'

There's a long moment's pause.

'That's not a happy childhood memory, Brandon,' I say gently.

'No,' he says, drawing breath. 'I don't have many – any – not ones which include Libby anyway.'

'I'm sorry to hear that,' I say.

'No need to be sorry,' he says, his tone suddenly becoming matter-of-fact. 'It's hardly your fault.'

'So, it's safe to say that you and Libby felt animosity between you.' It's a statement more than it is a question, given what he's just told me. 'That you didn't like one another?'

He shakes his head. 'I know what you're trying to get at,' he says. 'You think I killed her, don't you? You think I killed Libby because I was jealous of her, that she was the favourite and because of that I killed her?' He looks at me.

'Brandon,' I say, 'your sister is dead, she's been murdered, her head brutally bashed in to the point of her being unrecognisable. I'm sure you want us to find the person responsible as much as we do. We just need your help. Can you do that?'

He nods, lowers his head. His knees are trembling, feet tapping the floor.

'The night of Libby's disappearance, the night of the dinner party, Libby left around 7.45 p.m.?'

He nods again, doesn't look up.

'You left the house just a few moments later, maybe five minutes after Libby, to deal with "a bit of business" you said, according to Evie's statement. Can you tell us where you went, what that business you needed to attend to was?'

'I... I went to make a phone call. I made a phone call, to a girl.'

'Which girl was that, Brandon?' Davis asks. 'What's her name?'

His eyes dart from left to right in quick succession, his knees bouncing up and down. 'Just some girl from uni that I know, that I see sometimes... no one serious.'

'I see.' Davis smiles. 'And how long was the duration of this phone call? By all accounts you re-entered the house around 9.45 p.m., some two hours later. Where had you been to... make this phone call?'

'Just out walking, you know... up and down and that... I didn't want anyone listening in, so I went out for some privacy.'

He's lying. And I think he knows we know he is.

'It was a very cold night to be outside making a phone call for two hours,' I say, and he looks at me, visibly swallows.

'Like I say, I just wanted a bit of privacy... Dad and Evie had guests.'

'Like you said, it's a big house... your room is on the second floor, isn't it? Pretty impressive from what I saw – own en-suite bathroom, sofa, TV... more than enough privacy to make a phone call to anyone.'

His solicitor whispers in his ear yet again and, childishly, I feel like telling him that it's rude to whisper.

'I just wanted to get out of the house. I didn't think Evie wanted me hanging about. She doesn't like me much.' He shifts in his chair, swishes a bit of his long hair from his face, a face that is no longer a boy's yet not quite fully a man's yet either.

'Why doesn't she like you?'

He shrugs. 'I dunno. Ask her. She's never liked me much.'

There's a pause.

'Brandon, did you follow Libby that night? Was she the bit of business you needed to sort out? Did you have a falling out, a discussion of some sort? Look, we know there was no phone call to a girl from uni, and you came back to the house inebriated according to witnesses.' I lean forward across the table but I'm careful not to appear too intimidating. 'We've checked your phone records. The last call you made on the night of the twenty-first was at 7.56 p.m. for the duration of eleven seconds. Do you remember who you called, Brandon? Who was that call to?'

He looks at Davis and me respectively, his face a mask of panic. If the boy is guilty then he's hardly a criminal mastermind – surely he'd know that we could easily cross-reference with the phone company, find out the number and trace the recipient – in this case, Libby, the victim.

I look at Brandon Drayton properly; study him. I try to imagine him bashing his sister's head in with a rock, smashing it down onto her face repeatedly until it was a mass of blood and tissue and brain and bone and I think about what he's just told me, the unhappy memory from his childhood, a memory that I suspect is not an isolated one. Sibling rivalry can run deep; I've seen it many times in cases where blood is most definitely not thicker than water. Years of resentment building up, festering like poison, growing like cancer, everyone has a breaking point and, in the end, people can – and do – just snap.

'Can I have a private word with my client please?' the bored brief addresses me, stiff in his smart suit.

I nod; sit back in my chair. Davis stops the recording just as Mitchell pokes her head round the door.

'Gov, a word.'

Davis and I leave the interview room.

'What you got, Mitchell?'

'CCTV, boss. The night of Libby's murder. Brandon is picked up on camera inside The Chapel around 8.35 p.m.'

'Alone?'

'Nope.' My heart starts galloping inside my chest. 'Talking to the same man that was with Libby on Wednesday.'

'You're sure?'

Mitchell nods. 'Same description, same tattoos.'

Davis glances at me.

'We got a name on him yet?'

She shakes her head.

I turn to Davis.

'Eight thirty-five... does that give him enough time to kill

Libby and get to The Chapel? He'd have been covered in her blood, wouldn't he? Have we got his clothes – the ones he was wearing on the night?'

'Yes, gov, they're with forensics.'

I look at Davis, her silent thoughts mirroring my own back to me.

'Let's get back in there. Thanks, Mitchell.' I nod at her.

'Hang on, gov, there's more. The skin, the DNA underneath Libby's fingernails – forensics says it's not a match. It's not Brandon's.'

'Right, well, he's not off the hook yet,' I say. 'He's lied about the phone call, about where he was. This bloke at The Chapel, we need to find him, find out who he is fast and what's his connection with the Draytons.'

'Gov.' Mitchell walks away purposefully.

Brandon's head is resting on the table when we re-enter the room. He looks exhausted. I'm sympathetic; I know the feeling. But I haven't got time for sentiment right now. I'm slightly cranky myself having not eaten or slept in over twenty-four hours

.

'Who did you go to meet at The Chapel on Friday night, Brandon?'

He lifts his head up from the table slowly like it's the weight of a bowling ball.

'We've got you on CCTV talking to a man, a man with tattoos, the same man Libby was seen with on the previous Wednesday. Who is he? Why did you lie about where you'd been? You called Libby on her phone at 7.56 p.m. the night she died. What for?'

He glances at his brief. 'No comment,' he says.

'Brandon,' Davis says, 'are you involved in your sister's death? Do you know what happened to Libby – who's responsible for doing this to her?' She takes some photographs from a file and slides them across the table. 'Look at her, Brandon. That's your sister, your own flesh and blood.'

He's barely able to raise his eyes but curiosity gets the better of him. In my experience, people never *want* to look but they can't help themselves.

He visibly flinches.

'That's Libby, what's left of her, Brandon, your own sister. Your dad and Evie couldn't even formally identify her she was in such a mess. Do you know who did this to her? Because if you do, if you have any part in this...'

He looks distressed and is running his hands through his hair and gritting his teeth.

'She brought it all on herself!' He stands abruptly, the chair falling onto its back with the momentum. His brief rolls his eyes wearily. 'Stupid bloody bitch brought it on herself!'

'You don't have to answer them, Brandon, remember,' his solicitor says.

'Yes,' I say, thanking him with a nod, 'he's right, Brandon, you don't, but how's it going to look, huh, her own brother refusing to cooperate with police after his sister's brutal murder? And what exactly did she bring on herself? You think she *deserved* this? That she deserved to die like this – to die at all?'

He looks like he might even be crying as he starts to pace the room. 'No comment.'

'Please, Brandon, sit down.'

He drags his hands down his face, pulls the chair up from the floor.

I pause for a moment, let him gather himself.

'We did a search of your house, Brandon, and...' I place the clear ziplock bag onto the table in front of him.

He stares at it. 'What is it?'

'You tell me,' I say. 'We found them in your drawer, in your bedroom at your dad's house.'

He cocks his head to one side, studies the bag, shrugs.

'It's Libby's underwear, Brandon – a pair of her knickers, unwashed by all accounts. Forensics have confirmed they belonged to her. Why would a pair of your sister's used knickers be in your drawer in your bedroom?'

Horror suddenly sweeps across his features like fire.

'What the...' He looks up at me, his eyes widening. 'You've got to be kidding me... I... Jesus Christ! No! No way... She... SHE put them there!' He's bellowing now, eyes bulging from their sockets, his earlier composure diminishing rapidly. 'No... NO!'

He stands abruptly again, though the chair remains upright this time. 'She's... oh God, fucking hell! This is sick!'

He looks around the interview room as though searching for backup from absent people. 'She's set me up! SHE put them there, I'm telling you.' Spittle flies from his mouth. 'She wanted it to look like... Oh my God!' He drags his hands through his mop of hair again, tugs at it in what looks like rage or frustration or both. 'You don't understand...'

'Try me,' I say, nodding at him to sit back down. 'Make me understand, Brandon.'

I sense real fear in him now, panic filling the room as the seriousness of the situation begins to dawn on him – of the evidence he's looking at and the potential implications it has for him.

'She's done this... she's done this to make it look like... to set me up.' His eyes search mine. 'I'm not some fucking pervert, you know!' He's wailing now, crying. 'I knew she was going to do something...'

'What? What was she going to do?'

'Something to stitch me up, something to try and ruin my life, ruin my relationship with my family, with my father... I didn't think... I didn't think she'd go that low though... make me out to be a sicko.'

'Why would Libby want to make you out to be a sicko, Brandon? Who is the man you met at The Chapel? Do you know him? Did he know Libby?'

He looks over at his brief again as though asking permission to speak. I can see he's been advised to go NC but is close to breaking. I had a feeling the underwear would be the tipping point.

'Yes. No. I don't know him, not really, and yes, he did know Libby. That's why I went there to The Chapel that night. I wanted to find him, warn him.'

'Warn him? Warn him about what?'

'About her.'

'About Libby?'

'Yes.'

'Why?'

'Why?' He looks at me, his eyes watery and fearful. He shakes his head.

'Why did you want to warn him about Libby? Had she done something?'

He almost throws his head back and starts to laugh but nothing comes out. He pauses for a second then leans forward across the table and meets my eyes.

'You really have no idea, do you, Detective?' he says. 'No idea at all.'

FIFTEEN

EVIE

———

'Mrs Drayton – Evie.' The woman approaches her, takes her hand and shakes it brusquely. 'I'm Chief Superintendent Gwendoline Archer. It's good to meet you.' The pause is too brief for her to respond. 'Firstly, I want to say how sorry I am, how sorry we all are, and I...'

Evie automatically tunes her out, something she's become rapidly adept at doing. Maybe it's the grief, or perhaps it's the drugs – the pills that Jim prescribed her, making her feel detached and distant, like she isn't quite present. Una had come round with a bottle of them the previous day – a mercy mission. As much as she knew she meant well and only wanted to support her, she hadn't wanted Una to come – hadn't wanted anyone to. She'd just wanted to curl up in a ball on her bed, holding Libby's hoodie, breathing in the scent of her daughter, watching day turn to night in an endless cycle. She hadn't even wanted Tom near her, had felt herself flinch when he'd laid down next to her on the bed that morning.

'Don't shut me out, Eve,' he'd whispered into the back of her neck. 'We can get through this. Remember all that horrible business with that crazy woman a few years back... we got through that, didn't we? We can get through anything.'

How could he possibly compare some psycho ex-employee who'd set out to ruin his reputation by making false accusations against him with their daughter's brutal murder? She couldn't offer him any words of reassurance in return. All she could see when she closed her eyes were images of Libby lying dead in the woods, her face smashed to pieces, unrecognisable... her daughter, her *pregnant* daughter.

'... I want to personally assure you that my officers are working round the clock, *round the clock*, twenty-four/seven to make sure that whoever killed your daughter is remanded in custody as soon as possible.' The superintendent's voice comes back into focus. *How long has she been talking?* 'I give you my word, Evie. I mean that. We've got the best there is working on Libby's behalf, to get justice for her, and for you and Tom too.'

Evie attempts to speak, but again the woman continues before she has the chance, or maybe her reactions are just unusually slow. Maybe it's the pills.

'Dan Riley is the best there is; he's an outstanding detective with an exemplary record. We'll make sure whoever did this goes to prison for a very long time, I assure you. Both of you.'

She nods at the woman, manages a perfunctory thin smile as she glances over at Tom, who's being fitted up with a microphone by a member of the production team, a young man who's clipping something to his shirt collar.

Evie makes to speak again, but the moment has passed, and she can't even remember what it was that she wanted to say now. Her brain feels like it's blipping, marinating in a thick soupy fog inside her head, her thoughts struggling to push themselves through the density and break the surface. *Who was the father of her daughter's child? Why hadn't Libby confided in her? Her own mother...*

'The CCTV footage of Libby at The Chapel with the

unknown man is being released to the press as we speak.' The superintendent is talking once again. 'We're hopeful that a member – or members – of the public – or indeed anyone from the bar that night – might recognise him and come forward with an identification. The more emotive the appeal, the more likely we are to get the names rolling in...'

Evie stares at her. Was she suggesting that she over-egg her grief, ham up a performance of a heartbroken mother? Was she suggesting that she needed to *act*?

Tom approaches them before she can articulate these thoughts. He looks like she feels, dishevelled and anxious, his cheeks sunken, worry somehow emanating from his pores. She knows he's worried for Brandon. He'd been pacing the kitchen all night, pulling at his hair, talking aloud to himself in disbelief.

'Not my son,' he kept saying over and over on repeat between gulps of whiskey. 'Brandon wouldn't do anything to hurt Libby... I *know* he wouldn't.'

She felt herself stuck in a new kind of hell somewhere between hatred and empathy.

'There's not going to be any mention of Brandon, is there, about him being questioned?' Tom says, twitching nervously as he shakes the superintendent's hand. 'The press would bloody love that, wouldn't they? My boy had nothing to do with it. He wouldn't harm a hair on her head – I know that and you know it too, don't you, Evie?'

He turns to her, but she's too zonked out on medication to challenge him, but the truth is she *doesn't* know. She doesn't know anything anymore.

'You should be out there searching for the real killer,' he continues, 'not persecuting our bloody family. We're already suffering enough. I mean, how could you even think—'

'They must have their reasons,' Evie manages to say. 'He couldn't account for those two hours on Friday, he lied about making a phone call and... and...'

She can barely bring herself to talk about what the police had found in Brandon's bedroom drawer. She can't think about it without feeling physically sick. Had Brandon been abusing Libby, or thinking about it? Had he made unwanted advances towards his sister and killed her when she'd rebuffed him? Was she taking drugs to cope with what was happening to her? Had *he* given her them? Maybe Libby had threatened to tell her or Tom or to go to the police and, backed into a corner, he had silenced her? Perhaps she'd told him she was pregnant – oh God! Maybe even with *his* child. As sickening and egregious as this thought is, Evie has to consider that this is possible.

Why had she not seen it? Or had she? Had she mistaken Brandon's sexual obsession with his sister for mere jealousy, sibling rivalry? They'd grown up together as kids; spent countless weekends together, holidays, events, birthdays, Christmases... surely she would've noticed, would've seen something over the years – a furtive glance, a meandering look...

'I realise this is a terrible time, Tom, a sensitive time, and we have to—'

'Look, for Christ's sake, Brandon would never have murdered his own sister! He's just a boy! He's *my* boy. The... thing you found in his bedroom, it has to be a mistake!' His eyes are wide and bulging, making him look manic. She can smell last night's whiskey on his breath and wonders if the superintendent can too. 'Maybe he picked them up by accident with his own washing or something. Lord knows, I've done the same thing once or twice in my lifetime – haven't you?' He holds his arms up to the sky. 'It doesn't prove anything whatsoever.'

Evie watches the superintendent closely.

'He's just helping us with our enquiries at this stage. I know this is difficult for you, for both of you, it's just procedure, part of the elimination process. Your son lied about where he went and what he was doing that night, so we need to establish why. We've taken his DNA and his clothing for forensic purposes.

We'll need to interview him again. There's not enough evidence to charge him currently...'

'Charge him! Charge him with what exactly?' Tom's shouting now and people are turning to look. 'He hasn't done anything... Evie!' Tom glances at her for support. 'This is madness... absolute madness, you know—'

'Listen, Tom, we'll speak properly once the appeal is over and—'

'Fuck the appeal!'

Evie looks at him but still says nothing – it's as if her brain has disconnected from her voice box.

'You're not going to pin this on my son! My daughter is dead, DEAD, and you're telling me that my own bloody son is responsible – I don't believe it... not Brandon... he may well have made the odd fuck-up but he's not some perverted maniac, for Christ's sake!'

'Please, Tom, let's just calm down...' The superintendent addresses him with a measured tone. 'Brandon was picked up on CCTV at The Chapel bar speaking to the same man Libby was seen with on the Wednesday. He may be able to lead us to this individual...'

'Wait... What?' Evie says, the woman's words finally reaching her brain. 'Hang on, the *same* man?'

'Yes,' she says. 'Which is why we're doing this appeal. We need to identify him. We think he may have some key information.'

'Yes and he may be the actual bloody killer!' Tom shoots back, the microphone on his shirt coming loose, dangling by a thin wire.

'That's why we need to find him. There are quite a lot of unanswered questions, Tom... Brandon was gone for two hours that night, hours that are unaccounted for.'

Tom has started pacing again, running his hands through his hair and puffing his cheeks.

'Yes, well, Brandon wasn't the only one who slipped away for a bit that night you know, the night of the dinner party...'

'Oh?' The superintendent looks at him, her interest piquing.

'No!' Tom's voice is high with emotion. 'He wasn't, was he, Evie?' He turns to her.

'I... I...' She struggles to think. The dinner party... all that preparation, all that anticipation. They'd been so looking forward to it, to seeing their oldest friends in the flesh after so long. Libby playing piano... she hears the concerto in her ears, the melodic twinkling of the notes whirling and echoing around her mind. *'I'll be back by 10.30 p.m. latest...'* She hears her daughter's sing-song voice as she leaves the room as though she's standing right next to her. They'd all drunk some wine... she was preparing the starter, the smoked salmon; Una was chatting – yes, they were talking about that poor woman, Sara Mendes, Harry's mother, the boy from Libby's class who'd killed himself just a few weeks earlier and... oh God, hang on...

Evie swallows, heat pricking her skin like needles as her mind gathers some clarity. A bolt of adrenalin rushes through her. He had taken a phone call, yes, that's right, had said the alarm had gone off down at the surgery and that he needed to go and switch it off. He'd left the house, been gone a while, longer than he'd said he'd be... Una had told him off and... a scratch... he'd come back with a scratch on his face!

'Oh God.' Evie places a shaking hand over her mouth as the camera crew give the superintendent the nod to let her know they're ready for them. *'Jim?'*

SIXTEEN
AUGUST. JIM

'Libby! What a lovely surprise! Wow! Look at you!' Jim stands as she enters his office. 'I didn't see your name on my list this morning,' he says, getting a waft of her perfume as she closes the door behind her. He recognises it instantly. It's the same perfume that Evie always used to wear. He can't remember the name of it now but it's very distinctive and he's always liked it. Una used to wear it too sometimes, though it hadn't smelled the same – or admittedly as good – on her.

'Good to see you, Jim!' Libby smiles. 'I can call you that, can't I? Seems a bit weird calling you Dr Hemmings.'

He laughs a little, feels a touch awkward though isn't sure why exactly.

'Of course, of course. Come on in. It's great to see you too! Gosh, it's been a while, hasn't it?' He can't recall the last time he saw Evie and Tom's daughter, not here at the surgery anyway, and she's never attended without her mother before.

'No Evie?' he asks. 'No Mum with you today?'

'No. I've come alone.'

He smiles, observing her. 'Ah, that's a shame; would've been lovely to see her, and I have to say you're the absolute spit of her when she was the same age – for a split second, when you walked in, I thought it actually *was* her.'

'Really?' She giggles. 'I can't see it myself.'

'Well, trust me, you're the image of her when she was around your age. Anyway, how are Mum and Dad? Haven't seen them in ages either. Your mother is well?'

'Evie? Yes, Mum's fine. And Dad, he's good – busy, you know...'

'The practice still doing well?'

Tom Drayton has his own private and very plush physio clinic in a very salubrious part of town where he treats wealthy clients, including a few famous sports and TV personalities that he never fails to find a way to 'drop' into a conversation – all rather glamorous, in comparison to Jim's own surroundings at least. Evie had helped Tom set it up a few years ago now, had funded it entirely with her late father's inheritance. Jim supposed he'd always been a tiny bit jealous of this fact, though not so as he would ever let it affect their friendship adversely. Tom was a good bloke, even if he always somehow managed to land on his feet. He'd always been the type to fall in shit and come up smelling of roses, even when they'd all been at uni together. He'd not secretly given him the nickname 'Golden Balls' for nothing.

Perhaps he'd been a tad unfair though. He supposed it hadn't always been plain sailing for Tom, what with Maggie, Brandon's mother, who'd borne a grudge against him that had stood for almost twenty years, seemingly never forgiving him for leaving her 'holding the baby'. Then, of course, there was all that unpleasantness with that woman a few years back, an unhinged ex-employee who had become infatuated by him and had made all kinds of accusations against him. Tom had, with Evie's help, successfully cleared his name and sued her for slander in the end, but it had been a very trying time for them both. Anyway, he deserved his success. *Tom has a great career and a wonderful wife and now*, he thinks as he looks at Libby, *a daughter who's blossomed into a beautiful young woman*. He couldn't deny him that, even though he's wished he could trade places on more than a few occasions.

'Great!' She beams. 'They're doing really great and the clinic is busier than ever.'

'Splendid... that's good to hear.' He pauses momentarily, wonders why she's here. 'Well... take a seat, Libby.'

'You look really well, Uncle Jim,' she says, crossing her legs as she sits, her lemon-coloured summer dress opening slightly as she does, exposing a flash of her slim thighs. He tries not to notice. 'Have you been away somewhere on holiday, you and Auntie Una? You look really well... healthy and tanned.'

The compliment surprises him. Only this morning he'd inspected himself miserably in the mirror, a new rash of fine lines seemingly appearing overnight around his tired eyes. He supposed when you spent as much time taking care of other people as he did, it didn't leave a lot left for yourself and he was conscious of having let himself go a bit. He felt old and unattractive, though he was sure he'd been handsome once. Maybe not strikingly so like Tom, but he remembered that Evie had once thought so, although that was many moons ago now.

'Goodness, I wish.' He chuckles, chuffed. 'Far too busy here, I'm afraid, although I expect Una will get her way and we'll end up booking something last minute before the summer's over. You know how much she loves a summer break, and we've all had a few of them together in our time, haven't we? Although you were much younger then of course.'

He suddenly thinks of that time in Tenerife, the time she'd fallen as a tot and fractured her skull. He remembers seeing her one moment and then the next... lying at the bottom of the steps, blood spilling from her head... hearing the panic and screams of the women... It was awful, just *awful*. They'd always gone on a yearly jaunt together, the six of them back then, usually a last-minute bucket deal somewhere hot and cheap. But after that accident, they had never holidayed together again. It had left a bad taste in all their mouths.

'So,' he says, 'what can I help you with today?'

'Well, it's my stomach,' she says. 'It's been aching for the past couple of days.' She shifts in the chair, swishes her long honey-coloured hair from her shoulders. He gets another waft of the perfume she's wearing, tries again to remember the name of it.

'I'm sorry to hear that. Can you describe it to me? Is it a sharp pain?'

'No.' She shakes her head. 'More of a dull pain, in my lower stomach.' She rests her slim hand onto her pelvis. 'Here.'

Jim is suddenly conscious of how warm it is in his office. It's a hot August day; he must tell Janet to switch the air con on – it's stifling. He sips at a glass of water on his desk.

'Any changes in your bowel movements? Constipation? Diarrhoea?'

She shakes her head, looks at him. Her eyes are green, a mossy colour, like her mother's – so much like Evie's that he could be looking into them.

'OK, could you have eaten anything bad perhaps – any changes in your diet? Something that hasn't agreed with you?'

'No,' she says. 'Nothing.'

'No nausea, vomiting, listlessness?'

She shakes her head.

'Right, well, best we have a look at you then,' he says, suddenly feeling overwhelmingly self-conscious. He wishes he'd worn his new linen shirt now instead of this old M&S one that made him feel his age. 'If you'd like to lie down on the couch...'

She smiles and pops behind the curtain while he goes to the sink. His hands are shaking a little as he washes them, making it trickier for him to put his latex gloves on. He purposefully looks at the green plastic curtain as he begins to palpate her slim stomach.

'About here?' he asks.

'Lower,' she replies softly. He can tell she's looking right at him, can see her staring at him in his peripheral vision. He swallows hard. From the corner of his eye, he sees that her dress has fallen open at the top of her thighs, exposing a glimpse of her white lace underwear underneath. He can see the small mound of her pubic area, a faint outline of the contours of her intimate area through the lacy fabric... His breathing begins to increase.

'That's a Lempicka, isn't it?' she says, her eyes still fixed upon his face.

'Sorry? A what?'

'The painting,' she says, 'the one on the wall there... the artist is Tamara de Lempicka.'

'Gosh.' He laughs a little nervously. 'Yes, it is... well spotted.'

'We learned about her in art studies,' she says. 'She was an exceptional woman, you know, as well as an incredible painter. Did you know that she slept with a man to ensure her husband's emancipation from prison during the Russian Revolution?'

'No,' Jim says. 'I didn't know that. How fascinating. And you said it wasn't a sharp pain – more of a dull ache?'

She sighs. 'That's true love for you, I guess, fucking someone else to guarantee your love's liberty... Liberty, ha! No pun intended!'

Fucking. The word hangs heavy in the air above them. He tries not to appear as shocked by her use of it as he feels. He's never heard her speak like this before. She sounds knowing, more grown up – different to when he saw her last, which was admittedly a while ago now.

'And it's definitely more of an ache,' she says. 'Very low down. More of a throb, I guess.' She takes his hand by the wrist and guides it towards her pelvis, towards her—

Jim snatches his hand away. Pulls the glove off and turns away from her.

'Well...' He clears his throat and loosens his shirt collar a little. Why is it so damn hot in here? 'I can't feel anything...'

'Really?' She sits up then, tucks her knees up to her chest, exposing her underwear again; the thin lacy white sliver of her crotch. 'You couldn't feel anything at all?'

Her head is cocked to one side, her eyes still focused on him. Is she... is she *flirting* with him? No. No. He's reading this all wrong. She's just a girl, for Christ's sake, a young girl, his best friend's daughter. He's known her since she was in nappies, since she was born. And he's old enough to be her father; in fact, he's slightly older than Tom.

'How is your menstrual cycle?' he asks, still unable to look at her. He begins to pretend to start typing on his PC, but his hands are shaking so much now that he's barely able to. Why is her presence affecting him like this? He feels uncomfortable, awkward, *aroused*...

'It's OK.' She shrugs. 'I don't get so much pain these days. Not since I've been... well, since I've had a boyfriend...'

'I see,' he says.

'Sex is supposed to help, isn't it – help ease the cramps? I read somewhere that having regular orgasms can also help with the pain.'

He isn't sure how to answer – isn't sure that he even should.

'Does your mother know you're here, Libby?'

'No,' she replies, her green eyes wide. 'And I'd rather she didn't know, if it's all the same to you, Uncle Jim. You won't tell her, will you?'

'No, of course not.' He gulps back some water from his glass.

'Good. Because I can keep a secret if you can.' She smiles at him, lowers her eyes a touch.

'I have to ask this, Libby – in light of what you've just told me, is there a possibility you could be pregnant?' He says the word quickly, once again pretending to type so as to avoid looking at her. 'Are you using contraception?'

'I was,' she says. 'But we broke up so... And I don't know, maybe I could be. Now you mention it, my breasts do feel a bit sore, a bit tender, around the nipples... that's a sign, isn't it? But then again, they always get sore around my time... Can you tell, as a doctor, just by touching them if they're swollen?'

'Well, it is one of many signs of a potential pregnancy,' he says, his voice sounding scratchy. He clears his throat again, takes another sip of water. 'But the best thing is for us to do a test, just to be sure. I can organise it with the nurse, maybe get her to take some swabs, rule out any infections, that sort of thing.'

'Can't you do that?' She looks at him imploringly with those green eyes again. 'I'd rather you do it; I'd feel more comfortable with that.'

Well, that made one of them at least.

'Should you check them, my breasts?' she says, beginning to undo the top buttons on her dress.

'Check what? No!' His voice sounds high and panicky and suddenly he feels embarrassed. Is she being inappropriate or is he the one thinking inappropriately? He really can't be sure. What he is sure of, however, is how aroused he feels. His toe begins to tap on the floor and she looks down at it.

'No... no need for that,' he says, dropping his voice back down to a normal tone. 'Libby, I don't want to pry, but does your mother know about your... your relationship?'

'That I'm having sex, you mean? Or that I was having sex. We broke up recently...'

'Yes, I'm sorry to hear that. Don't you think you should talk to your mum? I'm sure she would give you some advice, help you...'

She looks a little tearful all of a sudden. 'I really miss him,' she says. 'I miss the intimacy we had... I miss him touching me, making love to me and... He was older, you see. I'm not really into boys my own age. I like mature men, men who've seen a bit of life, who know how to love a woman properly and make her feel special – a man who knows how to make a woman cum.'

The buttons on her dress are still open, and he can see the swell and curves of her breasts, the matching white lace on her bra. He doesn't want to look, doesn't want to think about how she looks and smells, how soft her skin would feel to touch...

'I... I... think,' he stammers, trying to hold it together, 'that we'll get you some tests done, a process of elimination, and then we'll see where we are... and I do think you should talk to your mother – you two are close, aren't you? You can talk to her, can't you?'

'Yes,' she says. 'We are. You were close once too, weren't you?'

'I'm sorry?' The words 'fucking' and 'cum' are circling around his head like a vulture. He consciously swallows.

'You and Mum, when you were at university together? You had a fling, didn't you? A relationship before she met Daddy.'

The candid question throws him off balance. She blinks at him, her face a picture of young, wide-eyed beauty, just as he remembers her mother back then. He honestly isn't sure how to react. Should he politely decline answering her or would that make him look like an old out-of-touch fuddy-duddy? It's an innocent enough question after all, isn't it? Maybe she's just being curious; young people are often curious, he tells himself. She's not a child anymore after all; she's a young woman.

'How do you know that, Libby?' He's flustered and is sure she can see this despite his best attempts to disguise it.

She smiles a little coyly. 'I overheard you all speaking about it once – once when you and Una were at our house having dinner, Daddy made a joke about it.'

Tom had always found his historical tryst with Evie quite

hilarious, and even though he'd gone along with the banter, this had always slightly irked him, as though it were a great big joke that Evie could ever have shown the slightest interest in *him*. He knew it made Evie squirm in embarrassment too, though he was never quite sure if that embarrassment was for herself or for him. Perhaps it was both.

'Well, yes, we had a brief relationship when we met at university – a very long time ago now.' He chuckles, but it sounds forced and disingenuous. 'We were just kids really, much like you now...'

He realises that this may have come across as patronising and instantly wishes he'd chosen his words more carefully.

'I'm not a kid anymore, Jim.' She looks at him intently, meets his eyes as he briefly looks up. 'I'm all grown up now.' She bites her bottom lip briefly and smiles at him. There's a pause that seems to go on forever. 'I'll wait to hear from you then,' she says finally.

'Hear from me? Oh! You mean about the tests... yes, yes, of course, of course. I'll get you all booked in with the nurse first thing.'

'Thank you, Jim.' She stands, her flimsy summer dress slowly sliding back down her thighs as she does. 'Thank you for seeing me. I really appreciate it, and I appreciate your discretion too.'

'That's perfectly OK.' Jim stands, goes to shake her hand, but she hugs him instead, pulls him into her and squeezes him. He can feel the contours of her body pressing against his own through the thin fabric of her summer dress, the feel of her strong slim thighs, the softness of her breasts against his chest, her silky hair brushing against his cheek and that perfume, *God, that perfume...* 'You can talk to me anytime, Libby – I want you to know that.' The words fall from his lips before he can prevent them.

'Thank you so much – thank you, Jim. Goodbye,' she says,

kissing him lightly on the cheek before leaving the room, softly closing the door behind her.

The morning surgery seemed to drag on forever. Jim had gone through the motions, umming and ahhing and making all the right noises as a revolving slew of patients with their varying ailments came in and out of his office like a carousel. But he couldn't concentrate, couldn't stop thinking about his encounter with Libby Drayton. He'd been struck by how much she'd looked like her mother. The moment she'd walked through the door, it was as if he was seeing Evie for the first time all over again. She had even smelled the same, reminding him of that moment all those years ago, recapturing that feeling of excitement – a frisson, like something magical was about to happen.

Images of her kept flashing up inside his head: the tilt of her chin, the lowering of her eyes, her use of the words 'fucking' and 'cum'. Why had she said those things? Was it inappropriate, given the context? Or was it just how the young speak these days – candidly, without a filter? He thought of her dress as it had fallen open at her thighs, the glimpse of her underwear, the outline of her crotch, the softness of her as he'd touched her stomach, her hand on his wrist, guiding it down...

Jesus! What in the Lord's name was he even thinking! *You're imagining things, Jim, you stupid old sod.* She wasn't flirting; she wasn't flirting at all. She's just a young girl, not yet self-aware. She was just being friendly, opening up to her GP – a close friend of the family who she's known forever – she was just being inquisitive about his and Evie's historic dalliance – there was nothing more to it than that. *Get a grip on yourself.*

He feels a twinge of self-disgust that he'd felt so aroused by her, by their encounter. He can still detect the faintest smell of her perfume on his shirt, lingering... What was wrong with him? Was he having some sort of mid-life crisis? As if she'd ever look at him that way – a beautiful, clever young woman like that with her pick of all the boys, no doubt. He was flattering himself, being utterly ridiculous.

But even as Jim tries to convince himself of this, he hears her voice: 'I like mature men... who know how to love a woman properly and make her feel special – a man who knows how to make a woman cum.'

He's grateful when his last patient of the morning finally closes the door behind her. He wants to get home, mow the lawn, maybe have a cold beer – and shower – do something to distract himself from these terrible thoughts he's having; indecent, improper images he doesn't want his mind to conjure up. Libby is Evie's daughter – his best friend's *young* daughter, and he's a married man, a happily married man, although admittedly he and Una haven't exactly been particularly active in that department for a while...

Stuffing some papers into his briefcase, Jim nods at the receptionist on his way out. 'See you tomorrow, Janet,' he says, 'oh, and can you make sure that the air con is switched on first thing tomorrow morning when you arrive. It was unbearably hot in my office today.'

She looks at him, perplexed. 'But it was on, Dr Hemmings – I switched it on first thing when I came in... Was it not working then?'

'Oh... I... Well, never mind, just make sure it's on tomorrow. Have a good afternoon.'

The heat hits him like a slap in the face as he makes his way outside the surgery towards his car and, flustered, he almost drops his briefcase as he unlocks the door with a click and beep. That's when he sees her. She's leaning up against his car door, smiling at him as she squints in the sunshine, her yellow dress matching it.

'Libby? What are—'

'I've been waiting for you, Jim,' she interrupts him. 'I'd like to talk to you *privately*. Will you give me a ride home?'

He begins to shake with the surge of adrenalin that rushes through him, stares at her in a state of arousal and shock, feelings that have not left him since she entered his office earlier that morning.

'Yes... er... yes, of course,' he stammers, opening the door for her almost instinctively. She slides into the passenger seat, the split in her dress once again opening to expose those lovely creamy slim thighs, and he gets another waft of that perfume again, Evie's scent. And it comes to him finally, the name of it, as he gets behind the wheel and starts the engine with shaking hands: Poison.

SEVENTEEN
PRESENT DAY. UNA

'I'm home!' Una calls out to her husband as she hurries through the front door into the kitchen, throwing the shopping bags onto the table with a clatter. 'Jim! I'm back!' She checks the time on the kitchen clock. Evie and Tom are going to be on the news any moment – giving their appeal – and she can't miss it. She lights a cigarette, switches the kettle on.

'You want tea, Jim?' she calls out to him a third time. 'Jim!'

Feeling cross, she stubs her cigarette out on a side plate discarded by the sink and struts into the living room to find him.

'Jim, switch on the TV... Oh!'

Her husband is sprawled out across the sofa, a glass of something in his hand. 'What are you... Is that... Don't tell me that's whiskey you're drinking?' She pulls a face. 'Why are you drinking whiskey at this time of day? *Jim...*'

He doesn't even look up. 'Give it a rest, woman. I just fancied a glass, that's all,' he mutters. 'Nothing wrong with that, is there?'

Una bristles but doesn't bite. Jim has taken Libby's death particularly badly; they all have – what other way could anyone possibly take such a dreadful, horrible tragedy? Her best friend's daughter has been murdered, brutally murdered. It was surreal, *unreal*. That she was actually dead was difficult enough to comprehend, although people did die – as a doctor's wife, she above most understood this: babies and children, young people, old people, middle-aged people, no one was exempt from illness, accidents and death, but *murdered*, her young life snatched from her in such a horrific manner – and for what reason? It was as if it hadn't really happened somehow, like it was all some sick joke, a nightmare that they would all eventually wake from, relieved that it had all been just a diabolical dream.

It hadn't properly sunk in, even when she'd been at Evie's the day before, doing her best to comfort her friend, giving her pills to help her sleep, putting on a wash for her and tidying up, doing the mundane, everyday things just to try and help, to do *something*. None of it made any sense whatsoever – who would want to kill such a young, beautiful girl in such a horrific way? Was it some random stranger? Was a maniac on the loose and Libby had just been in the wrong place at the wrong time – or was there more to it than that?

She could barely get a straight answer out of Evie who had looked so ill that it had shocked her; it was as if she'd aged ten years overnight and was so thin and pale, like she was disappearing. Una hadn't known what to say to her exactly, which was something of a first when she thought about it because finding the right words in the right moment had, she'd always liked to believe, been one of her personal strengths. But what could she possibly say to console her?

People always attempt to say helpful things in tragic situations; it's human nature. She remembers when she was going through rounds of IVF, her period turning up each month with regularity like a baddie in a fairy tale. 'It'll work next time,' 'I'm so sorry,' 'Keep the faith, don't give up,' or, even, 'If it's meant to be it will happen' – she'd really hated that one, as if people were somehow implying that if it didn't happen then it wasn't ever supposed to and that she wasn't destined to become a mother.

Evie had been such a huge support during that dismal, disappointing time in her life; she'd never rolled out the clichéd one-liners after each failed attempt like most people had. She hadn't attempted to make her feel better with empty words and statements; she'd simply held her hand and cried with her, poured her a glass of wine, *been there*, which had only ever compounded her guilt.

Guilt was an insidious, unrelenting emotion; it had a way of creeping up on you just when you'd thought you'd forgotten. It was perhaps one of the only things that didn't seem to diminish with time, like Japanese knotweed taking root inside you, snaking its way around your conscience and strangling it as it grew. Sometimes she felt it, tangible in her stomach, as though she'd swallowed poison and was going to throw up, purge it all out from inside her. She would feel better afterwards she felt sure, but that feeling wouldn't last. Nothing good would ever come from it. A confession would be a purely selfish act to appease her conscience. And so instead she lived with it, had learned to, not altogether unsuccessfully either. But occasionally it reared up inside her, reminding her, taunting her. And yesterday, seeing Evie in that state, it had returned with a spiteful vengeance, to the point where she'd been unable to look her in the eyes.

Una watches as Jim takes a sip of whiskey from his glass.

'Brandon has been arrested,' she says, sitting down on the edge of the sofa and looking at him gravely.

'What?' Jim sits up immediately, almost sloshing the whiskey onto the sofa with the momentum. 'Brandon? Arrested? What on earth for?'

Una sighs. 'Oh God. It's a terrible mess. Evie thinks

Brandon might've been' – she can barely stomach saying the words aloud – 'abusing Libby, you know, *sexually* abusing her. The police took him in because it transpires he lied about where he was on the night of the dinner party, and about the phone call. He was picked up on CCTV at that bar – The Chapel or whatever it's called – was seen talking to a man there, the same man Libby was seen talking to a few days earlier... God only knows what's going on but it doesn't look good...'

Jim is upright now. 'No... no...' he says over and over again, rubbing his temples with his thumb and forefingers. 'Brandon hasn't got anything to do with this... This is insane... They can't have arrested him; he's just a boy... He didn't kill her, he didn't kill Libby, it's not possible. Oh God...'

Una watches as her husband unravels. He looks so distressed that she instinctively reaches for his hand.

'I know... I know... it's just awful, all of it. I mean, I can't believe it myself, but then Evie told me, well...' Her voice lowers an octave. 'The police found something in his bedroom, in the drawer while they were searching the house...'

'Found what?' Jim drains the dregs of his glass, goes over to the cabinet and pours himself another whiskey.

'Oh Jim, do you really think that's such a good idea...' Una is careful to keep her tone light. She can see that her husband is on edge and doesn't want to nag; it might cause him to flip.

He repeats the question. 'Found *what exactly?*'

'A pair of her knickers... used underwear.' She drops her head, doesn't want to think about it.

Bizarrely, Jim starts to laugh, a manic, horrible sound. Una stares at him in shock, wonders if he's having some sort of breakdown.

'It's not funny,' she says, horrified by his reaction. 'I mean, what if he *is* guilty? I don't want to believe it myself or even think such a thing – Brandon's a lovely boy, we've known him his whole life, been on holidays together, birthdays, Christmases... and I can't believe for a second he would ever do something so... so depraved... so awful. She was his sister! But... but you have to admit, it doesn't look great, does it? Him lying about where he was and... her underwear... the man at The Chapel? Maybe he's involved somehow... after all, we both know he was jealous of her, or so Evie has always said anyway, and they were never exactly close, were they, like a real brother and sister?'

Jim is still laughing, shaking his head. 'They've got it wrong,' he says. 'This is all so bloody wrong!'

'She was pregnant too,' Una says quickly. 'Evie told me yesterday. They did an autopsy and... Oh God, Jim, Libby was *pregnant.*'

She watches as the glass slides from his grasp, sees it happen almost in slow motion. It bounces onto the carpet, the contents forming a dark brown pool on the pristine cream Axminster. She's not long had it cleaned.

'Jim!' Suddenly she feels frightened, not of him but *for* him.

'How... how...'

'How what?' Una bends down to pick up the glass, but he snatches it up before she makes it, goes and pours himself another.

'How pregnant was she?'

Una doesn't move for a moment. Sighs before sitting back down on the sofa.

'I don't know exactly. Not very – eight or nine weeks, something like that... Poor Evie is in absolute shock. She had no idea, no idea that Libby even had a boyfriend, let alone that she was having sex and... taking drugs apparently too...'

He's laughing again, shaking his head and muttering. Maybe he's drunk.

'I mean *Libby*... she wasn't that kind of girl, was she? She and Evie were close... I think that's what's upset her the most, that Libby kept it all from her.'

'Ha! And the bloody rest!' Jim shouts, making her jump.

Before Una can ask him what he means, Evie's and Tom's faces appear on the TV screen.

'Turn it up,' she says, reaching for the remote. 'They're on, look, they're on the news... the appeal...'

They watch in silence as the policewoman addresses the camera; someone called Superintendent Gwendoline Archer, a formidable-looking woman with notably good hair and teeth. She's explaining how Libby was found, how she was bludgeoned to death in 'the most savage attack'. CCTV footage of a man appears on screen and she's asking for people to come forward, to help identify him.

The camera switches to Tom. Una watches, almost too scared to breathe, as he asks for the public's help in catching Libby's killer, his 'beautiful, talented daughter with a bright future ahead of her'. The camera switches to Evie, her gaunt face and sunken cheeks. Her eyes look grey and puffy, the pain in them practically transmitting through the TV into their living room.

'Libby was an angel, my beautiful angel, my only daughter; my only child has been taken from us in the most terrible way. She was loving, and kind, bright as a star... wasn't she?' She turns towards Tom and he squeezes her arm, lowering his head lightly onto her shoulder for a second.

'She was so loved by everyone who knew her...' Evie's voice sounds low and hoarse. She looks almost unrecognisable. 'If anyone knows anything, knows who did this, why they did this to my little girl, why they took her from us... please... please come forward and contact the police. Please.' The camera pans in close to Evie's face, red raw with tear stains. 'Imagine if it was your child, your own daughter... someone somewhere must know something, must know what happened... If it was you, if you did this, please, I'm begging you, begging you as a mother... as a human being, ple—'

'Turn it off, Una.' Jim stands suddenly. 'I can't bear to watch it; I just can't bear it.'

Una ignores him, unable to take her eyes from the TV. A photo of Libby flashes up on screen, her beautiful face smiling back at them. She really had been a stunning little thing, so young, so beautiful, and such a talented girl too. It was all just so sad, so horrendously sad. Una had loved that girl too, adored her like she'd been her own. She had always hoped that one day she'd have a daughter just like her, prayed to the gods that she too could be gifted such a wonderful child. But when she'd accepted that this would never happen, Libby had become even more special to her she supposed... the daughter she never had, never *could* have.

'TURN THE FUCKING THING OFF!' Jim snatches the remote from Una's hands and shuts off the TV.

'Jim!' Una can feel she's going to burst into tears at any moment. 'What the hell is wrong with you? Tell me what's going on, what's got into you? Why are you behaving like this? I'm really worried about you, you're—'

The doorbell rings and she cuts off to go and answer it, wiping her eyes with her fingertips.

It's the police. She recognises one of them from the night of the dinner party, that fateful awful night...

'Mrs Hemmings? Una Hemmings?'

'Yes?'

'I'm DC Parker and this is DC Mitchell.'

'Yes, yes, I recognise you,' Una says, doing her best to muster up a small smile.

'Can we come in?'

'Of course,' she says, ushering them into the hallway. 'Have you got some news about Libby? We've just seen Evie and Tom on the news, the appeal for witnesses. It was almost unbearable to watch,' she blathers. 'This whole thing is a nightmare, it really is... we've known the Draytons for over twenty-three years, you know – they're our best friends –

and for something like this to happen to them, it's just tragic, you know, tragic, we're all in such shock. Jim, my husband, he's taken it particularly hard and—'

'Actually, it's your husband we've come to talk to, Mrs Hemmings. Is he in?' the male officer interjects.

'Jim? Yes,' she says, a sliver of unease settling upon her. 'He's through there, in the living room.'

They begin to walk towards the door.

'Why do you want to talk to him?' she asks, her unease increasing with each step.

'Jim?' The young policeman addresses him as he walks into the living room. 'Dr Jim Hemmings?'

He nods. 'Yes, that's me.' His tone sounds weary. He drains his whiskey glass and places it on the side table.

'Jim, we'd like you to accompany us down to the station to answer a few questions. Would that be OK?'

'What?' Una is looking at them and Jim simultaneously. 'Questions about what? What's going on?' A feeling of dread engulfs her like flames.

'It's OK.' The female officer turns to her. 'We just need to ask your husband a few questions, Mrs Hemmings, about the night Libby was killed. Clear a few things up.'

'Can't you ask them here? Why does he have to go down to the station?' She can hear the panic in her own voice, suddenly wonders if there's a police car outside and if the neighbours are curtain twitching.

'It's just a routine thing, Mrs Hemmings; it's better if your husband comes down to the station.'

Jim is already putting his coat on without objection. He's not speaking. Why does it feel to her like he was expecting this? Why doesn't he appear alarmed or shocked or outraged?

'It's OK, Una,' he finally says, gently touching her arm with his fingers. 'It's OK.'

She blinks at her husband as a thousand questions explode like a mushroom cloud inside her head.

'Oh God, Jim.' She looks at him, fighting back tears. 'What have you *done*?'

EIGHTEEN

DAN

'We've had to release Brandon Drayton, PFI,' I address the tired faces of my team in the incident room to low murmurs and groans. We've all been at it for almost three days straight now and frustrations are beginning to show, not least my own, although I'm careful to conceal them. It's my job to keep momentum going, keep the team upbeat.

I gulp back some hot, sweet black coffee that Davis has thoughtfully brought me from the machine. I reckon at this rate, if they cut me open, I'd bleed neat Nescafe.

'I know, I know.' I feel their disappointment. I'd have liked it to be as cut-and-dried with 'the jealous brother did it', but the more time goes on, the more uneasy I'm beginning to feel about this whole case – and about who Libby Drayton really was. It's quickly transpiring that she wasn't quite as innocent and naïve as her parents believed and regrettably that (empty) gut of mine tells me there's more to come.

'Davis...' I nod for her to take over. My voice is hoarse and scratchy through exhaustion and I need to rest it – there's a lot to get through.

'Well, Brandon claims that Libby came to him some weeks

before her murder asking him to help her procure drugs – and we're not just talking for personal use either; we're looking at a fairly substantial amount. He says she threatened to blackmail him when he refused, threatened to tell his parents he'd dropped out of uni – something they wouldn't be best pleased about. Clearly, there was no love lost between them. In fact, we got the distinct impression that they hated each other. In interview, Brandon referred to Libby as "a calculating, manipulative, psychopathic bitch", said she had the parents totally fooled, that they believed she was this role-model daughter, grade-A student, sensible, butter-wouldn't-melt type – but what they didn't know was that behind the façade, she was frequenting bars, fraternising with men and, it would seem, dabbling in drugs.'

'Well, boss, you'll be happy to know that we've got a name already, the guy from The Chapel on the CCTV,' Mitchell pipes up. 'Phones have been off the hook since the Draytons' appeal this afternoon – and it looks as though we've come up trumps.'

'Go on, Mitchell...' My heart begins to gallop in my chest, aided and abetted by the caffeine.

'Cody Phillips, twenty-eight, small-time drug dealer from South London – pretty low down on the food chain by all accounts – and a regular at The Chapel.'

I recall the manager, Dick, telling Davis and I how he didn't recognise him and smile to myself. I'm not naturally vindictive but I might just have him nicked anyway for obstructing a murder enquiry – and for being a misogynistic, unhelpful bastard.

'He has previous for possession and with intent to supply, plus possession of an offensive weapon, and GBH. There's an APB out on him now, boss, and uniform are checking his known addresses.'

'Brilliant – that's fantastic news.' This is a shot in the arm. I've got a feeling this Cody fella could be a vital missing link.

Davis continues: 'Brandon admits that he followed Libby the night of the murder, but when he tried to catch up with her down the path in the woods, she wasn't there. So he headed to The Chapel, assuming that's where he would find her. He wanted to tell her to back off, that he knew she was up to no good. He was asking punters if she'd been in – if they knew her – and that's why he's seen talking to Phillips on the CCTV. He never got his name apparently, but Brandon claims Phillips asked him why he was asking after Libby, and he told him he was her half-brother – and to stay away from her, for his own good, and that she was, in his own words, evil.'

'But that gives him a window,' Harding says. 'He could've killed her, then made his way to The Chapel as part of an alibi. Sounds like he had motive – and enough time.'

'Only there wasn't a drop of blood on him,' I interject. 'The nature of the murder as we know was pretty brutal. He'd have been covered in her blood – it would've been all over him – and both Evie and Tom corroborate that the clothes he left the house in that night were the same ones he returned in, not a speck of anything on them – and CCTV at The Chapel seems to back this up. CSI found nothing at the scene. He'd have had to have an identical outfit to change into – trainers, T-shirt, jacket, jeans... replicas – and he would've needed to dump the bloodied clothes somewhere and wash up before going to The Chapel.'

'Well, you'll be pleased to know that forensics are down at The Chapel now, gov – they've sealed the place off.'

I think of Dick again and the inconvenience this will cause him and can't help feeling a touch of malicious glee.

'Plus,' I add, 'his demeanour on CCTV and when he returned home... he wasn't agitated, didn't seem particularly nervous... not like someone who'd just bludgeoned his little sister to death with a rock anyway. His clothes are with forensics but I'm pretty sure they'll come back clean.'

'What about the underwear, boss?' Baylis asks. 'Libby's used underwear that was found in his bedroom drawer?'

I open my palms. 'Brandon claims she planted them there deliberately, that she had some kind of plan to stitch him up, wanted him out of the way and to get back at him for refusing to help her. It was no secret that Evie had a tricky relationship with Brandon, and Libby knew it wouldn't take much for her to believe the worst of him.'

'Jesus, that's pretty calculating,' Baylis says. 'And do you believe him?'

I gulp back some more of the hot black liquid that's become my life fuel these past few days. It tastes bitter and sweet, which pretty much sums up my mood. Davis glances at me, seemingly as keen to know my thoughts as Baylis.

'It's looking more and more possible,' I say carefully. 'Clearly, there was more to Libby Drayton than met the eye.'

'Do you think her death was drug-related? They found Xanax in her system, right, the autopsy?' Parker joins in. 'Maybe she developed a drug habit, an addiction, got involved with the wrong people... Maybe she owed them money and that's what got her killed.'

I shake my head. It's a sensible assumption from a sensible and promising PC, but my instincts tell me that's not why she's lying on a mortuary slab right now – that it's something else, something more complex, more personal.

'If she owed money to a dealer then they might've put the frighteners on her, roughed her up a bit, scared her into paying up, but to bludgeon a seventeen-year-old girl to death? We can't rule it out but... none of her friends we've spoken to corroborate that she was a drug user; in fact, they all say she was pretty anti-drugs.'

'Yeah, and she had a healthy bank balance in her account,' Mitchell says. 'In fact, she had more than I've got in mine!'

'Well, that wouldn't be too difficult on our salary,' Harding snorts and the team titters.

'What's interesting is that in the past couple of months there's been at least three transfers of quite substantial amounts into her account.' Mitchell hands me some statements from her desk, has circled the transactions. 'There are three recent deposits of a thousand pounds each.'

Suddenly I'm reminded of the night of Libby's murder, when I'd spoken to the Draytons about what she'd been wearing when she disappeared. They'd reeled off a list of designer gear: Gucci, Balenci something or other – top names, expensive brands. I'd assumed at the time that she must have had a job but Evie had said otherwise, that she got an allowance, so where was she getting the money to buy all this stuff? It couldn't all be from her allowance surely.

'Look who the transfer comes from.' Mitchell nods at the statement.

I look at it – Mr T. A. Drayton. She raises an eyebrow. 'Her dad, Tom.'

'Evie did say they gave her a monthly allowance.'

'A thousand pounds a month, that's a pretty generous allowance for a seventeen-year-old, don't you think, even with their money? And what's more, referencing back through her past statements, it seems that her usual allowance was only £350 a month, and then, a couple of months before her murder, it suddenly jumps to £1,000 a month.'

My brain starts to tick over. I can see that Mitchell's is too because she has that enigmatic look I've come to recognise, a look that suggests she's onto something.

'So, I've done a bit of digging into Tom Drayton's background – mandatory stuff really.'

'And?'

'Might be nothing, boss, but some years back, a former employee of Drayton's filed a complaint against him for sexual harassment, someone by the name of Tina Molten. It went to a tribunal and he was eventually acquitted. It wasn't left there, however; *he* then took *her* to court and sued her for slander – and won.'

The ticks in my head are getting louder.

'Possible vendetta?'

I nod. 'Worth pursuing. Dig a little deeper – you have an address for this Tina woman?'

'I'm onto it, gov.'

'Nice work, Mitchell.'

Often in murder cases, when I ask people if they know of anyone who may want to harm their loved one – anyone who may hold some kind of grudge or reason for wanting them out of the picture – it's almost always an unequivocal 'no'. But then you start to dig, to peel back those layers like an onion, like an archaeologist brushing away thousands of years of dirt, layer upon layer to uncover a rare artefact. In my entire career investigating murders, I've never encountered a victim who had an entirely clean past, and by this, I mean sometimes they weren't even aware of having an adversary – a former disgruntled employee, a secretly jealous friend or a greedy relative they'd always thought highly of. People who bear grudges – particularly covert ones – are not to be underestimated.

I turn to Parker. 'So, I believe we've brought Hemmings in for a chat?'

'Yes, sir... sorry, boss,' he corrects himself. He remembered. He's a quick learner.

'At the appeal today, Evie Drayton mentioned to Superintendent Archer that Hemmings left the house on the night of the dinner party and was gone for the best part of an hour – said he had to sort out the alarm down at St Saviour's GP surgery; he's a partner there. When he returned, he had a scratch on his face, told the other members of the party that he'd had problems switching it off and that he'd needed to call the local police station for assistance.'

My ears prick up like a dog's. 'And this has been corroborated?'

Parker raises his eyebrows, almost triumphantly. 'No call ever came through, gov, no record of anyone going to assist. We're taking DNA samples now. He's in interview room four. So let me know whenever you're ready for him, boss.'

I glance at Davis and then back at Parker. 'I was born ready.'

NINETEEN

SEPTEMBER. LIBBY

'I told you I wouldn't let you down, didn't I?' She throws herself onto the bed, swigs the bottle of beer she has in her hand, spilling a little onto the duvet. She doesn't suppose it matters. This place is a shit hole, a grubby bedsit somewhere in the deepest bowels of South London.

'Watch it,' he says. 'That's clean on today.'

She pulls a face, looks around the untidy room with barely concealed disgust. 'So, this is where you call home, is it?'

He's rolling a spliff at the table, has his back to her. 'What, not posh enough for you, sweetheart?'

'Not posh enough for a rat,' she retorts. 'But don't worry, you'll be out of here soon enough. *We'll* be out of here.'

She takes another swig of beer, watches him from the bed.

'We?'

'Well, you can't get rid of me now, can you? You need me.' She can tell he's smiling even though he has his back to her. 'Besides, I know too much.'

'OK. I admit it, I'm impressed. The girl done good, came up with the goods, just like she said.' He throws the large plastic ziplock bag containing the drugs onto the bed. 'So what did you do, rob a chemist?'

She curls her feet up underneath her, rests her head onto her elbow.

'Even better than that,' she says, grinning.

'Oh yeah?'

'Yeah. And there's plenty more where that came from, *plenty*. Once we've knocked that lot out, I'll be able to get more.' Frankly, it had been like taking candy from a baby.

He turns to look at her then, licks the ends of the cigarette paper. 'Are you serious?'

'Deadly.' She smiles at him. 'As long as you keep selling it, then I can keep supplying it, and then you'll be able to move out of this dump and we can get a place together, an apartment somewhere with a concierge and a gym and a rooftop swimming pool, somewhere overlooking the Thames...'

'Easy, tiger, we've only known each other five minutes and you're talking about moving in together. We haven't even' – he nods at the bed – 'you know – yet.'

'So what are you waiting for then?' She looks at him with a lascivious grin, stretches herself out across the bed provocatively. 'You're the big man now, Cody.'

He shakes his head, laughs a little as he lights the spliff. 'You really are serious, aren't you? So are you going to tell me how you got all this or am I supposed to guess?'

She sits up, tucks her knees into her chest and looks at him sweetly. 'What you don't know can't hurt you. All you need to know is that there's an endless supply.'

He sucks on the joint, pops a beer open and leans forward to chink her own. 'You're something else, do you know that?'

'I do.' She knocks his bottle with hers, feels pleased with herself.

'Here,' he says, pulling open a drawer under the small

rickety old table and pulling out her Pandora bracelet, 'before I forget to give it back.'

He throws it to her on the bed.

'Why don't you come here and put it on for me.'

He laughs. 'It don't suit me. Tried it on already.'

'Very funny.' He thinks he's clever. Maybe he is. But she's cleverer by half.

'Where do you even live? What do you do? I know nothing about you. I'm still not convinced you're not undercover filth.'

'Oh, I'm filth all right.' She takes her top off, flings herself back down onto the bed. He's laughing and she's pleased that she amuses him.

He acquiesces, joins her on the bed and begins to undress himself. She inspects his body carefully, a body that is predominantly covered in tattoos, black ink scrawled all over him like a canvas. She's read somewhere that tattoos are a form of self-harm and she deduces, this being true, that Cody must therefore be racked with deep unresolved psychological issues. Still, they are impressive, and he lacks nothing if not dedication to turning himself into a walking work of art.

The sex is quick and rough, almost painful as he flips her onto her front, pulling at her hair, biting the back of her neck. The encounter lacks tenderness but not passion. Harry had been 'tender', all scattergun kisses and gentle soft strokes, and it had repulsed her – at least this way she actually feels *something*.

Her chest begins to heave as she feels the power of him, his strength, his *anger* as he thrusts himself into her, sweat from his body beginning to drip down onto her skin. In this moment, she realises that he possesses the physical strength to kill her should he want and choose to – in a split turn of a second he could wrap his hands around her neck and crush her windpipe, extinguish her life, but instead of feeling vulnerable by such a dark thought, she feels exhilarated, her climax closing in...

He lights a cigarette afterwards and she waves the smoke

away. She has always hated the smell, which is even more intense in his poky little bedsit. They're silent for a moment.

'What's your first childhood memory?' She turns to him, props her head onto her elbow and wafts the smoke away from her again.

'What?'

'Your earliest memory as a child... or a vivid one will do. You've probably fucked your long-term memory anyway with all those drugs...'

He laughs, sniffs. 'Yeah, I probably have. But sometimes there are things you don't want to remember.'

'Like what?'

He glances at her. She can see he doesn't want to answer her and that the subject has immediately put him ill at ease, but she'll press until he does.

'I don't really want to talk about my childhood,' he says flatly. 'All you need to know was that it was shit. My mother was an alcoholic and a drug user, my dad did the off before I was even born, and I spent the best part of it in and out of care and foster homes – like I said, shit.'

She watches him intensely, can sense his emotional discomfort bouncing off the four walls of his shitty bedsit.

'I'm sorry.' She touches his arm. That's what people do, isn't it, when they're sorry?

He visibly swallows; she can see the movement of his prominent Adam's apple. The question has triggered an emotional reaction that he's clearly at pains to try to hide. *How exciting.*

'Yeah, well, don't be. It taught me that you've only got yourself to rely upon in this life and that ain't no bad thing, trust me.'

'Do you hate your mother? Do you hate her for being an alcoholic, a druggie, for neglecting you, leaving you in care, for not caring enough?'

He swallows again as she begins to trace one of the tattoos

on his arm, a scythe with droplets of blood spilling from it, the weapon of the Grim Reaper.

'I don't want to talk about my mother,' he says, rising abruptly from the bed and pulling his boxers on. 'Why don't you tell me about yours instead? You're always asking me questions... answer one yourself.'

'I thought you'd never ask,' she says, stretching back onto the grubby sheets he claims are clean on. '*My* earliest childhood memory is of my mother trying to kill me.'

'Eh?' He turns to her briefly.

'I could've only been around four or five years old at the time. She pushed me down some concrete steps while we were on holiday and I fell, smashing my skull open.'

He's staring at her now, his eyes wide. 'You're bullshitting me.'

She shrugs. 'It's true. I remember the feeling of the hot sun, the smell of the beach and sand on my skin, the ice cream I was holding, melting onto my fingers, sticky... I recall the feel of her hands on my shoulders, the force of the shove... and the scent of her perfume – Poison by Christian Dior, strong and sweet... I've hated that smell ever since.'

He blinks at her. 'Your *own* mother tried to kill you as... a *baby*? And you remember this? At four years old? Nah...' He shakes his head. 'You're bullshitting me.'

She smiles. 'I'm not. I remember it vividly, flashes and snippets, sensations... She had post-natal depression allegedly, stupid bitch, sent her off her head apparently. I was too young to articulate what she'd done, but I do remember it. I remember being pushed, the smell of that perfume...'

He looks sideways at her, unsure.

'I've never told anyone that before,' she says. 'I've never wanted to.'

He shakes his head. 'Man, that is some fucked-up shit...' He starts to build another spliff. 'Do you want a Zanni?'

She looks at him blankly.

'A Xanax – it'll help with that memory, trust me.'

She shrugs and he throws her one from the bag on the table.

'Have you ever wanted to kill anyone?' She swallows it, is curious to know how it feels, if it will change anything, if it will stop the dark thoughts and the headaches...

He laughs, swigs his beer. 'Yeah, daily.'

'I'm serious. Have you ever thought about killing anyone?'

He lights the spliff, takes a large toke, his face disappearing in a huge plume of fragrant smoke. 'Thought about it, yes... I suppose so. I've wanted people dead.'

'Your mother?'

'Yeah... I dunno, I guess so. But there's a difference between wishing someone dead and actually killing them, you know – like twenty years inside difference.'

'But if there wasn't... if there was no way of getting caught, of any repercussions' – she raises her eyes – 'then would you do it? *Could* you murder someone?'

He blows a smoke ring above his head, looks up at the water-stained ceiling, the peeling paint above.

'Probably, maybe... I dunno, it's not really something I've thought about much.'

'What about for gain; monetary gain? How much would you kill for?'

'Fuck me, this is a weird conversation.' He pulls his chin into his neck. 'Why you asking me this?'

She shrugs one shoulder. 'Just hypothetically, if, for example, my parents and brother died, I would inherit everything; they're rich, they have a huge house, cars and two other properties, one in Portugal and another in London they rent out. My dad has a successful business and plenty of savings. I reckon they're worth a couple of million at least; maybe three, four, maybe even more.'

She watches him, can tell he thinks she's playing devil's

advocate, or maybe that she's trying to trip him up. He's looking at her suspiciously.

'Are you saying you want to kill your parents? That you want *me* to kill your family?'

She curls her knees up into her chest. 'I'm just having fun, asking questions, you know, like the game, "Would you ever...?"'

He relaxes, sucks on the spliff and passes it to her. She shakes her head. She doesn't really smoke weed – it's a bum's drug.

'You're one weird little fucker, do you know that?'

She does. But she also knows that he's fascinated with her already. His body language tells her as much.

'Well, would you?'

'Would I what?'

'Kill people for money, a lot of money...?'

He switches the TV on. He's not taking the question seriously.

'That sort of money?' He shrugs. 'I'd consider it maybe, if it was foolproof.' He turns the volume up a little, relaxes back onto the squalid single bed. 'You should chill, you know, let the Zanni take effect, relax.'

She sighs softly, rests her head on his chest. There's work to be done here but she's hopeful. *He's definitely the one.*

'How would you do it?' she says after a pause.

He's watching TV now, his mind elsewhere. 'Do what?'

'Kill them?'

'Who? Your folks?'

'Or anyone, yes.'

'Why would you even want them dead... I mean, I know you said about your mum... but what's your dad done, and was it a brother you said you have?'

'Half-brother,' she corrects him. 'And he's been sexually abusing me since I was a child and my father knew and turned a blind eye. They've never cared about me, none of them. A mother who tried to kill me, a brother who molested me and a father who let it happen.'

He switches the TV off then. Sits up and looks at her. She can feel the effects of the pill he's given her start to take effect. She feels warmer, softer, like her bones are made of marshmallow. But her thoughts still feel the same.

'Jesus, babe.' He puts his hand on her arm and she knows by this small gesture that she's got to him, touched something in him that he can relate to on a painful level.

Her phone beeps, startling her, and she rolls over to reach it from the floor next to the bed.

'Holy fuck,' she whispers aloud as she reads it, sitting bolt upright.

It's a message from Katie. Katie hasn't really spoken to her since the night she met Cody at The Chapel. The night that big-mouthed bitch Georgina had told her that she'd driven past Harry's house during the early hours one morning and seen Libby sneaking out of it. She'd vociferously denied it of course, said that she'd been mistaken, that Georgina was a liar out to cause trouble, to ruin their friendship because she was jealous.

'How could you? You've known for ages how much I like him, Libby,' Katie had whined down the phone during the tense conversation. 'You can have anyone you want... why him? When you know how I felt, how I feel about him... why would you do that to me? You've never shown the slightest bit of interest in Harry... you've always told me you thought he was "a dickhead".'

She'd spent a good ten minutes on the phone to Katie denying and protesting her innocence, maybe not enough to one hundred per cent convince her that Georgina was lying, but enough to put doubt in her mind and undermine her version of events.

Still, Katie had returned none of her calls since.

Harry is dead. 💀 He killed himself last night. His sister Emily found him hanging in his bedroom. I think it was because of him getting into trouble with the police and his dad dying and everything. I wish he had talked to me. 😢 I can't stop crying and am heartbroken 💔. Did you know?

Fear prickles her skin like needles, adrenalin rushing through her. She is frozen for a moment, her mind starting to race. Had Harry told anyone about them? He'd gone silent after she'd dumped him, and she'd thought that was the end of it, hadn't given him any more thought. During their 'relationship' they'd been communicating on a secret pay-as-you-go phone and, as agreed, they always deleted every message they'd sent to each other afterwards. Would there be a trace? Would the police look into his suicide? Investigate? She doubts it. He was depressed, on medication, emotionally fragile. She can't be traced back to him, can she? Only perhaps on Katie and big Gob Georgina's unfounded accusations, and even then there's no proof, no evidence, she can simply deny, deny, deny...

'Fucking hell, Harry!' she says aloud. 'You stupid idiot!'

But as she says it, the fear begins to dissipate into something else, a feeling she hasn't experienced before, one she doesn't recognise. It's not glee to be exact, not euphoria, though it's edging towards it – more of a sense of power, power that she has held such sway and influence on someone's decision to choose between life and death, that she alone is capable of creating such emotion in someone else that they would take their own life because of her. *How... intoxicating.*

'Bad news?' Cody asks casually, nodding at the phone.

She can feel the effects of the Xanax much more potently now mixed with her adrenalin. It's not an unpleasant sensation, just an unfamiliar one.

'Nothing to worry yourself about.' She smiles, placing her phone back down on the floor. 'What's on telly?'

TWENTY

JIM

What you cannot change, you must accept. These are the words running through Jim Hemmings' mind as he sits in the airless, soulless box room waiting to be interviewed by the detectives. But the mind is a powerful governess with its own agenda, and as hard and as desperately as he tries not to let them through, other thoughts, dark and despairing, slip between the hairline cracks in the protective walls he's tried to erect around himself.

'Dr Hemmings? Jim Hemmings? I'm Detective Inspector Dan Riley, and this is DS Lucy Davis. Thank you for coming in. I know you're a busy man.'

He stands as they enter the room, shakes their hands respectively. He remembers them both from that fateful evening, remembers immediately warming to Riley. Whatever else he now was, he had always been a good judge of character – nearly always anyway.

They take a seat opposite him and he returns to his own with a looming sense of a fait accompli.

'We wanted to ask you a few questions about the night of the dinner party at the Draytons' house – the night Libby was murdered... There's just a few things we need to clear up so hopefully this won't take too long.' Riley smiles at him apologetically, as though he's sorry he has to take up his time. 'The DNA sample we took from you, it's purely for elimination process, you understand – we're not accusing you of anything or suggesting that you're guilty of—'

'It's OK, really,' he interrupts. 'Whatever you need...'

Detective Riley gives a small smile of gratitude.

'So that night... during the dinner party... you left the Draytons' house for a period of time, said something about an alarm going off down at St Saviour's Surgery, the surgery you work at, and that as a designated key holder you had to go and switch it off. Is that correct?'

Jim nods. His throat feels tight.

'You left at approximately 8 p.m. and were gone for around an hour?'

He nods again, unable to speak.

'You mentioned,' the female detective interjects, 'something about needing police assistance to turn the alarm off. That you'd struggled with it...'

She looks down at a piece of paper on the table then back up at him. Jim closes his eyes.

'Only when we checked this, Dr Hemmings, there was no record of any call being logged and no attendance by police recorded at the property. Can you explain this?'

Jim exhales. He's rehearsed this moment over and over inside his head, what to say, how to explain it all, but now isn't sure where to start.

'I lied.' The words come from him almost compulsively. He has never been an accomplished liar.

He watches as the expressions on the detectives' faces shift, the briefest exchange of a glance between them. There's a pause.

'And why did you lie, Dr Hemmings?' Detective Riley says evenly.

Jim's face falls into his hands. 'I wanted her to stop,' he says eventually, dragging his fingers down his cheeks. 'I just wanted it all to stop.'

'By "her" you mean Libby? What did you want her to stop, Jim? I can call you that, can't I?' Riley leans into him across the table a little, but not so far that it feels intrusive.

Jim exhales loudly in a bid to expunge the flux of adrenalin that is making his breathing laboured.

'Yes... Libby. I... I...'

'Take your time Jim. It's OK...'

But he knows it isn't – it isn't OK, any of it.

'It was all planned,' he blurts out. 'I... I realise that now of course,' he stammers.

Riley maintains eye contact with him. 'Tell me what happened, Jim.'

'She came to see me.' His voice sounds thin and reed-like, quite unlike his own. 'At the surgery... some months ago now... said she had a stomach complaint.' He pauses. 'But that wasn't the real reason she'd paid me a visit at all.'

'So what was, Jim?' the female detective says.

He shakes his head. He doesn't want to say it. He knows how it will sound, how it will make him look.

'She... she... came to seduce me.' He says it quickly then looks up, attempts to gauge their reactions. 'Look, I realise how that sounds... how it looks... a pretty young woman like Libby...' He gives a little incredulous snort. 'I mean, look at me... but you have to understand...' Jim's voice trails off. Who is he kidding? They'll *never* understand. He doesn't even really understand himself.

'Go on...' Riley says.

'It was all about getting drugs at the end of the day. That's what she really wanted, drugs... And I'd had a thing you see, with Evie, many, many moons ago now, while we were at university together, before she met Tom, before I met Una. Evie was my first love...'

His memory wanders back two decades, to the first time he'd seen her, her dazzling smile as it had lit up the room, the scent of her perfume leaving an indelible imprint on his heart and soul.

'She reminded me so much of her mother, that day when she came to my surgery...'

Riley is watching him intently.

'Look, I'm not a pervert, Detective Riley, I... I... can't explain it... but somehow she just knew what to say, how to get under my skin... all those memories resurrected.' He feels engulfed by hopelessness as he attempts to explain the events of that afternoon, their conversation in his office, how she had waited for him by his car and what had taken place in it between them.

'I was racked with self-loathing and disgust afterwards – you have to believe me when I say this. I mean Libby was... she was my goddaughter, the child of my best friends... I was old enough to be her father...' He wrestles back the guilt and shame he feels, but the emotion is simply too powerful to overcome and he buries his face in his hands again. 'God help me.'

Riley graciously affords him a moment to compose himself before he continues.

'Did you follow her that night, Jim? Did you make the excuse that the alarm had gone off and go after Libby?'

'Yes,' he replies quickly – there was no turning back now. Maybe that unrelenting ache in his chest will soften if he just tells them the truth. 'She started blackmailing me, you see. The... the... *encounter* that took place inside my car... she covertly filmed it on her phone. She said she'd go to the police, tell them I'd been... that I'd been *abusing* her.' He shakes his head. 'She threatened to make the video viral, send it to Una, to my colleagues...'

Images of their sexual encounter flash up inside his mind, making him feel sick.

'She knew I had access to drugs, you see. As a trusted partner at the practice, I have access to the pharmacy.'

'Did she tell you why she wanted them, the drugs?'

Jim shakes his head.

'She wouldn't tell me, though I suspected they weren't for her. Libby never touched drugs, or at least not that I knew of... she wasn't that kind of girl...' But as he says it, he realises ironically that he had no idea what kind of girl she really was at all.

'The scratch,' the female detective says. 'Witnesses report that you returned to the Draytons' house with a scratch on your face. Can you tell us how that came about, Jim?'

He sighs. 'I followed her,' he says, pinching at his nose with a thumb and forefinger – it's started to run. 'The night of the party, I made the excuse about the alarm so that I could go after her, try and talk to her, to reason with her, make her see sense. They do audit checks, you know, at the surgery, and it would come to light that drugs were missing. There would be an enquiry, an investigation and... I just wanted to talk to her.'

'So you caught up with her, down the path?'

'Yes. And I was begging her, pleading with her to stop all this nonsense, told her that it would ruin my life, my career... that people would be hurt, Una, her parents...'

'And what did she say, Jim?' Riley asks. 'Did she listen to you?'

He looks up at the detective. 'She *laughed* at me.' He winces as he recalls the moment she'd mocked his despair, the sound of her mirth echoing through the woods musically. 'She told me I should've thought of that before I'd...'

He drops his head. He can't bring himself to say it. 'Look, I thought if I complied with her, agreed to get her the drugs just once then she would have what she wanted and that would be the end of it. But she kept coming back for more... and I was just so desperate, I didn't want anyone to get hurt; you believe that, don't you? I was trying to protect my wife, my friends, my...'

'Self, Jim? You were trying to protect yourself?'

Jim lowers his eyes. 'Yes,' he says, 'and also myself. I made a mistake, a terrible, dreadful error of judgement, a moment of utter madness. I let myself down, I let everybody down, and I realise it was selfish, to want to protect my career and livelihood, my reputation, my marriage – everything I love and have worked so hard for and dedicated my life to, but...' Jim tries to finish the sentence, but it all just sounds like self-serving excuses and justification, no matter how he tries to explain it.

'Did it make you angry, that Libby had mocked you? Did you become aggressive towards her?'

Jim clenches his fists. 'I'm not going to lie,' he says. 'Lord knows there's been enough of that. In that moment, in that briefest of moments, yes, I wanted to hurt her, to kill her even, but that's all it was, I swear to you, just a fleeting flash of anger, of despair. I would never have hurt her – ever.' He briefly glances at Riley, wonders if he believes him, but his expression is giving nothing away.

'She started to walk away from me and I reached out, grabbed her by the forearm and that's when she swung round and scratched my face.'

Jim recalls the sense of doom he'd felt in that moment, as black as the night that had surrounded him. He'd realised then that there would be no reasoning, no rational discussion and no end to the nightmare.

'So what did you do then?' Riley's voice is respectful but firm – reminiscent of his own when he speaks to his patients.

'I went back to my car,' he says flatly. 'I was shaking, crying, choked up by it all. I thought about ending my own life, Detective, right there and then – swallowing some pills, or running a pipe through the exhaust...'

Jim can feel his eyes welling up and rubs his thumbs into

them in a bid to stop the tears from slipping out. 'I sat there, numb, not knowing what do, what to think, how to begin to resolve such a dreadful mess... I'm not sure how much time passed – five minutes, ten, possibly more. I can't be exact. That's when I heard the scream.'

'A woman's scream?' Riley's eyes are fixed upon him intensely.

'I wasn't sure. I thought that perhaps it might've been a fox at first – there's plenty around the woods.'

'Did you go and investigate?'

'Not immediately,' he says. 'I was too emotional, too over-whelmed by everything... and, well...' Jim shifts in his seat uncomfortably. 'I was scared, I suppose. But eventually I got out of the car and made my way back down the pathway again, using the light on my mobile phone to help me see where I was going. And that's when I found her.'

Jim squeezes his eyes tightly shut, tries to block out the image that has flashed up inside his head. He sucks air in through his teeth, his feet manically tapping the floor.

'Take your time, Jim,' Riley says softly.

'She was lying on the pathway. I Instinctively knew she was dead just by looking at her. I gasped, stumbled backward, I think, almost lost my balance completely.' The tears have come now; he can no longer fight them. 'I dropped down next to her – I remember how cold the ground felt against my knees – and, oh God... oh my God...'

'You're doing really well,' the female detective says encouragingly.

'Her face... I saw the damage to her face, what was left of it.' Jim wipes mucus from his nose. 'I grabbed her wrist, checked for a pulse, but there was nothing.' He shakes his head. 'Nothing at all.'

He looks up at the two pairs of eyes in front of him, unblinking as they hang on his every word. 'I put my ear to her chest but found no heartbeat either. There was nothing I could've done for her; you must understand this.' He looks at each of them respectively. 'I'm a doctor, for Christ's sake. If there had been anything, anything I could've done... but there was no hope – she'd gone.'

Jim exhales loudly, sits back in his seat. There. He's said it now.

'And what happened next?' Riley says.

Jim clutches at his head in distress. 'I went to dial 999, I absolutely swear I was going to call you, call the police but then... Oh good God, forgive me, please forgive me.'

'Then what, Jim?'

He can feel the tension in the room, the pressure of it almost palpable.

'Well, she was dead, wasn't she? I couldn't bring her back. I thought that if I called the police then understandably they would want to know why I was there in the woods and would ask questions. Obviously I realised it would look suspicious, like I had something to hide, which of course I did.' His nerves are causing him to blather. 'And I know it's absurd, I know that now, but at the time I just wasn't thinking rationally, and so I thought that maybe, just maybe, I could pretend that I hadn't seen the body – a body I couldn't bring back to life – and that maybe, just maybe, none of what had happened would come to light and that even if I couldn't spare Evie and Tom the grief of losing their daughter, I could spare them the grief of knowing what had happened between us, about the drugs and the blackmail and the whole abhorrent mess.'

He draws breath; wringing his hands in a bid to stop them from vibrating. 'I know what you're thinking, that I'm a self-serving coward, that I was thinking only of saving myself, but it's simply not true.' But even as he says it, he isn't even convinced himself.

'What did you do then?'

Even now Jim cannot understand why he did what he did next. It was instinctive, he supposes, because he can't remember consciously making the decision.

'I took her by the arms and pulled her further into the woodland. I was terrified, shaking so hard I barely had the strength in me.'

'You *moved* her body?'

'Yes. God forgive me, I did.'

'Why, Jim?' Riley leans towards him, meets his eyes imploringly.

'I... I just don't know,' he says. 'I was in shock, running on adrenalin and fear and panic...'

'Did you interfere with her clothing in any way?' the female detective interjects.

'Undress her, you mean?' Jim feels horrified by the idea but realises he's hardly in a position to take affront. 'Good heavens, no! I think her tights became ripped as I pulled her through the brush, her skirt rolled up around her waist...' He feels nauseous. His confession sounds even more damning spoken aloud than it does inside his head. He's going to go down for murder – he knows it. 'I tried to cover her a little, with leaves and branches, tried to protect her from the elements, from the animals...' He hears how pathetic he sounds, how spineless and weak and pathetic.

'And then what did you do, Dr Hemmings?' Riley says, addressing him formally now.

In that moment Jim realises with such brutal clarity that his life is over – it feels as if he's been cut in half. He looks up from the table. He can barely bring himself to make eye contact with the man in front of him, such is his all-consuming shame.

'And then,' he says, 'I got in my car and went back to the Draytons', just in time to make the second course.'

TWENTY-ONE

EVIE

She has lost all concept of time. Daylight is disappearing outside, casting a dim grey glow through the window. She gauges it's probably around fourish, four thirty, though time is irrelevant. Still, she'll be glad for the changing of the season when it comes; darkness is all she sees around her now.

Libby's bedroom is just how she left it. The bed is half made – a corner of the duvet pulled back, a little crumpled, the cushions mostly upright though one appears disturbed. There's a cardigan draped over the side of the pink velvet tub chair, a pair of trainers abandoned on the floor next to it, the physical remnants of her daughter's haste as she left her bedroom for the last time. Evie vows never to move them, but instead keep them there in that exact position, forever frozen in time. Stood still, like a shrine, a mausoleum.

She pads barefoot over towards the dressing table, an ornate shabby-chic one that Libby herself had chosen, and consciously refrains from looking at herself in the mirror above it. She doesn't want to see her reflection – can't bear to see the person she has become now, broken and bereft, an unkempt, unrecognisable stranger. The police have taken some of Libby's things –

books and clothes and her laptop. They'd scoured her room, rifled through her drawers, her wardrobe and personal things. She knows it's their job; they have to search for evidence, for something that may lead to the reason why any of this has happened, but somehow it has tainted everything.

Evie picks up a bottle of perfume from the dressing table, realises that it's her own, Poison by Christian Dior – her signature scent, or used to be anyway, many moons ago. She wonders why it's here in Libby's room. Libby had always said she hated the smell of it, that it made her feel sick and brought on her headaches. That's why she'd stopped wearing it in the end. She automatically squirts a little onto the back of her hand, brings it up to her face. The smell instantly transports her back to her own youth, to a time when she'd been at university, where she'd met Jim and Una and Tom. Back to carefree days when she'd been shyly hopeful about life, about love and the future, the glorious, exciting future she'd planned for herself that had stretched out before her.

She replaces the bottle back on the dressing table, rearranges it exactly where it was, with the lid next to it, just as her daughter had left it. She runs her fingers along the edge of the table, lightly touches the jewellery box and opens it. The police had returned Libby's Pandora bracelet as soon as possible – she had insisted upon it. Libby had lots of jewellery, some of it precious, most of it costume; junk stuff that reflected the trends, but that particular piece was special. She'd had the bracelet since birth, and it had been modified as she'd grown.

Evie smiles through the tears that begin to drip down onto the wood below, staining the whitewashed surface grey as she touches the myriad charms, each one representing an achievement, a milestone, a birthday, a Christmas, an occasion... there were so many. A teddy bear and a baby shoe Tom had bought her when she'd been born. A birthday candle, a dreamcatcher to ward off childhood nightmares, a sea turtle when she'd first learned to swim, a rainbow, angel wings, a good-luck horseshoe for an exam she'd gone on to pass with flying colours, a ballerina, a tiny piano, an owl, a little birthday gift box and...

Hang on, where was the spinning heart that had 'mother' and 'daughter' engraved on each side, the one she'd bought her for doing so well in piano lessons and, well, simply because she'd wanted to?

She studies them all carefully again, frantically goes through them one by one. No, it's definitely not here; it's missing. She wonders if it's somehow fallen off, come loose after being handled by police. She makes a mental note to ask Dan Riley about it when she next speaks to him; she'll be cross if they've mislaid it – it was the last gift she'd ever given Libby. Evie wraps the bracelet around her wrist and snaps the clasp shut. It's all she has left now.

She sits on the edge of her daughter's roughly made bed. Grief has paralysed her mind these past few days, but gradually it's re-awakening and in turn starting to ask questions. Who did this? Who would want her darling daughter dead? *And what might she have done to make them feel that way?* Someone somewhere knew something. Someone somewhere always does. Nothing is a secret when you really think about it, even if you're the only one keeping it.

Suddenly she thinks about the flowers and condolence cards that are covering half of her driveway. Would there be a clue in them? Killers sometimes leave them, don't they, their 'heartfelt' condolences, hoping to put police off the scent? She stands with purpose. She hasn't been out of the house since it happened. Hasn't opened the door to anyone, hasn't been able to, has left it to Tom to deal with all of that.

She looks out of the window. A majority of the journalists have dispersed now. Clearly enough time has passed. Libby is already yesterday's news – for now, at least.

Tom has brought some of the flowers and condolence cards

into the house, left them in the hallway. She's been unable to touch them until now. But now she feels as if she needs to see them, in case there's something, something the police have missed, something in those cards and flowers that will give her some understanding in all of this. She almost runs downstairs, suddenly propelled by a feeling she can only describe as intuitive. A little out of breath, she stares at the sea of flowers, the blooms of many beginning to curl up at the edges, tinged brown.

She snatches up a random card and reads it; it's from an old acquaintance of theirs... the next, the school and all its pupils, the scrawl, ironically, almost illegible. Like a maniac, she plucks the cards up, reads them and then discards them one by one onto the wooden floor... friends, family, the local shop from up the road, work colleagues, a card from Harry Mendes' mum... that poor woman who lost her husband and son within mere weeks of each other to suicide. She stops and reads it. '*I'm so sorry. Sara and Emily. x*' She places it down onto the side table. Where are the flowers and card from Susan and Katie... Libby's best friend and a woman she's known since they were at antenatal classes together, pregnant and blissfully naïve? Surely they would've sent something...

She opens the front door, starts rifling through the bouquets, looking for Susan and Katie's names to appear, but they don't. Why haven't they sent anything? She feels angry, aggrieved, like they've snubbed her daughter, snubbed *her*.

Paranoia sets in and suddenly she wonders if Katie knows more than she's letting on. She'd told police that she'd had no idea where Libby was going that night, no idea that she had used her as an alibi. She'd claimed they hadn't spoken in a while, which now suddenly strikes her as odd. Had there been a falling out? Libby hadn't mentioned it, but if there was then about what? Surely Libby would've confided in her best friend if she'd been sleeping with someone – if she was pregnant. She and Una had told each other everything when they were younger, confessing all their secrets, but Katie had said there was no boyfriend that she knew of. Was she lying?

Suddenly, she has to know. She'll call Susan. No, better still, she'll go round there, unannounced, catch them off guard. She'll demand to know if Katie is holding something back. She'll know just by looking at her – she's known the girl all her life.

Spurred on by a sense of purpose, Evie runs inside the house and slips some shoes on, grabs her keys, handbag and phone and opens the front door. But then her phone rings.

'Evie? Hi, this is DS Davis, Lucy Davis. Have you got a moment to chat?'

Evie's heartbeat begins to accelerate in her chest.

'I was just going out of the door, but of course,' she says, a little breathless. 'Has... has something happened? Do you have something to tell me?'

'Actually, Evie, yes, I do,' DS Davis says. 'It's about Jim.'

'Jim?' Evie swallows dryly. She immediately senses she won't like what the detective is about to say. 'What about him?'

'He's been arrested,' she says. 'On suspicion of murder.'

TWENTY-TWO

DAN

'I was hoping never to hear that son of a bitch's name ever again!'

Tina Molten – Tom Drayton's ex-employee, who he'd formerly accused of slander – bristles, one hand on her hip, chin raised in defiance as she stands in the kitchen of her small but immaculate apartment.

'I appreciate it was a difficult time in your life, Tina,' I say, 'and I'm sorry to have to rake it all up again, but as I'm sure you've seen on the news, we're investigating the murder of Libby Drayton, Tom Drayton's seventeen-year-old daughter, and we need to get as much background as possible...'

'Background? You'll have your work cut out then!' She gazes out of her kitchen window.

I stare at her. She's attractive, petite with long brown hair and I'd say, in my spectacular lack of accuracy on guessing women's ages, that she's somewhere around her late thirties.

'And yes.' She turns back to face me. 'I did see it on the news.' Her tone is bordering on terse. 'And I feel sorry for the girl, of course, maybe even feel sorry for her mother, but not for *him.*' She hisses the last word. 'Some people might even say it was karma.'

Davis raises an eyebrow. 'Karma for what, Tina?'

'Call me a heartless bitch if you like – I've been called far worse thanks to him – but let me tell you this.' She narrows her eyes. 'That man *ruined* my life; he absolutely *destroyed* it.'

A sense of unease settles upon my empty stomach as I witness the woman's unfettered hatred. It's fair to say that Miss Molten is clearly not Tom Drayton's number one fan.

'You worked with Tom Drayton as his PA at his physio clinic back in 2018? Can you tell us about that? How well did you know the Draytons?'

I cut to the chase because I'm conscious of time. We still have Jim Hemmings in custody and less than twenty-four hours to hang on to him before we charge him with anything – *if* we charge him, that is.

Archer was ecstatic when she heard the news of his arrest, however.

'Marvellous work, Dan,' she'd said, and for a moment I thought she might come round from behind her pristine desk and hug me, which was not an idea I relished – nor one I'm sure she would've either, seeing as though I haven't showered in days. 'We'll get a statement sent out to the press as soon—'

'Ma'am,' I interrupt her with gentle caution, aware I'm about to piss on her fireworks. Admittedly, I used to get a tiny sliver of perverse satisfaction whenever I did this with Woods, my former super, but it's not quite the same with our Gwen here, or 'Cupid' as the team calls her on account of her surname.

'At this stage we don't have enough to charge him with anything...'

She smiles at me but I can tell she's masking the first flutters of irritation. 'Oh come on, Dan. He's confessed to being in an inappropriate relationship with her, says she was blackmailing him with video footage, threatening to show his wife, his colleagues... go public, which would have had devastating consequences for him both personally and professionally. He has a very clear and strong motive.' She draws breath. 'It's obvious what happened...'

'Is it?' Her question makes me wonder how people like Archer reach the lofty heights they do in this line of work, or if by reaching them they forget the very open-mindedness that may well have got them there in the first place.

'Yes, it is.' She clarifies her position in a measured tone while managing to exert her authority at the same time. Suddenly, the rumours circulating around the nick about her being responsible for killing off both her previous husbands don't seem so outlandish.

'He killed her in a fit of rage and panic after she'd been blackmailing him... perhaps he didn't *mean* to kill her; maybe he simply lost it in a moment of madness. Anyway, he'll plead diminished responsibility, no doubt, and as a man of previous good character...'

I look at her, wonder if it's something to do with the swivel chair she's inherited, wonder if somehow my old super's residue has rubbed onto her because it's like I'm having déjà vu and that I'm opposite Woods again – a man who seemed more obsessed with results than the absolute truth, a man who appeared to have forgotten the very fabric of police procedure, eschewing it in favour of the end result and the reflected glory that inevitably brings.

'I believe Hemmings' story,' I say, knowing that it'll go down like the proverbial pork pie at a vegan convention. 'I believe he's telling the truth.'

Her earlier demeanour – affable, convivial and congratulatory – stiffens somewhat. Her hair – not one strand out of place – doesn't move, even as she shakes her head.

'Oh, you do?' she says, rhetorically.

'Yes.'

There's a pause.

'Are you being deliberately contumacious, Dan?'

Contumacious? No idea what it means. She's trying to use fancy words to throw me off balance!

I style it out.

'No, ma'am. I'm not being... *contumacious* at all. I'm simply presenting the facts, and, admittedly, going on my intuition.'

'Ah yes,' she says with a degree of sarcasm. 'The talent that precedes you, Riley.' She eyes me carefully. 'Even the best of us can get it wrong sometimes.'

I raise my eyebrows. *Best of us?* I'll take that as a compliment.

'I wouldn't know, ma'am.' I smile affably.

She gives a little snort of what I detect is incredulity.

'Look, what I *do* believe is that Hemmings went after Libby that night. I think he confronted her about the blackmail. I also believe he found her body and moved it. But I *don't* believe he was the one who killed her, inflicting those savage wounds on her. He'd have been covered in her blood for one thing – his clothes would've been soaked with it, and when he returned to the Draytons' house there wasn't a speck on them, or him, aside from the scratch. It doesn't make sense, or add up. It was the same with the brother, Brandon – he also had motive - and he too followed her that night, but his clothes also came back clean.'

She makes to speak but I continue. 'The timeline suggests that he did exactly what he told us he did, and that after he found her body, he panicked, moved her, and then drove straight back to the Draytons' house, back to the dinner party. There would have been no time for him to dispose of his clothes and drive home to retrieve identical clean ones.'

'Even so, Riley,' she cuts me off sharply. 'He went back to

the Draytons' and continued eating, drinking and being bloody merry. Surely that shows a level of callousness, an indication of his true character. And why, if he found her body, did he not simply call the police, call for an ambulance? The man's a doctor, for goodness' sake – wouldn't it have been second nature to him even more than most?'

She has a point, of course, but something tells me – something told me during Hemmings' interview – that he was telling the truth about why he didn't. Truth is, no one knows how they will react when under extreme duress, not with one hundred per cent certainty anyway.

It all needs to be checked out of course: the timeline, witnesses and forensic evidence. Hemmings claims that Libby sent him a copy of the video footage she'd secretly shot on her phone of the two of them together in his car and that he'd deleted it in a state of panic. His phone has been sent off to tech, to see if it can be retrieved. The tyre marks and footprints will be cross-referenced, and we'll obtain a warrant to search the Hemmings' property and impound his car. I have a feeling that it will all come back conclusive and that it will be very damning for Dr Hemmings, and whatever way it's not looking good for him. And yet I believe him when he says he didn't actually kill Libby Drayton. Hell, he may have wanted to – Lord knows, most people might've if his version of events is genuine – but my gut tells me unequivocally that while his actions are at best cowardly, contemptible and lacking integrity, he's not our killer.

'And basically, Dan,' Archer continues, 'this whole black-mail story could simply be fabricated. It could all be a cover-up for the fact that he may have been abusing the girl and killed her when he found out she was pregnant.'

'It's possible,' I reluctantly agree. 'But Hemmings is...'

I struggle to find the words I'm looking for without coming across as condoning his behaviour. 'He's a family man, devoted to his wife and his patients. There's no history of violence what-soever. Quite the opposite in fact – everyone we've spoken to says what a gentle, caring individual he is... and anyway, he claims Libby had told him that she had a boyfriend, that she'd been sleeping with someone when she visited him at the surgery – she didn't say who, only that he was "an older man", and that she preferred "older" men. He claims she was the one who made inappropriate sexual remarks to him...'

'Well, he would, wouldn't he?' Archer scoffs. 'She was seventeen, for heaven's sake, Dan. Anyway, he can say anything he wants to now she's dead.'

I nod. As uncomfortable as it makes me feel, I suspect that alongside her musical and artistic talents, Libby Drayton could add master manipulator to the list. Slowly, it's beginning to tran-spire that she was a young lady of some persuasion, one with an agenda. Not that this makes her brutal death any less atrocious or more deserved, but it's beginning to paint a bigger picture as to why she may have met the ending she did – and it's that 'why' which I'm sure will bring me closer to finding – and catching – her killer.

'I worked for him, for a couple of years,' Tina says now, gesturing for us to take a seat on the kitchen stools. She opens the fridge, takes out a half-full bottle of white wine and pours herself a glass. 'I need this if I'm going to have to talk about that bastard.' She swigs a large mouthful back, almost half the glass in one hit. 'It started off OK. He was nice, you know, friendly, a good boss. I felt lucky to work there... initially anyway. I needed the job at the time, like, really needed it, you know? I was strug-gling financially, trying to make ends meet. I was ecstatic when I got that gig.' She swigs more wine as she recalls, clearly with some degree of bitterness. 'Ha! Little did I bloody know.'

Davis glances at me but we both stay silent, let her tell her story.

'He was funny, likeable, used to have a bit of banter with the staff and that. I liked him.' She shrugs. 'And yes, I suppose I thought he was quite attractive for an older bloke, although I didn't fancy him. Funny, isn't it,' she says, shaking her head, 'how someone's good looks can vanish once you realise what a cun—' She stops herself. 'What kind of a person they are.'

She pours the rest of the wine into the glass, making sure she doesn't miss a drop. 'Basically, he came onto me one night, when everyone else had gone home of course – was never stupid enough to have witnesses around. I was staying late to finish the new filing system, get it up to date. He got take-out pizza and wine while we cracked on. Honestly' – she looks up at me, eyes wide – 'I hadn't seen it coming, but looking back now... well, I was a bit stupid, you know, naïve.' She takes a deep breath. 'Anyway, I was shocked, taken aback. I rebuffed him of course – he was my boss and he was married. I mean, sod that! I'm not the type to get into all that kind of drama – even if I'd have fancied the pants off him.' She screws her nose up, adding, 'Which I didn't.'

'And he didn't take kindly to the rejection?'

She raises her eyes. 'You could say that! Bastard almost raped me. I had to fight him off, physically push him off me, kept telling him, no, no... NO!' She downs more wine. 'He ripped my tights...'

Davis shoots me a sideways look. *Ripped tights.*

Tina visibly shudders as she recalls. 'I was terrified, properly terrified... I really thought he was going to...' She closes her eyes.

'It's OK, Tina,' I say gently. 'Take your time.'

She exhales. 'Anyway, he started shouting and that, saying I'd been leading him on and that I was "a little cock tease" – his words. He reckoned I'd been giving him signals for weeks – "the green light", he called it, but I swear... I'd only ever been nice to him, in a boss capacity, you know? I had a boyfriend at the time too, though he fell by the wayside when all the trouble started... couldn't handle it.'

'Trouble?'

She snorts again. 'Afterwards I went home and tried to forget about it, put it behind me, pretend it hadn't happened. I needed that job – it was a good job, best-paid job I ever had. I didn't tell anyone. I hoped it was just a one-off, thought that maybe he was a bit drunk, you know, and that things would just go back to normal, but they didn't.'

She finishes her glass and goes to the fridge again, pulls out a new bottle. Her hands are shaking as she opens it.

'He started a hate campaign against me after that, pulling me up on the smallest things, picking fault in my work, in everything I did, even things I wasn't responsible for. If I was a minute late back from lunch, or if the phone wasn't picked up within three rings, he'd be on my case. He started making threats, you know, to sack me, and I was beside myself, running rings around him, trying to hold on to my job, a job I desperately needed. I tried to appease him, tried to talk to him, but that only made it worse. He told me if I ever mentioned what had happened to anyone, then he'd *"make me wish I'd never been born"*. That's what he said to me.' She shakes her head.

'And he was good on his word too,' she adds bitterly. 'A week later he accused me of stealing the petty cash – £250 from the safety box – and he sacked me. He got the police involved and everything. He had me arrested, *arrested* on suspicion of theft.'

'Was it proved?'

Her eyes flash up. 'Was it fuck!' she spits. 'Sorry.' She shakes her head. 'I'm sorry, but, well, that was just the start of the nightmare...'

I glance over at Davis and our eyes meet. I can tell she's

thinking what I'm thinking – this is potentially a whole new insight into Tom Drayton.

'There wasn't enough evidence to convict me, but I told the police everything, about him sticking it on me, almost raping me! I wasn't going to be labelled a thief by that lying, arrogant pervert who couldn't take no for an answer.'

'Good for you.' Davis smiles, unable to disguise her solidarity.

'They spoke to him, questioned him about it...'

My brow furrows. Why hadn't we picked up on this sooner? It's a serious accusation, attempted rape.

'But he's a clever bastard, twisted everything around, he did, convinced them that *I* was the one who'd been trying to seduce *him*, that *I'd* made it all up because *he'd* rejected *me*! He told them I was infatuated with him, had been stalking him and everything! I mean, I couldn't prove it – I had no injuries, there were no witnesses, nothing... he told them I was being malicious, trying to blacken his reputation by crying rape... or attempted rape... and... and they believed him! Said I'd been wasting police time! They even threatened to nick me for it! That's how convincing he was – that's how manipulative that evil bastard Tom Drayton is.'

Davis lowers her eyes slightly, her reaction mirroring my own thoughts. Tina Molten clearly feels very let down by the system and in this moment – assuming she's being truthful, and I think she is – I can't say as I blame her.

'He took me to court – can you believe that? *He* took *me* to court for slander, said I was a malicious fantasist who was trying to damage his reputation.' She shakes her head. 'I mean, I couldn't afford all the barristers and legal eagles like he could. I wasn't even working at the time! He made a big song and dance about it, desperate to clear his name. Turned up in court with his glamorous wife by his side, looking down on me like I was some low-life nutjob, made me out to be this mentally unbalanced stalker... It was...' She places her head in her hands momentarily. 'It was awful. Like, the injustice was unbearable. Victim shaming, they call it – that's what it was. I was the victim yet somehow he managed to turn the tables on me and make himself out to be the one who was wronged. My name and picture were in the papers and everything.'

She wipes the rims of her eyes with her thumb. 'He won of course. I was forced to retract my allegation and apologise to him. I was made to apologise for him attempting to rape me! Can you believe that?' She looks at Davis and me respectively. 'Can you?'

I shake my head, genuinely sorrowful. 'No, Tina,' I say. 'I can't.' But the truth is I actually can believe it. Men like that – narcissistic men – are master manipulators and have been known to fool everyone – their families, friends, police and even judges. It strikes me that if Tom falls into that category then perhaps the apple didn't fall far from the tree after all.

Suddenly, I think of Evie, wonder how she's doing, how she's coping. I need to talk to her again. As much as I'd like to talk to Tom Drayton.

'I had to pay his court fees – judge ordered me to, over £30K! I didn't even have thirty quid, let alone thirty grand! My parents remortgaged their house to pay it off.'

I can see she's really struggling not to cry now and I gently place my hand on her arm. She stares at it for a moment before looking up at me.

'The irony is, I did become a nutjob after that... had a full-on mental breakdown, couldn't sleep, couldn't eat, couldn't work... everyone believing I was the type of girl to cry rape because I'd been rejected... some vindictive bunny boiler. Who was going to employ me or have a relationship with me after that? Mud sticks, you know.'

Tears are falling down her cheeks now, and I struggle not to wipe them away, not to feel the injustice of it all for her.

'Anyway.' She pulls her arm away, attempts to regain her composure. 'It was almost four years ago now. I've moved on, tried to rebuild, you know? What doesn't kill you makes you stronger and all of that,' she says unconvincingly. 'But if you're asking me to feel sorry for that piece of shit... I don't. Whatever's coming to him is due, let me tell you. *It's long overdue.*'

TWENTY-THREE
EVIE

She isn't surprised when the doorbell rings early that morning.

'Come in, Dan,' she says, leaving the door ajar as she hurriedly returns to the warmth of her kitchen, wrapping her dressing gown around her.

'Sorry it's so early.' Dan nods at Tom as he enters the kitchen. Tom barely lifts his head in acknowledgement. He'd taken the news even worse than she has. 'I know DS Davis spoke with you on the phone yesterday but I wanted to come round in person, keep you both in the loop and up to speed. I know it must've come as a terrible shock to hear the news about Jim's arrest...'

'Well, that's a fucking understatement!' Tom snaps, and Evie shoots Dan a look of apology on his behalf.

'And I'm even more sorry to say that I'm afraid we're going to have to let him go, for now at least,' he says, quickly adding, 'He's still a suspect, but we need more time, more evidence if we're going to charge him.'

'If? *If*? This is bullshit!' Spittle flies from Tom's lips as he spits the words out. 'Jim bloody Hemmings... of *all* the people... He had *sex* with her, with *our* daughter, with his *own* goddaughter! She was seventeen, for God's sake – it's sick! *Sick!*'

He starts pacing the room and she feels exhausted just watching him.

'He killed her... he must've... he's made it all up, this black-mail business... it's all nonsense! It's obvious he was abusing her, he groomed her, then when he found out she was pregnant, he bloody killed her!'

Tom breaks down and starts to cry, bringing his hands up to cover his face and Evie realises that this is the first time since Libby's body had been found that she's seen him do this. Her own tears have run dry.

'Do you think he's telling the truth?' She turns to Dan, her voice barely a whisper. 'Jim, when he said he didn't kill her? Is it possible that, like he said, he simply moved her body...?'

'Well, this is what he's claiming, yes,' Dan says.

That's not what she asked him though.

'But do *you* think he's lying?'

'Of course he's fucking lying!' Tom's shrill voice cuts right through her. 'Don't you see, Evie, he's been duping us for years, sniffing around our little girl all this time... all that Mr Nice Guy act for all those years. He bloody murdered our daughter! This is insane...'

Only that was just it, she thought. Can someone really put on such an act for all those years? Evie knew Jim – she'd known him before she even knew her husband and Una. They'd met at university and had had a very brief and clumsy romance before she'd decided they were better as friends – and that's what they'd remained ever since. She'd even been the one to intro-duce Jim to Una, a far better-suited match, she'd thought. Jim was a good, decent person and the idea that he was capable of harming anyone, let alone Libby, just seemed so... preposterous, so unreal. The man was a philanthropist, for goodness' sake, a GP, a *caring* doctor dedicated to helping the lives of others.

Dan Riley is watching them both simultaneously.

'Jim mentioned that Libby had told him about a boyfriend, a boy she was seeing who she'd recently broken up with... Do you know who this boy, or man, might've been?'

'No,' she says. 'I have no idea.' And in that moment Evie realises that she has no idea about anything, no idea who her daughter really was, who she'd ever been. She hadn't known her at all.

'Surely you don't believe him,' Tom addresses her incredulously again. 'You *can't* believe him!'

Evie shakes her head. It's not that she *can't* believe it, it's that she doesn't *want* to.

'Actually, there was something I wanted to ask you, Tom,' Dan says, 'about some transactions that went from your bank account to your daughter's. Namely three transactions of £1,000 each over approximately eleven weeks.'

Evie looks up from her lap. Transactions? She knows nothing of this.

Dan starts searching through a notebook. 'One on 11 August, another on 1 September and the last one dated 28 October. Can you tell me what these were for?'

'Tom?' She blinks at him.

'It was her allowance,' he says dismissively.

'But her allowance was only £350 a month,' she replies, a trickle of unease settling upon her empty stomach. 'Why did you give Libby £3,000? What for?'

'Oh... I don't know.' He waves a hand. 'I can't exactly remember now...'

'You can't remember what you gave her £3,000 for?' Evie hears her own voice rise an octave.

'It was for something or other she wanted... you know what she was like, always after a new handbag, or trainers or something... all those designer labels she was into.'

She feels confused – and suspicious. They'd agreed upon

their daughter's £350 monthly allowance as 'more than enough' for the things she needed day-to-day. If she'd ever wanted for anything, they'd always made a point of discussing it between them first before agreeing.

'It's just that Libby's bank statements don't tally up...' Dan continues. 'She didn't make any large purchases before she died – no handbags, no designer goods.'

'Well... I... I don't know. That's what she told me she wanted the money for...'

'Why didn't you tell me?' Evie looks at her husband. 'Why didn't you square it with me first? Three thousand pounds is a lot of money, Tom.'

'I didn't think I needed your permission to give my own daughter money – money that *I* earn,' he snaps back.

Evie blinks, startled. Why is he being so defensive? He's lying. She can tell that he isn't telling the truth, and she suspects Dan Riley can too. Nothing makes sense anymore. Has *everyone* been lying to her? Libby, Jim and now her own husband too?

'I went to see someone yesterday,' Dan says. 'A former employee of yours, a lady by the name of Tina Molten.'

Tom swings round. 'What? Why on earth did you do that?' His eyes widen. 'Lady? Ha! Hardly! That nasty, spiteful bitch tried to ruin me!'

'That's funny,' Dan replies. 'She said exactly the same about you.'

'Yes, well, she bloody well would, the mad cow! Hang on, do you... are you saying you think *she* might've had something to do with Libby's death? God...' Tom starts running his hands through his hair. 'You don't think *she* could be responsible, do you – that she killed our daughter out of some kind of revenge, to get back at me?'

'We have to explore every line of enquiry, Tom,' Dan says. 'But as it stands, no, I don't believe she had anything to do with

Libby's death – her alibi checks out. She did, however, claim that the allegations she made about you were correct, and that in a bid to silence her and save your reputation, you falsely accused her of theft and of being an infatuated fantasist.'

Tom snorts in incredulity. 'Jesus, man, you don't believe that surely? The woman is unhinged, mad as a box of frogs and a vindictive lying bitch with it, and the judge agreed with me!'

Dan stares at her husband, pauses.

'Jesus... this is madness, absolute bloody madness, man! What are you trying to say, Detective Riley?' Tom's demeanour has turned. He suddenly seems angry, *aggressive*.

'Fuck this!' He grabs his car keys from the table. 'I'm not standing here listening to this crap! I'm not sure what it is you're trying to suggest, Riley, but I won't stand for it! I'm going to the station to talk to your superiors. I want someone else on this case – someone competent, someone who's actually committed to finding out who killed our daughter, not someone who's more interested in digging up dirt from the past and looking in all the wrong places.'

He stomps from the kitchen, slams the front door behind him.

There's a moment's silence before Dan pulls up a chair opposite her.

'I'm sorry, Evie,' he says. 'We have to look into every possibility, and this sometimes means picking over old scabs, for want of a better description. Do you understand?'

She nods but suddenly she understands nothing. All that dreadful business with Tina Molten and the court case some years back – it had been such a stressful time. She hadn't even thought to question her husband's version of events, never had reason to. She'd simply believed him implicitly, taken him entirely on his word. They had a happy marriage. Tom wasn't a womaniser, and he'd never cheated on her, not ever. As far as Evie was concerned, Tina Molten was just an unstable young woman who'd become obsessed by her older, attractive boss and became vindictive when he'd refused her advances – she'd felt sorry for her. But now... now tiny fragments of doubt begin to introduce themselves to her thoughts. Had Tina been telling the truth all along? She tries to push this unsettling idea away, but after all she's learned, she's beginning to question everything, question her own reality.

'Listen, Evie, I wanted to ask you more about an old injury that Libby had – one the pathologist picked up at the post-mortem, an injury to her skull.'

'Yes, the holiday,' she says. She feels so exhausted that she hardly has the strength to push the words from her lips. 'In Tenerife, with Una and Jim and Brandon... like I told you before. Libby was just a tot really, not even five years old.' She's instinctively begun smiling at the memory of her daughter when young. 'God, she was so adorable, so... innocent and adorable, you know, like they all are at that age, into everything, finding their feet, their independence...'

Dan smiles and nods. 'I have an eighteen-month-old myself,' he says, and she sees the pride in his eyes as he speaks of his own child.

'I took my eye off her for a second, just a second,' she says, the memory of it traumatising her all over again. 'It was terrifying... turning round and seeing that she'd gone, that she wasn't there. And then suddenly all this screaming... people running, panicking... and blood, oh God, seeing her blood on the pavement below...' Evie can feel her heart rate increase as she recounts the accident again, feels her body temperature spike with adrenalin just like it had done in that dreadful moment.

'We were all walking along a promenade, the six of us, going to get an ice cream. There were these steps that led down to the beach below, huge concrete steps, at least thirty of them, I'd have said, and she just...' She closes her eyes. 'She must've just lost her concentration, too busy with her ice cream probably, and toppled down them. She fell from top to bottom, hit her head on the pavement below.' She winces as she remembers the sound of the impact, of her daughter's tiny head connecting with the concrete. 'But I didn't realise it was her until... the screams...' She takes a sharp intake of breath.

'She was taken to hospital in a helicopter. I was beside myself, hysterical, inconsolable... we all were. I thought she was going to die that day and that I was going to lose my baby girl. The medical staff at the hospital were amazing. They took such great care of her. She'd suffered a fracture on her skull. I remember bursting into tears as the doctor showed me the X-rays, crying hysterically, but he assured me that it looked worse than it was and that she would heal. They did brain scans and all sorts and, sure enough, well, he was right, she did heal and she did get better. We flew home fourteen days later.'

'And she made a full recovery?'

'Yes. Although her life was plagued by headaches, I'm sure as a result of that injury. And then there were those episodes when she was younger... although the doctors couldn't positively attribute them directly to the accident.'

'Episodes?'

'Yes. Libby started having seizures – terrifying they were. Her eyes would roll back in her head and she would start to convulse violently, even foam at the mouth.' Evie shudders at the memory. 'I would have to restrain her until the ambulance arrived, literally hold her down while she lashed out, kicking and screaming and shouting, calling me terrible names... words I couldn't believe she even knew because Tom and I – well, we were always very careful with our language around her. It was like she'd been possessed. And she was so strong, for such a tiny girl – she had the strength of ten men while she was fitting.'

Evie pulls her dressing gown tight around her again like armour. 'The doctors couldn't really get to the bottom of why she was having them. They thought it might be epilepsy at first, but then they ruled that out and well... then they stopped, went away on their own... and she never had one again.'

Her eyes drop to her lap. 'Why do you ask about this again, Dan?'

He looks hesitant, like he's not sure how to answer her.

'It was just an awful, dreadful accident. I never forgave myself for it, for taking my eye off her for that split second. I felt I'd failed her, that people were looking at me and thinking I was negligent and that I was responsible. The guilt was overwhelming, on top of the depression I already had...'

Dan looks at her. He has such kind eyes. The kind you don't see too often anymore. 'You had depression?'

She immediately wishes she hadn't mentioned it.

'Yes, I did for a few years, after I had Libby – post-natal depression. But I got through it, you know; the doctors prescribed me antidepressants. I had some therapy too, and gradually the clouds lifted, and I felt like myself again. I was a happy mum after those initial few years; I loved being at home with her and taking care of her. I was a good mum...' She sounds like she's trying to justify herself.

'I don't doubt that for a moment, Evie.' Dan smiles gently. 'I don't think anyone could ever dispute that.'

Suddenly she remembers about the bracelet, about the missing charm on Libby's Pandora bracelet.

'Actually, I wanted to mention something to you myself.'

'Oh?'

'Libby's bracelet, the one she always wore, the one with all the charms. There's one missing from it, a little revolving heart with "mother" and "daughter" inscribed on each side. It was the last thing I ever bought her...' Her voice trails off. 'I knew every charm on that bracelet, you see; each one represented something in her life: a birthday or an achievement, a special occasion. I counted them all – went through each of them – but that one is missing. It couldn't have fallen off,' she says. 'The charms link through the actual bracelet itself, through a little hole in each one that threads onto it, so I wondered if perhaps it had somehow been mislaid, maybe while it was with forensics? Could you look into that for me? I'd really like it found – that bracelet is all I have left...'

'Of course, I'll look into it for you. I promise I—'

The doorbell rings again and suddenly she hears Una's voice through the letterbox.

'Evie... Evie... you have to let me in!' she's screaming, making a scene, typical Una. 'Evie, please... let me in. I need to speak to you; I must speak to you!'

She's rapping the letterbox and ringing the bell simultaneously. Evie wants to cover her ears with her hands.

'I'll speak to her.' Dan nods in understanding. 'I'll tell her that now isn't the time.'

Evie winces as she hears the kerfuffle taking place in the hallway – Una screaming her name, Dan attempting to prevent her from entering the house. She buries her head in her hands, wants it all to stop. She can't face Una right now – she doesn't know how she feels, how she should act.

Eventually the histrionics stop and she hears the front door close.

'She doesn't like to take no for an answer, does she?' Dan returns to the kitchen, a little ruffled.

'She doesn't,' Evie says, sadness jabbing at her heart as she realises her friendship with Una has irrevocably changed now too.

Dan's phone rings and he stands to take the call.

'Great... that's brilliant news, Harding, bloody brilliant. Hold him there, yes... yes I'm on my way... Good news,' he says to her, hanging up. 'The man from the CCTV footage down at The Chapel – the one that you did the public appeal to find – well, we've got him. I'll have to go.'

'Yes... yes of course... Do you think he's the man Libby referred to when she told Jim she had a boyfriend?'

'I don't know,' Dan says. 'But hopefully we're just about to find out.' He turns to leave. 'I'll call you as soon as I have anything to tell you, OK?' He lightly touches her arm.

'Thank you,' she says, suddenly not wanting him to leave, to be left alone with nothing but her dreadful thoughts.

TWENTY-FOUR

DAN

Cody Phillips is slumped back in the plastic chair opposite Davis and I in interview room five. The duty solicitor, Elaine Markham, is seated next to him, and while I detect Cody is no stranger to this process, I can still sense the fear coming off him at ten paces.

Davis switches the machine on, cautions him, goes through the motions – motions I suspect Cody is regrettably all too familiar with.

'I want to make a deal,' he says.

'A deal?'

He sniffs loudly, crosses and uncrosses his legs. 'Yeah, a deal.' He pauses, looks directly at me. 'Come on, you lot know what I do for a living, right? Well, I want a guarantee that there ain't gonna be no charges brought against me, you know, for possession or dealing or anything else you lot wanna do me up for.' He sits up slightly.

'We don't want to talk about your profession, Mr Phillips,' I say. 'We're not interested in that. We want to talk about Libby Drayton, a young lady who was brutally murdered last week – a young lady who we believe you knew. Can you tell us about that, about your relationship with the deceased?'

He meets my eyes with his own, narrows them. 'I want a guarantee first.'

'I'm afraid I can't give you any guarantees of anything, Mr Phillips,' I say. 'But I can give you my word that we're not interested in your... career.'

He shakes his head, huffs. His body language portrays arrogance, on the surface at least, but I detect the fear in him – the real him that he's so at pains to disguise.

'You came here today of your own accord, Cody,' Davis says. 'Why is that?'

He looks at her as though she just came down with the last shower.

'Why do you think? Saw meself on telly, didn't I... face in the papers and all that. Look.' He leans forward again. 'I didn't even know the girl was dead until a couple of days ago, I swear down.' He holds his palms up in protest. 'When I saw that footage, I shit myself, thought here we go, they're gonna try and pin this shit on me... and that ain't happening right.' His tone hardens a little, though I suspect it's no more than flimsy bravado. 'Because I ain't killed no one, *no one*, and I ain't got nothing to hide so that's why I'm here now.' He looks genuinely spooked underneath all that sincerity.

'Did you know how old Libby Drayton was when you met her?'

'No,' he says quickly. 'She told me she was twenty-two.'

'And you believed her?' Davis says.

He shrugs. 'Yeah. Come on, you saw her, right? She looked a lot older than seventeen.' His beady eyes dart nervously between Davis and I. 'I wouldn't have touched her if I'd known she was only a teenager. I ain't no fucking nonce.' He scowls.

'When did you last see Libby?'

I've instructed Davis to undertake most of the interview so that I can largely observe, get an intuitive feel for our man here. I've met the likes of Cody Phillips many times during my career – small-time dealers with a big-time attitude, guys on the peripheries of the big league, usually with a charge sheet the length of a toilet roll that began in their often-troubled youth and an inherent disregard and hatred of the law and police – in that order. Cody is no exception, a young man who's been let down in so many ways by so many people, in and out of care homes since he was seven years old, a stint in youth offenders, his story is sadly not uncommon; his profession almost a foregone conclusion given his life so far – a life where he's seen rejection and addiction and violence from an all-too-young age. I understand it; the arrogant swagger he exudes is regrettably little more than a learned defence mechanism in order to survive.

'Few days ago...'

'When exactly?'

He shrugs. 'Wednesday maybe.' He sniffs loudly.

'I see. So what was your relationship to Libby exactly?'

He leans further back on his chair, but I can see that he's nervous, *very nervous*. Cody Phillips may be trying to appear cocky and confident, but he's been around the block enough to know that he's potentially in it up to his neck.

'Look, I hardly knew the bird, right. We started knocking around together a bit after I met her at The Chapel one night.'

'When was that? When did you first meet?'

'Few months ago maybe... I ain't good with dates... bad short-term memory, see – too many of the old Persian rugs... you know? She approached me at the bar one night and asked me for some drugs.' He pauses. 'It was nothing serious, just a bit of fun, you know what I mean?' He looks Davis up and down, adding sarcastically, 'Or maybe not.'

'So the relationship became a sexual one?'

He shifts in his seat. 'Yeah, well, you know... I'm a man, she was a woman...'

'A very *young* woman,' Davis reminds him.

'Like I say, I never knew she was only seventeen, right? She was a good little liar, I'll give her that. I ain't done nothing wrong,' he protests. 'She wasn't underage or nothing, and trust me,' he adds, 'she was the one doing all the running. I weren't really that interested, to be honest. It was only cos she said she could help me...'

'Help you?'

'Yeah. The night we met. I owed some money to some people and she said she could help me, said she could get hold of some drugs that I could sell to pay the debt off.'

'Did she say where she could get hold of these drugs?'

I'm listening intently, wondering if he's about to corroborate Jim Hemmings' story.

'She wouldn't tell me. Just said that she could get hold of them and that there was plenty more to come. I didn't think she was being serious at first. I mean, I was suspicious of her – she was a bit on the posh side, you know, thought she might even be undercover filth... police at first, trying to stitch me up. Anyway, she reckoned she could get a couple of grands' worth of gear by the following Friday and that she'd meet me with it. She gave me some expensive bracelet to hang on to as a sort of guarantee...'

'What kind of bracelet?'

My heart starts to accelerate, and Davis and I exchange glances.

'Silver one, big, loads of charms on it. She said I could sell it if she didn't come up with the goods.'

'Why would she do that, Cody? She'd only just met you; she didn't know you from Adam. Why would she offer to pay off *your* dealing debts, procure drugs for you, and then give you her bracelet when she hardly knew you?'

He looks at us both and shakes his head incredulously. 'Look, I'm fucked if I know just as much as you lot are. I thought the same thing meself, but she said it was because she wanted to.'

He blinks at us, realises how outlandish it sounds. 'Look, I ain't as stupid as you lot think I am. I know no one does anyone a favour without wanting something in return. I thought she must have an agenda somewhere along the line, but I was in the shit big time with a supplier and I weren't gonna look a gift horse in the mouth, was I?'

'So she delivered on her promise? She met you the following week with the drugs?'

He nods. 'Yeah, she did as well. Turned up with a ziplock bag full of shit, prescription stuff – bennies, vallies, barbs, methodone... a shed load of them. I asked her again where she got them from but she wouldn't tell me, and to be honest I didn't really care. Ask no questions and you'll get no lies.'

'Did you give her the bracelet back?' I ask.

'Yeah.' He nods. 'We went back to my place that night. It was in the drawer in me bedroom and I gave it straight back to her. I weren't gonna stitch her up after she delivered.'

I think about Evie and the missing charm she mentioned, the mother-and-daughter heart.

'You never took any of the charms? Never took anything off the bracelet?'

'No.' He shakes his head. 'I slung it in the drawer after she gave it to me and never even looked at it again until I gave it back.'

'You didn't think about selling it?'

He looks up at me for a moment. 'Look, I ain't a complete bastard. I wanted to give her the chance to come good before I flogged it – and she did.'

'You're all heart, Mr Phillips,' I say, and he snorts in response.

'That night, that Friday night when she came back to your place, did you have intercourse? Did you have sex with Libby?'

He shifts awkwardly in the plastic chair again. 'Yeah.' He nods. 'It was the first time we did it.' He looks at us both respectively again, quickly adding, 'It was consensual... I never forced her. It was the other way round if anything. The girl was no virgin – she knew what she wanted, what she was doing.'

'Did you use contraception?'

'Eh? No... no, we never. I didn't think about it. Well, you know, that's a girl's thing, ain't it? Why? What's that got to do with anything?'

Davis raises an eyebrow. 'Did you know that Libby was around eight weeks pregnant when she was murdered, Cody?' she says. 'And looking at the timeline, there's every possibility that you could've been responsible for that pregnancy. Did she tell you she was pregnant?'

He looks shocked, confused, starts shaking his head as he leans back into his seat. 'Hang on... Nah... Nah... She never said nothing to me about no pregnancy!' His voice rises an octave. 'We only met up a few times after that, and it was always much the same: she brought the drugs, I sold them, we went back to mine, had a few beers, smoked a joint, swallowed a couple of barbs, and, you know... went to bed...' He glances at his brief.

'The night she died – the night of the murder – you were captured on CCTV at The Chapel around 9 p.m. Can you tell us your movements prior to this? Had you agreed to meet her there that night?'

'Yeah,' he says. 'Only she never showed up, did she?'

'You were seen talking to someone that night, a young male at the bar. Do you remember him – remember who it was?'

He nods. 'He'd come in looking for her. I asked him why he was looking for her, who he was and that... he said he was her brother, told me to stay away from her, that she was bad news, that she was some psycho. I thought he was having a laugh at first, overprotective brother and all of that... but as I'd got to know her a bit, I sort of understood what he was getting at.'

'Getting at?' My interest has piqued again. 'What was that, Cody?'

'Well, she weren't the full pound note, was she? I knew it pretty much from the off, something... I dunno, something a bit strange about her, couldn't quite put me finger on it. Didn't fully trust her... something a bit off. And then she started telling me all this stuff... coming out with all this weird shit.'

'What weird shit was that?'

'I dunno, some story about being abused, since she was a kid and that... felt a bit sorry for her, you know? I know what it's like... I've been in care.' He turns away slightly, looks down at the floor.

'Did she say who had been abusing her?' Davis says.

He shakes his head. 'I dunno. The brother, I think. I was a bit high, you know... she never went into any details, just said that her parents knew about it, didn't do nothing about it, let it happen and that. And that's why she hated them.'

'She told you that she hated her parents?'

'Yeah, really fucking hated them – her mother especially – wanted them all dead.'

Davis and I exchange glances.

'She wanted her parents dead?'

'Yeah. She said something...' He pauses for a moment, rubs his temples. 'Something about her mum trying to kill her when she was a kid... pushing her down some stairs or whatever...'

I feel my stomach lurch.

'I didn't take much notice. I mean, we've all got horror stories from our childhoods, ain't we? Me own mother was a cun — Well, she was no angel herself, so I thought she was just mouthing off, like you do. But then she started talking about how she'd like to do it, or more like how she wanted *me* to do it...'

'To do what, to kill her parents? Libby asked you to kill her parents?' A chill runs the length of my spine.

'I didn't think she was actually being serious, but yeah, she talked to me about it on a few occasions. Told me that with them all gone she'd inherit everything – the houses and cars and her dad's business and all of this money... she said if they weren't around, we could have the lot and fuck off and live the life of a king and queen in some penthouse together...'

He pauses for a second, gauges our reactions. 'I mean, I thought she was just fantasising about it at first, but... but... I dunno, she started talking about it more and more, every time I see her, know what I mean? She talked about the best ways of how to kill someone and get away with it, talked about arson, about setting fire to the house with them all in it and I thought... Hang on, fuck me, this bird's being serious... and she's sounding me out, wants to see if I'm game.'

'And were you?'

He puts his hands down onto the table. Looks directly into my eyes.

'I might not always have been a model citizen, boss,' he says sagely. 'I've been a bit naughty in my time, I'll admit that, but murdering someone's entire family... are you off your nut? My life might be a shower of shite, but I value what little there is of it, and I value my freedom. I ain't being banged up for the rest of me life in some five-by-six for some random mad bird – you got to be having a laugh. Anyway, it felt like she was...' He looks away then, almost embarrassed.

'It felt like she was what, Cody?'

He laughs a little awkwardly. 'Like she was grooming me, you know... getting hold of drugs for me, because she had some plan... some mad idea that I was gonna kill her fucking parents for her or something. I dunno... She never asked me outright, only in a roundabout way. I mean, she had me in her pocket by then, didn't she? I owed her. I started to feel a bit...' He drags his hands down his face, pulling the skin around his eyes. 'A bit freaked out by her – wasn't sure what she was capable of.'

The door opens and Mitchell pops her head through it. 'Need a word, gov.'

'Let's leave it here for a moment,' I instruct Davis, and she switches the recording off.

'What you got, Mitchell?' I ask once I'm outside. I feel a little light-headed with adrenalin, or perhaps it's lack of food and sleep – probably the hat trick.

'The GP surgery, gov, the one where Hemmings works... it transpires it was robbed a couple of months ago. A young lad broke in and stole some prescription drugs from the pharmacy, bit of an amateur affair, practically caught red-handed. Someone called Harry Mendes.'

'Mendes... Harry Mendes... Why does that name ring a bell?' I squint in a bid to concentrate, search my memory. I've heard that name before, I feel sure of it...

'He was at school with Libby Drayton – they were in sixth form together.' Her eyes widen. 'According to classmates and friends, Harry Mendes' father had committed suicide some months earlier but everyone we interviewed said he and Libby weren't close, that they didn't have much to do with each other, but it's possible, gov.'

The trickle of fear I felt earlier accelerates into a gush as it comes to me. Evie had mentioned him the night Libby disappeared... said she'd been a bit upset by a death or something.

'Get a warrant to search Cody Phillips's place as soon as possible,' I say. 'Get anything you find down to forensics straight away. And get me Harry Mendes' home address.'

'Boss.'

She cranes her neck slightly to get a look inside the interview room. I sense Mitchell would like to have been part of the interview process and make a mental note to consider it next time. I feel she's more than ready.

'What do you think, gov?' she says, nodding in Cody's direction. 'Can Archer book a hair appointment for the press conference already?'

I try not to smile – don't want to encourage her – but one escapes anyway.

'Let's see what the search comes back with first,' I say, noncommittal. But yet again, my instincts are screaming at me that as unsavoury, as unscrupulous as Cody Phillips might be, he's telling the truth. I think about what he's just told me, about Libby wanting her family dead, about her mother attempting to kill her.

My thoughts feel tangled up as I return to the interview room; this case is becoming more and more complex with each passing day. I have more questions than answers, and while the questions seemingly keep coming, the answers are becoming more and more elusive. I feel frustration burn my earlobes. I'm missing something, a vital cohesive link that will bring everything together.

TWENTY-FIVE

EVIE

Evie pulls up outside Susan Parsons' house and stares at the front door. She'd wanted to visit earlier but the news of Jim's arrest had floored her. So many things weren't right, so many things didn't add up or make sense. It was becoming more apparent to her that her daughter had been leading something of a double life, a life she hadn't been remotely aware of, one that included men and sex and drugs and secrets, and now that the shock of learning this is beginning to subside a little, she wants answers.

'Evie! Gosh... I... I wasn't expecting you.' Surprise registers on Susan Parsons' face as she answers her front door.

'Can I come in, Susan?' she says. 'I'd like to speak to you, and to Katie too – is she home?' She detects Susan's reluctance almost instantly.

'Um, well... yes... yes she is – she's upstairs...' She pauses briefly before opening the front door a little wider. 'Of course, come in.' She smiles thinly but doesn't make eye contact. 'I was just going to make some tea, unless you'd like something else... something stronger. A glass of wine maybe? You know, I've... I've really been meaning to call you, Evie,' she says as she walks with her back to her into the kitchen, though it's evident that she's clearly embarrassed that she hasn't.

'I just thought,' Susan continues, 'what with everything you have going on, that it would be best to... well, that... that you might just want some peace and privacy, that's all. Tea?' She still has her back towards her and is filling up the kettle at the sink.

'Actually, I'll think I'll have that glass of wine.'

Susan nods, puts the kettle down and goes over to the fridge.

'Think I'll join you,' she says, taking out a bottle of Chardonnay and filling two glasses before bringing them to the kitchen table. There's no toast.

'God, Evie, I'm so sorry. I'm just... God,' she says again, sighing heavily. 'It's just so hard to know what to say. I mean, it's all so shocking, so awful. I've known Libby since she was... well, since forever. I just couldn't believe it, can't believe it...' Her words sound sincere enough but she doesn't reach for Evie's hand like everyone else seems to do. 'I can't imagine what you must be going through, you and Tom. I'm just so, so sorry...'

The mention of her husband's name reminds her of what Detective Riley had said earlier. Why had Tom given Libby £3,000? Why hadn't he told her about it? She pushes the question away, needs to focus on the job in hand.

'Not sorry enough to call or send a text or a bunch of flowers though? We've known each other seventeen years, Susan. You've known Libby all her life...' The words have left her lips before she's had time to stop them.

'Oh, Evie... I... I... I meant to... I was planning on coming in person, once things had... well, once... The shock has been terrible.'

She can tell this is excruciating for Susan. She waves her hand, lightly shakes her head. 'It's fine... Please, just ignore me. I'm sorry – I'm not in a very good place right now.'

Susan manages a weak smile. 'God, of course you're not, of course...'

There's a pause and Evie knows that Susan is wondering why she's really here.

'Can I speak to Katie?' She cuts to the chase. 'I'd really like to see her. Ask her a few things.'

'Things? What things?' Susan asks.

She's still affable, but Evie detects slight caution in her inflection.

'The police have been here three times already, you know,' she says. 'They've questioned her *three* times. She's told them everything she knows, answered every question they've put to her. Honestly, Evie, there's really nothing more she can say that she hasn't already.'

She blinks at her with bespectacled eyes that suddenly look far steelier than Evie has ever noticed.

'She was at her grandparents' that night, that whole weekend when Libby was...'

She can't bring herself to say it. No one can. Everyone seems to stop just short of saying it, like if they don't say the word 'murdered' then it hasn't really happened.

'They hadn't spoken for a while apparently. She had no idea that Libby had said she was supposed to be going out with her that night and, well, as I'm sure you remember, St Saviour's was closed and there was no band on... I was never picking them up because they were never together that evening. There's really no more she can tell you, that either of us can.' Susan takes a gulp of wine. She looks like she needs it even more than Evie does.

'Yes, but Katie's her best friend,' she says. 'Was her best friend. I think... well, the police think... Look, Libby was hiding things, had a secret boyfriend maybe. I mean, did you know that they'd been hanging out at this place, that bar, The Chapel?'

Susan visibly stiffens. 'No,' she says. 'I didn't. And I wasn't best pleased about it either when the police told me. Katie says she only went the one time. Libby had really wanted to go and check it out and had persuaded Katie to go with her...'

Evie feels the emotion rising up through her diaphragm. It was clear that Susan was suggesting that Libby had led Katie astray, and even though she's beginning to accept that this was probably the case, she still has a primeval instinct to protect her daughter's memory and resists the urge to throw her wine in Susan's pious, sanctimonious face.

'Well, I'm sure she didn't drag her there kicking and screaming,' she retorts, gripping her wine glass.

'No.' Susan gives that weak smile again. 'Look, Evie, I'm sorry. Katie's dreadfully upset. If there were anything – anything at all – that she knew that could help you, then she would've already told the police. After all, Libby was a...' She pauses for a brief second, sips at her wine, which Evie reads as a bid to buy time to find the right words. 'She's known her – knew her a long time.'

'Yes,' she says, 'but it really would give me some comfort to see her, Susan. Katie was her best friend... they've been best friends since...'

An image of a photo she had taken on their first day at primary school flashes up inside her head, the pair of them standing together in the hallway of her house, their hair neatly braided, their uniforms pristine, and their nervous smiles – all missing-tooth grins. She fights back tears, but a couple escape from the corners of her eyes and she brushes them away.

'How are you and Tom coping?' Susan changes the subject. 'I *was* going to call, you know, but it's so difficult to know what to say and...'

Was it though? Evie thinks. *Was it so difficult to pick up the phone or send a text or a bunch of flowers?* She's sure it's what she would've done were the boot ever to have been on the other foot.

'Have the police come up with anything new?' Susan continues. 'I heard on the news that they'd made an arrest. That's good news, isn't it?'

She's talking to her like she's a child, and no – it isn't bloody 'good news' that one of her closest friends – a man she's known and trusted for most of her life – is under suspicion of killing her daughter.

Evie tries not to think of Jim, tries desperately not to allow those sickening, disturbing images of him and Libby on the back seat of his Toyota to enter her head. She doesn't want to imagine them, to imagine that this ever took place between them. She wants it to be a lie – a disgusting, depraved and deceitful lie that Jim has concocted in a bid to cover up his deviant, despicable and deceitful behaviour, but as hard as she tries to stay stuck in denial, her mind slips out of gear and begins to skid off road.

'Yes.' She nods. 'If you could call it that.'

'So do you know who he is, this man they've arrested?'

Evie resents Susan's fishing for information, especially as she's not exactly being forthcoming herself. She's not here to talk about Jim Hemmings.

'I can't say much at this stage,' she says, deflecting her. 'Look, Susan, I really would like it if I could speak with—'

As she says it, Susan looks up and Katie appears in the doorway of the kitchen.

'Katie!' Evie stands, her emotions rising with her. 'Oh, Katie...'

She rushes to her, throws her arms around her. Katie's a similar size to Libby, a little taller and heavier perhaps, but still it's like she's holding her daughter again and she begins to cry.

'Oh, Katie...'

She feels her body stiffen in her embrace and after a few moments she drops her arms.

'Hi, E-Evie.' Katie smiles ruefully, looks down at the kitchen tiles beneath her.

'Look, this is exactly why I didn't want you to see her,' Susan says with a hint of crossness as she herself stands. 'As you can see, she's very upset.'

She was upset! Evie places her hands on Katie's small shoulders, stoops a little to make eye contact with her.

'Katie, darling... Oh, Katie, what happened? What happened with you and Libby? Do you know something you're not telling me, not telling the police? Please, Katie, if there's anything... anything at all, because it doesn't make any sense... all this stuff, this stuff about Libby and drugs and men and... Did she say anything? Did she tell you anything? You were her best friend, perhaps her only real friend...'

Katie looks like a deer caught in headlights.

'Yes, well, there's probably a good reason for that,' Susan mutters under her breath, but they both hear it.

'Mum!' Katie says.

'What do you mean by that, Susan?' Evie feels herself grow taller suddenly, her maternal instincts kicking in.

She turns back to Katie. 'What does she mean by that, Katie?' Now she's convinced there's something she doesn't know.

'Nothing... it's – it's nothing,' she stammers, glancing over at her mother again. 'I've told the police all I know. I'm sorry... I'm so sorry, Evie. I miss her, even after everything she did, I miss her and... it's like I can still see her, like she's still here and—'

'Everything she did? What do you mean, Katie? What did she do?'

She starts to shake her a little, as if by doing so the truth may just drop out of her like the last penny in a piggy bank.

'Evie, I'm sorry.' Susan comes towards her. 'I know you're upset, I know this is a dreadful time, but I want you to leave now. Katie is distraught and this won't help. It won't help anybody, so please, can you just leave?'

Evie translates her request as the instruction it was clearly intended to be but isn't about to be fobbed off. She wants the truth, she wants answers and she's not leaving until she gets them.

'Katie, please,' she implores. 'Libby is dead. She was murdered in the most brutal way, her head caved in, battered beyond recognition. We couldn't even identify her body... She was meeting someone down at The Chapel. You went there with her. Who was she meeting? Did she have a secret boyfriend? Did you see her take drugs? Did she confide in you about being pregnant?'

Katie's eyes widen then and instinctively she shakes her head.

'Evie!' Susan's voice cuts through the atmosphere like an axe. 'I'm not asking you, I'm telling you to leave now, before I call the police! This is harassment! I want you to leave her alone. LEAVE MY DAUGHTER ALONE!'

Evie drops her arms from Katie's shoulders. She's hyperventilating, her chest heaving up and down, her lungs crying out for oxygen, adrenalin shortening her breath. Susan's body is close to hers, practically pushing her in the direction of the front door. She turns back towards Katie, stunned and crying in the kitchen.

'*Your* daughter?' Evie cries. 'What about *my* daughter? Libby is dead, Susan; she's DEAD. You still have your girl. I'll never get to see mine ever again.'

She's on the front doorstep now, Susan having successfully evicted her from her house. She hasn't the physical strength to fight her.

Susan leans out of the half-closed door. 'Your daughter was a bad egg, Evie. Everyone knew it deep down, everyone but you. I'm sorry for you for that, I truly am, but I won't allow you to come to my house and upset my daughter like this... I am sorry, Evie,' she says again. 'Truly. I've always liked you and you don't deserve this.'

She shuts the door in her face, leaving Evie shaken on the step. She stands, frozen, waiting for her breathing to regulate. Turning, she sees a neighbour looking out of her window. She drops the curtain once she realises she's been spotted.

Attempting to compose herself, she walks unsteadily across the road and gets into her car, where she collapses onto the steering wheel and lets the sobs come – wretched, heart-wrenching sobs that hurt her chest and cause her to hiccup violently and—

A tap on the window startles her. Katie's young face, a picture of grief and fear, is peering through it. She looks nervously behind her as Evie opens the window.

'I'm sorry,' she says, 'about Mum... what she said. She's out of order...'

'But she's right, isn't she?' Evie says, wiping the mucus and tears from her face onto her hands. 'And you *do* know something, don't you, Katie? Something you're not telling...'

Katie opens the front passenger door and gets inside.

'I didn't know about the pregnancy, I swear,' she says. 'Libby never told me. She never told me anything really. I never understood why she did—' She pauses, fiddles nervously with her fingers in her lap.

'Why she did what? Oh please, Katie, please... just *tell* me.'

'Why she could be so mean, so horrible. Like, sometimes she was nice, you know, and then other times... other times she said bad stuff, did bad stuff...'

'What bad stuff did she do, Katie? I know about the drugs... about the sex.'

'Like, well... she always said bad stuff about you.'

Evie's heart drops to the footwell of her car. 'Bad stuff about *me*?'

'Calling you a bitch and that... calling you horrible names. I... I never understood it because, well, because I knew you were a good mum, that you loved her and did everything for her, and

I used to tell her that!' she adds, becoming more animated. 'I didn't understand why she seemed to hate you so much, why she hated *me* so much.'

Evie's throat feels tight, like it's closing up. Her own daughter hated her?

'She didn't hate you, Katie. You were her best friend.'

Katie exhales. Shakes her head. Pauses.

'I had a thing... this thing, you know, for a boy we knew,' she says awkwardly. 'Well, it was more than just a thing, I suppose. I was... I was kind of in love with him and had been for a long time. Libby knew all about it – I confided in her, told her how I felt about him... that I was too shy to let him know.' She shakes her head again. 'I mean, Libby could have her pick of all the boys. They all fancied her – she was the prettiest girl in the class, maybe even the whole school.'

She smiles then and Evie manages one too though it cracks into another sob.

'But it turned out that she was... well, she was seeing him behind my back.'

'Seeing him?'

'Someone told me that they'd seen her coming out of his house in the early hours of the morning. I was devastated, felt so betrayed... I confronted her about it and she denied it, but I knew it was true.'

She pauses. 'Thing is – the worst thing is – I know she didn't really like him, that she was never really interested in him. She told me she thought he was a pussy, a geek, bit of a dickhead... s'cuse my language.' She looks down, a little embarrassed. 'And I realised that she'd only started something with him because she knew it would *hurt me* if I found out, like she got some kind of sick pleasure out of secretly betraying me, letting me go on about how much I loved him while she was... well, while she was doing what she was doing with him. She didn't care about him, not really, and she didn't care about me either. I stopped speaking to her after that, didn't want anything more to do with her, couldn't get over it, why she'd done it. And then... well, then it all went badly wrong.'

'Badly wrong how?'

Evie feels sick but she wants to hear it – she needs to, to try and understand who her daughter was, who she really was.

'He was such a nice person.' Katie is crying now. 'He... he was vulnerable, you know. His dad had just died and... well, he got into trouble, did something stupid, tried to rob a chemist and got caught. No one could believe it. I mean, he wasn't like that... he was nice, you know. He wasn't one of those sorts of boys; he was quiet and gentle, kind. He...' She wipes her eyes, sniffs loudly. 'I never told the police that I suspected anything about him and Libby, you know, being together.'

'Why? Why didn't you say anything, Katie?'

She drops her chin again, sighs. 'His family, I suppose.' She shrugs. 'What's left of them. They'd been through so much already and...'

Evie doesn't understand. 'Been through so much? What? What had they been through?'

'I thought that maybe she had something to do with it – that she'd somehow convinced him to rob the chemist, and so I was protecting her too, protecting them both really I suppose... the memory of them both... because although she betrayed me, I still didn't... I still don't want people to think badly of her... of both of them.'

'Both?' Evie's head is throbbing as she tries to make sense of what Katie's saying. She rubs her temples subconsciously.

'Yeah,' Katie says, her voice soft with a sadness that's so palpable it's all Evie can do not to open a window and release it. 'You see, not long after he was done by the police, he...' Her voice catches in her throat. 'Well, he killed himself. Hung himself in his bedroom from the light fitting. His little sister found him.'

Evie blinks at her then gasps suddenly. Oh God. Realisation slaps her so hard across the cheeks that she thinks she can feel the sting of it.

'He was in our class at school,' Katie says. 'His name was H—'

'Harry,' Evie says, finishing the sentence for her. 'Harry Mendes.'

TWENTY-SIX

EVIE

Deciding that there's no time like the present, Evie swings her car into reverse and does a U-turn as Katie's words resonate inside her head. *'She always said bad stuff about you... calling you a bitch and that... I don't understand why she seemed to hate you so much...'* How could Libby ever have said such things? Evie had adored that girl, loved her so deeply, unconditionally. Libby had been her life; she had admittedly, in hindsight, almost vicariously lived through her daughter, her triumphs and her disappointments becoming her own.

She thinks of all the time they'd spent together. They'd been so close hadn't they, like best friends? People had even commented on it, admired their intimate bond. And Libby *had* been a loving daughter. She had been tactile and affectionate, always hugging her, telling her she loved her, sending her little jokes or memes and texts with emojis to brighten her mother's day. She had felt that from her. It had been real – hadn't it? How was it possible that she'd secretly felt those things towards her, had said such hateful words about her own mother? It didn't make sense. But moreover it hurt. Dear God, how it *hurt*.

The Mendeses' house looks unoccupied as she pulls into

the driveway. It's a nice house, modest but well kept, the garden neat and tidy. Icy gravel crunches underfoot as she makes the few steps up the drive to the front door and rings the bell.

A few moments pass and she presses it again – once, twice more. Nothing. As she's about to turn away she sees the warm orange glow of a light flick on and hears footsteps, the creak of stairs.

Sara Mendes opens the door.

'Hi... Sara?'

She takes a step backward. 'Yes?'

'I'm sorry to call round unannounced like this, and I know it's a little late... My name is Evie... Evie Drayton and—'

'I know who you are.' Sara's voice is tentative, unsteady.

'Yes. Of course.' She supposes everyone knows her now. She's the mother off the telly, the one with the drug-addled, pregnant daughter who was murdered. That's who she's become.

'Come in,' Sara says after a brief pause. 'I'm sorry it took a while to answer the door,' she apologises. 'Emily, my daughter – I have to sit with her until she's asleep. She suffers from night terrors and somnambulism, you see.'

Evie nods though she has no idea what somnambulism means and doesn't want to show her ignorance by asking.

'I have to keep a close eye on her sometimes. It's got a lot worse since... well... it's got worse lately,' she says with a nervous smile. 'Do you want to come through to the lounge? I'll make us coffee, something to warm us up. So cold out tonight.'

'Thank you,' Evie says, nodding. 'Coffee would be nice.'

'Go through. I won't be a moment.'

It's dark in the lounge and she switches the light on, sits down on the edge of the sofa, her heart beating loudly in her ears.

It's a pristine room, homely but very neat and clean. There's a coffee table with tea roses in a glass vase, a soft rug on wooden flooring, a table lamp and a tub chair with a bright cushion, and a feature fireplace – above it is a large selection of family photos in frames on the mantelpiece. Instinctively, she goes over to look at them.

There's one of Sara and her husband on their wedding day, her head tilted back in laughter, his hands on her small waist as he looks lovingly into her face – a beautiful, joyful moment captured in time. There are baby pictures – a boy, around four years old at a guess, and a baby girl, and one of them both together – Harry and his sister, she presumes. There's a picture of the four of them together, the sort that you can have done in shopping centres against a cloudy backdrop where everyone looks a little posed and awkward.

There are more of the children through the ages: the girl with a toothy grin, the boy on the verge of becoming a young man... She fingers them carefully, a visual documentary of a family in happier times, times when they were no doubt hopeful and content, blissfully unaware of what the future held. Photographs were such bittersweet trophies sometimes.

'That was the last one ever taken of him,' Sara says as she walks through into the lounge carrying a tray of fresh coffee in a pot with two cups. 'That I know of anyway,' she adds, her hands shaking as she pours the dark liquid into the cups.

A flush of embarrassment warms Evie's face. 'I hope you don't mind me looking. I...'

'Not at all,' Sara says, spilling a little of the coffee as she hands Evie a cup. 'They're all I have left now really,' she says, 'those memories caught on camera. Well, that and my Emily – just the two of us now.'

Evie's heart tightens inside her chest. Sara Mendes has lost both her husband and son to suicide in a matter of months, a horror so egregious that to suffer it once would be enough to break most people, but to suffer it twice – and in such quick succession – that must be another kind of hell altogether. It's little wonder the poor woman's a nervous wreck.

Sara sits down opposite her in the tub chair, her long hair falling in front of her face like curtains.

Evie's unsure how to start the conversation, how to begin to ask the questions she seeks answers to without causing Sara any more upset. But she is just in so much pain herself.

'I'm... I'm truly sorry about your daughter,' Sara says, her voice as shaky as her hands. 'I know the pain you're going through. I know *exactly* how it feels to have a child *taken* from you.' Her eyes drop back down to her lap. 'The emptiness,' she whispers, 'like your heart has been carved out of your chest with a knife, leaving nothing but a black hole where it used to be.'

Evie gulps back some of the hot coffee. Does Sara Mendes really know *exactly* how she feels? As tragic as it was, Harry hadn't had his life taken from him; he'd taken his own. It wasn't the same, was it? Suddenly, she feels guilty for thinking this. Of course this woman knows how she feels.

'Thank you... thank you,' she says, taking a breath. 'And I'm sorry too, about your husband... about... about Harry. I know Libby was upset by his death.' She searches for Sara's eyes, but she doesn't look up at her.

A strange shiver ripples through her. It's probably the cold.

'I suppose I should explain why it is I'm here, Sara. I...'

'I know why you're here,' she says quietly, without looking up. 'I knew it would only be a matter of time... Incidentally, how did you find out?'

So it was true then, what Katie had suspected about Libby and Harry being in a relationship.

'It should never have happened.' Sara finally raises her head. Her eyes are wide and glassy in the low light. Evie thinks she may be crying but she can't be sure.

'You know, just as sometimes two people meet and the stars collide and magic happens, it can also be the opposite, a bad thing, something evil... something that should never have happened.'

Evil? Evie's throat feels scratchy and dry, and she takes another gulp of coffee, but it doesn't seem to help.

'I want you to know, Evie' – Sara's voice sounds lower now, grave – 'that I never wanted this, for any of us. I tried to stop it, I really did try, and I *did* put a stop to it many times, but... but...' She pauses, looks away, doesn't finish the sentence. 'Anyway, I'm just thankful, just grateful that you're willing to listen to the other side.'

Unsettled by Sara's words and demeanour, Evie feels a flutter of confusion and something else... fear perhaps? She's not sure.

'When did it start?' she asks. 'How?'

'I've asked myself that same question over and over again. How do these things ever start?' She looks at her intensely, which somehow only adds to Evie's discomfort. 'Some people, they sense vulnerability like a predator senses a wounded animal in the wild, don't they, Evie?'

'Yes, I suppose so.' She's not entirely sure what Sara is trying to tell her.

'Anyway' – Sara straightens up a little – 'I should've known better. I should've just put my foot down, been stronger about it, but with everything that was going on at the time... I knew it was wrong. I knew it in my heart. I'm not a bad person,' she says. 'You do believe that, don't you?'

'Yes,' Evie says, 'of course. I haven't come here to upset you, Sara. I just want some answers, that's all.'

'Of course you do,' she says, 'I don't blame you at all.'

She drops her head again in that submissive way she seems to possess. 'None of this is your fault. None of what it led to was anything to do with you, you had no idea what was going on; you've been innocent in all of this. As much as you might not believe me,' Sara continues, 'I want you to know that *he* instigated it, *he* did all the pursuing and chasing and the wooing...'

'Did he?' Somehow hearing this gives Evie a small modicum of comfort. So far everything she's learned about Libby has portrayed her daughter as being the instigator, calculated and manipulative, certainly not the role of a victim.

Sara nods. 'That's not to say it was right. I'm not trying to exonerate myself, I... I... Oh! Emily!' Sara jumps up so suddenly that Evie involuntarily splashes a little of her coffee onto her jeans in surprise.

The young girl is standing in the doorway, her long hair hanging lankly around her face, and she's wearing a nightdress with unicorns on it. Sara rushes over to her, quickly starts backing her out of the room.

'Em... Can you hear me, Em?'

She looks back at Evie nervously. 'She's sleepwalking again,' she explains. 'She's been doing it since she could walk, but it's got so much worse since her dad passed and now, well, since Harry... it's practically every night. Sometimes she goes out of the house... has walked for miles before we've found her. We've tried locking the front door but she found a window and climbed out of that. She's quite resourceful really – and it's not always easy as she's – well, you can see for yourself – she's a big girl for her age, and she's incredibly strong.'

'How old is she?' Evie asks.

'Twelve,' Sara replies as she struggles to remove her from the room. 'The doctors have given her lithium now. They don't usually prescribe it to children but they're trying her on it, see if it stops her from... well, see if it helps her.'

'That must be terrifying,' Evie says, staring at the girl. Sara is right; she's big for her age, almost the same size as her mother. Her eyes are wide open yet she is statue still, her arms straight by her sides, her face expressionless, like a ghost somehow, eerie and unsettling.

'If she wants to join us, I really don't mind...'

'No, no,' Sara says quickly. 'Em... Em, come on now, back to bed, sweetheart; let's go back upstairs...'

Evie watches as Sara wrestles with her daughter and wonders if she should offer to help.

'She must've heard our voices in her subconscious and has come to investigate,' Sara explains. 'The nightmares have been dreadful, just awful, since she found her brother. He meant the world to her...'

Of course, it was the sister who found him, wasn't it, hanging in his bedroom? She remembers Una talking about it on the night of the dinner party, the night her life changed forever.

She looks over at her again, that poor girl, so much loss and devastation in her young life already. Suddenly, Emily turns her head and seems to stare straight at Evie, like she's about to walk towards her. Instinctively, she pulls back in her seat, startled.

Sara frantically blocks her daughter's path. 'Em... Emily! No! Wake up now... wake up!'

'Isn't it dangerous to try and wake her?' Evie says, suddenly fearful. 'I'm sure I've read somewhere that it's dangerous to wake someone when they're sleepwalking.'

'Oh no, no... she's not dangerous,' Sara reassures her. 'You're not dangerous at all, are you, my love? Wouldn't hurt a fly this one, absolutely not. Come... come on now, poppet... back to bed...'

Evie watches as Sara finally manages to usher the girl from the room and suddenly she wishes she hadn't come here, hadn't had an insight into Sara Mendes' depressing and sad life.

She returns a few moments later. 'There. All fine now. She's settled again.'

She takes a seat and smiles, but it belies how visibly shaken she appears. 'Hopefully that will be it for tonight, though I can't guarantee it. Sometimes she's up four, five times...'

'That must be very difficult,' Evie sympathises.

'Yes, well, I'm used to it now.' She smiles ruefully. 'She's a special girl, is Emily. I guess they're all special really in their own way, aren't they?'

'Yes, they are.' Evie pauses. 'Um, you were saying something, Sara, something about how *he* was the one who instigated everything?'

'Oh... yes... I'm sorry, I'm not trying to minimise my part in any of it, you understand that. I accept I was also to blame.'

'To blame?' Evie's confused now. 'What for, for not stopping them from being together?'

'Them?' Sara returns her own look of confusion.

'Was it that they were no good for each other, brought out the worst in each other? Was it her who convinced him to rob the pharmacy? Did Libby ask Harry to do it and it led to him... to him taking his own life? Was that it? Was that what happened?'

Sara stares at her. 'I... I think... Oh God, Evie, I'm sorry, we seem to be talking at cross purposes here.'

'Cross purposes?' Now she is *really* confused. 'I'm talking about Libby and Harry. They were together, yes, in a relationship – a bad relationship? That's what you're talking about, isn't it?' Flickers of fear start dancing inside Evie's guts.

'No... no... Oh God!' Sara looks up to the ceiling. 'Oh God...' she says again. 'Not Libby and Harry. As far as I know they were never together or had any kind of relationship. She's never been here to the house; they hardly knew one another from what I knew. I... I was...'

Evie tries to swallow but it feels like her throat has closed up.

'Then who are you talking about, Sara?' she asks, hysteria rising up through her body. She starts to shake.

Sara's eyes are closed as she sucks in a breath.

'Tom,' she says. 'I was talking about Tom and I.'

TWENTY-SEVEN

EVIE

'You've got it all wrong, Eve.' Tom stands opposite her in the kitchen of their home, concern – and perhaps, she thinks, a touch of panic – etched across his wrinkled brow. He'd been in bed asleep when she'd returned from Sara Mendes' house and she'd woken him, surprisingly calm as she'd asked him to join her downstairs in the kitchen to 'talk'. Clearly, he'd sensed by her tone and body language that something was wrong, *terribly wrong*, because he'd followed her almost immediately, not even bothering to get dressed, asking, 'What's happened, Eve? Has something happened – something to do with Libby?'

The short drive home from Sara Mendes' house had been a blank, so much so that Evie can't even recall getting into her car or how she'd managed to drive at all. She'd been on autopilot, the shock of Sara's confession rendering her numb, her mind paralysed as though to protect her.

Her whole body is shaking with trauma and shock as she stands in her kitchen opposite her husband. She feels it consuming her, taking her over, cell by cell. Her mouth is dry, her heartbeat fast and erratic in her chest. Disbelief, confusion, horror, it's all here again, like the night the police came to tell her their daughter was dead.

'It's really not what you think, whatever she's told you...' He throws a hand up in protestation. 'The woman's mad, Eve...'

He's watching her carefully, studying her reaction. Does she believe him? Is she going to lose it, start throwing and breaking things, lash out at him?

'Why were you even there, at her house? What were you doing going over to see her?'

She wants to answer the question but the squeezing, the knotted cramping in her stomach, is so intense that she thinks she might be sick and it's all she can focus on, preventing the contents of her guts from rising up and spilling all over the kitchen floor. *This is what betrayal feels like.*

'Eve, look, whatever she's said, whatever that woman has told you, it's bullshit, OK? Lies and bullshit.'

But she can see from his expression that he knows – by her own – that she doesn't believe him and that he's going to need to do a lot better than this to convince her.

'Jesus.' He drags his hands through his hair, looks up at the ceiling. 'We don't need this, Eve. Our daughter was murdered last week... She's dead, we haven't even been able to bury her body and now *this*...'

He's talking like this is somehow something *she* has done, something she has created, but still she is unable to speak.

'We should be focusing on Libby's case, on finding out who killed our daughter, not worrying about the ramblings of some mad, obsessed woman... Jesus, for all we know maybe *she's* the bloody killer – it wouldn't shock me if she was. That woman is unstable; she's mentally unhinged. Her husband killed himself, for fuck's sake... Makes you wonder why, doesn't it? What was going on to make him do something like that... and then the son as well? C'mon, the whole family aren't right.'

Evie takes a crystal tumbler from the cabinet with shaking

fingers and somehow manages to pour herself a large brandy. She swallows it back in one hit.

'A mad, obsessed woman? Unhinged, unstable?' She finally manages to find her voice, though it sounds as shaky and as unsteady as she feels. 'What, like Tina Molten was too, you mean? You've been very unlucky, Tom, I have to say. Just how many mad, obsessed, unhinged women have there been exactly?'

She can't look at him. She can't look at his face. She doesn't want to see, doesn't want to witness the man she loves lying to her. She cannot bear it.

'Tina Molten... Jesus, why are you bringing that bitch up? Is it because that bloody detective went to see her, fishing for dirt when he should've been doing his job? You *know* what happened there...'

'No,' she says flatly. 'I don't, Tom, not anymore.'

He snorts, incredulous. 'Yes, you do! The woman was off her head, a fantasist. You saw her – she made it all up just to get back at me because I sacked her.'

'You're a liar, Tom.' Her voice is low and calm, which somehow makes it sound all the more sinister. She wants to believe him. She really wants him to convince her – she needs him to because surely this will finish her off, to know for certain that her husband is a cheat and a liar, an adulterer who's been duping her all this time.

'Sara told me everything. She told me how she initially came to the clinic with a back complaint. How you saw the vulnerability in her, how you took advantage of her, to seduce her.'

Tom shakes his head. He looks distraught, perhaps even more distraught than when he heard the news that his own daughter was dead.

'And you believe that?' His voice has risen to a shriek. 'You actually believe a woman you hardly know, one who clearly has mental-health issues, over me?'

She turns away from him, still unable to look directly at him for fear of what she might see.

'This is me you're talking to, Eve. Tom, your husband...'

'Please, Tom.' She closes her eyes, squeezes them shut. 'Please just tell me the truth. I can live with the truth; it's the lies I can't stand. Please, just the truth...'

Truth. She wonders what the definition of the word really is – for truth is not fact; it's simply one's interpretation of them. It's subjective, seen through the eyes of the individual, tailored to suit an individual narrative. She's read somewhere that the most authentic-sounding lies are ones that are interwoven with a modicum of truth in them, a hybrid mix of both, truth diluted by lies, or vice versa. Would she know if her husband was lying to her? Would she instinctively be able to tell? She's not so sure anymore. She trusts, she *trusted* Tom implicitly. He was, *is*, her husband. There had been no secrets between them – had there? Their marriage was built on the firm foundations of trust and integrity, on mutual respect and love. But he hadn't told her about the money he had given Libby, he had kept that from her – he had lied. And it all makes sense now, diabolical sense, and those foundations – the solid concrete ones she's always believed that her life, their life together, was built upon – are made from nothing but sand.

'I'm telling you, Eve... she's lying to you. That's not how it happened. She was the one all over me.' His voice is high-pitched with protest. 'She kept coming into the clinic with injuries that didn't really exist just so that she could find excuses to see me. I...'

'He was beating her, wasn't he, her husband?' she interrupts him, can't bear to listen to it. 'You saw the bruises and you asked her about them – you knew what was going on in that house, in that marriage, and what he was doing to her and you took advantage of that, of an abused, battered woman who was desperate for comfort, for protection, for a kind word. You showed her attention, affection, offered to help her. She was a sitting duck...' She struggles to catch her breath. 'A year on and off, she said, *a year*; sex at the clinic on the physio table, at her home while her husband was at work, once in a hotel room, the Premier Inn no less, *you cheap bastard.*'

She turns away from him and suddenly she understands in that moment how people *do* kill each other, how when pushed, all that anger and hate and pain builds up and spills over into murder, and she wonders if it was the same for her own daughter's killer. Had he been pushed to his limits too and simply snapped? Perhaps he wasn't driven by evil, after all, but by pain, such dreadful pain and anger.

Tom's head is hanging forward, his hand on his brow. 'I swear to you, that's not how it was, Eve. She wasn't... she isn't as innocent as she's making herself out to be. You have to believe me.'

'No,' she says tightly. 'I don't *have* to believe you, Tom. And I don't believe you. I don't believe a word you're saying.'

Sara Mendes had presented as a gentle, softly spoken woman who'd suffered terrible tragedy and losses in her life and was doing her best to stay strong for her only remaining child, a child she clearly lived for. She certainly hadn't come across as some femme fatale out to seduce other people's husbands. She'd seemed so vulnerable, sad and lonely, her disposition a little on the nervous side. And she'd been remorseful, terribly so. Had it all just been an act? *Was everybody lying to her?*

He's pacing the kitchen floor now, his hand still attached to his forehead, as though he's thinking about what lie to tell next in a bid to minimise the damage, salvage something of himself in the wreck of their destroyed lives. It's suddenly so clear to her now, like a veil has been lifted, like a blind man who can see for the first time – a miracle. He moves towards her but she backs away.

'Don't come near me,' she warns him. 'Do not come anywhere near me, Tom.'

He retreats, holds his hands up. 'OK... OK... I'm sorry.' His chest is visibly heaving with adrenalin.

She pours herself another brandy. The initial impact of the shock has ever so slightly begun to wane and she can feel it coming – the pain and the grief, the heartbreak and betrayal, the anger, the disbelief, the sadness and regret, the humiliation and shame – all of it at once – and she wills it back. She doesn't want it to come, doesn't want to feel it on top of the pain that's already there. It will surely kill her.

Tom must sense her despair, identifying the opportunity to capitalise on it, because he boldly takes a step towards her.

'You were always busy with Libby.' He sighs so heavily that his body sags. 'She always came first, always came before me, before *us*...' he says. 'I'd been working so hard, all my time and effort put into the business. I... just lost my way... let my physical feelings cloud my judgement. Eve, please... It all meant nothing, nothing at all. I didn't love her... I don't love her. I love *you*.'

Her eye wanders to the knife block on the work surface and she imagines herself taking the biggest one from it and plunging it into his chest, piercing his cheating heart and watching him bleed out all over the oak table. He was trying to blame her, to blame their daughter, their *dead* daughter, and blame the business she'd helped him create by funding it entirely out of her father's inheritance for his deceitful lies and behaviour, for betraying her, for betraying their family, for destroying everything she'd thought they were. She's been tricked. It's all been a lie, a deception and fake.

'It was partly the reason for his suicide, wasn't it?' she says. 'Why Victor Mendes hung himself. He found out about you, didn't he? Sara told me. He found out about the affair and knew it was all going to come out, about the domestic abuse, about you and her... and he couldn't live with it, couldn't live with himself or the shame. So he killed himself, and the boy found him, found his own father swinging from a beam in the garage.'

Tom collapses onto one of the kitchen chairs, rests his elbows on the table and buries his head in his hands.

'Come on, Eve, I wasn't to know he was going to top himself, was I? Look, apparently he was in a lot of debt, drinking too much, suffering with depression... He was giving her a battering on a regular basis, taking everything out on her...' He exhales heavily. 'I felt terrible after it happened, but I shouldn't be held responsible for what he did.'

It was true, she supposed. Victor Mendes had made his own choices.

'No, you probably shouldn't blame yourself, Tom,' she says. 'But I'm going to do it for you anyway.'

She takes a seat opposite him and leans forward across the table. '*You* helped him make that decision, Tom, you. *You* as good as handed Victor Mendes that rope. You're a predator, Tom, a liar, a manipulator and a cheat and... that's why you gave Libby that money, isn't it? The three grand Dan Riley told us about.'

Sara had told her there was nothing going on between Libby and Harry – that she knew of anyway – but this would explain it. Libby had seen her father and Sara together, at the Mendeses'.

'Did she blackmail you, Tom, or did you pay her off?'

Tom's head drops in defeat. 'Does it matter?' he says resignedly.

'Yes, it does.' She wants to know if Libby was blackmailing her own father or if he'd simply offered to buy her silence, the latter being marginally the lesser of two evils. *Libby*. Libby had known about the affair, she had known and hadn't told her. It was yet another fracture to her irreparably shattered heart. 'Well? Which was it?'

'I don't know... a touch of both really.' Tom sighs again. 'OK, so she saw me there one night. I'd gone round to end things, to tell Sara to stay away and that it was over for good, and she got upset and... I saw Libby as I left. She opened a window – the bathroom window above – I looked up and we made eye contact. I guessed she was there to see Harry. We never spoke about it afterwards but she mentioned something about needing some "extra funds", about increasing her allowance... I knew what she was getting at... I wanted to explain to her that it wasn't what she thought...'

'Only it was, wasn't it, Tom? It was *exactly* what she thought it was. You made our daughter lie for you, *lie to me* and cover up your dirty tracks for you by giving her money. And you never said a word to the police, about seeing Libby at Harry's house.'

All these lies, all this subterfuge and deceit, she's been living among it all for so long, blissfully ignorant, totally in the dark to all of it. She feels ridiculous, humiliated – a stupid, blind, gullible idiot who's been played.

'Libby, she wasn't the angel you always thought she was, Eve. Trust me,' he says, somewhat ironically. 'I loved that girl with all my heart, God help me, I did, but there was another side to her, a side you never saw, never knew about, one she kept well hidden.'

Evie laughs. 'Well, I guess the apple didn't fall too far from the tree then, did it, Tom?'

She feels like she's been dismantled bit by bit. Every part of her reality has been exposed as fraudulent, a smokescreen for what was really happening underneath. Her child, her husband, Jim, people she thought she knew intrinsically, people she loved so deeply and trusted, they had all been nothing but strangers to her.

'Did you kill her, Tom? Did you kill our daughter because she threatened to expose your affair?' Evie would never have dreamed of asking her husband such a thing as little as a couple of hours ago, but now it feels like a legitimate question that merits an answer.

'What? Jesus... Eve... for Christ's sake.'

He looks at her, his face crumpled in disbelief, and she wonders who he's most horrified for, her or himself. This time her money is on the latter.

'How could you even ask me that?'

He looks like he's about to burst into tears – tears she's convinced would be shed solely for himself, for being exposed for who and what he truly is. The mask has been ripped off, the façade that carefully concealed his catalogue of manipulation and lies, his dishonesty and deceit shattered, exposing the bald, ugly truth beneath.

'Quite easily now,' she says. 'I don't know what you're capable of, Tom. I don't know you at all.'

'But you *do* know me, Eve,' he whines, 'you do! Look, it was just a mistake; I made a mistake! I'm just a man, for God's sake. I'm not the first man to fuck up and I won't be the last. I'm just a selfish idiot who made a stupid mistake.'

'Mistakes plural,' she corrects him. 'This wasn't a one-off, Tom. A year, she said! A whole year while you were coming home to me, to your wife. You talk about mistakes... What about Jim Hemmings then – he made a mistake too, didn't he? Funny, you don't seem to reserve the same empathy for him as you afford yourself, Tom.'

'Ah come on, Eve... that was different, *is* different. Sara's an adult; she's not an impressionable young teenage girl like Libby was. It's... hardly the same thing.'

But actually it wasn't so different, was it? She imagines the times her husband must have come home to her after being with Sara Mendes, greeting her with an affectionate kiss and cuddle, chatting about his day, showing an interest in hers, acting perfectly normal... and all the while he was hoodwinking her, carefully covering his tracks, the scent of another woman on his skin...

'I could never have harmed Libby.'

Tom looks utterly crestfallen, pitiful even, and she has to remind herself not to feel empathy towards him. *He is not the man you think he is.*

'You know that, *you do*. I know you do. I could never have killed my own daughter... our daughter, and besides, when would I have done it, eh? I never left the house that night. I was here, with you...'

The fact that he's even attempting to defend himself depresses her further.

She thinks of Una then, wonders if Jim has been released yet and if, like her, she's currently standing in the kitchen of their home and looking at her husband like she's just met him for the first time, like he's a stranger to her, one who's capable of such deception and lies.

Tom runs his hands through his hair, takes a swig of the brandy on the table straight from the bottle.

'So where do we go from here, Evie?'

He looks at her, silently pleading with her, only perhaps this is a lie too, nothing but an act for her benefit. Tom Drayton, devoted family man, dynamic, handsome and successful, a man with integrity – a man with morals and ethics who can be relied upon – everybody's friend, a *thoroughly decent guy*. Reputation means everything to Tom – 'a man's reputation is what he trades on' is a phrase he often likes to use. It would crush him for people to know the truth and that the 'thoroughly decent guy' was nothing more than an adulterer, a pathological liar who could compartmentalise his double life and hide his true self from his family.

Had Sara been the first? She doubted it. Maybe Tina Molten had been telling the truth all along actually; maybe more than maybe – yes, she almost certainly had been. Evie burns with shame as she thinks of what happened to Tina – she believes now that Tom mercilessly destroyed the young woman's career and character, making her out to be a vindictive fantasist, making *her* apologise to *him*. That was perhaps the worst part of it all. It wasn't enough that she'd lost her job for daring to rebuff his advances; he'd wanted to humiliate her further, destroy her character, her credibility and her life. That took another level of cruelty altogether. How had she not seen it, not seen through any of it?

'I love you; you're my wife. I don't want anyone else, never have and never will. Eve, look—'

He stretches his hands out across the table towards her own. She wants so much to take them, to hold them, her husband's hands, so familiar and reassuring, but instead she clenches her fists tightly into little balls, her knuckles digging painfully into the wood.

'We've just lost our daughter – the worst thing that could ever happen to us, to any parents. We need to be strong for each other, stand together, united... That thing with Sara, it ended a long time ago... I haven't seen her for weeks, months, and have no desire to. I regret every single moment of it, and I regret more than anything hurting you. I just want a chance to make it right, please,' he says. Tears are rolling down his cheeks now, cheeks she's kissed a million times over, probably more.

'I just want a chance to make it up to you – to us. I just want to be able to prove to you that it was a one-off, a slip-up, and that our marriage is everything to me. You're everything to me, Eve, everything. I need you, to get through this. We need each other. We've lost so much already. Please, baby, I just need another chance.'

Evie stares at him. It all sounds so genuine, so heartfelt, and habitually, instinctively, she feels the familiar pull of him, her husband, the father of her beloved daughter, the man she loves, her darling Tom. She wants none of it to be true, wants to rewind back to the time before the dinner party, a time where she'd been blissfully unaware, ignorant, in denial, *happy*. Pain skewers through her, sharp and brutal, an ocean of sadness threatening to pull her under, starve her lungs of oxygen until she drowns. Death seems inviting in that moment, anything, anything to stop the relentless misery and pain that keeps finding her.

'You've told me what *you* want, Tom. Now let me tell you what *I* want,' she says. He looks up at her, blinking back those crocodile tears, ones she imagines he's conjured up for just such an occasion as this one.

'And what's that, Eve?' he says, his tone bordering on hopeful. 'I'll give you anything. I'll do anything to make this right. Just tell me, baby – tell me what it is that you want...'

'A divorce, Tom,' she says, placing her brandy glass down onto the table. 'I want a divorce.'

TWENTY-EIGHT

DAN

'Forensics has come back on the tyre marks found at the scene,' Harding says. 'They're Jim Hemmings'.'

'There's nothing at the house though, gov,' Mitchell interjects. 'We did a thorough search but nada... we took the clothes he'd been wearing that night and sent them to the lab; they'd been washed by the wife, but they came back negative – no DNA, nothing. Libby's DNA was found in the car, but he's admitted to her being in it. No traces of blood, nothing at all. Archer wants him charged with perverting the course of justice – for now anyway. She's still convinced he's our man, gov, and to be fair to her, he's our most likely suspect.'

'Thanks for that observation, Mitchell,' I say. 'Parker?'

'Same with Cody Phillips, sir... sorry, boss,' he corrects himself. 'DNA found at his bedsit, but nothing came back on the clothes. Witnesses at The Chapel all corroborate his statement about the time he was there that night, what he was wearing... Oh! And he was picked up on CCTV, on the high street, around the time of Libby's murder.'

'So we rule Phillips out,' I say, though in all fairness I'd pretty much done this already.

'We need to start looking closer at Tom Drayton.'

'The dad, boss?' Harding looks at me in surprise.

'I don't trust him. He's a bit of a slippery bastard, and I sense he's not been telling us the whole truth. He was evasive when I asked him why he'd deposited large sums of money into Libby's bank account...'

'Maybe Libby was blackmailing him?' Harding says.

'Seems like it was a prolific hobby of hers,' Mitchell says.

'It does,' I agree. 'Libby Drayton appeared to get some kind of kick out of extorting people, even her own family and friends.'

Davis addresses the team: 'Cody Phillips alluded to the idea that Libby wanted her family dead. According to him, she'd mentioned it a few times, sounded him out about it, talked about how it could be done... in this case, setting fire to the house with her family in it.'

There's a smattering of gasps from the team.

'You serious?' Baylis says.

'Deadly,' I reply, 'assuming you believe Phillips's account.'

'And do you, boss?' Parker says. 'Do you think he's credible?'

'Phillips is a small-time drug dealer with a fair few convictions behind him, not the sort I'd want my own daughter mixing with, but in this instance, yes, I do. He may have the street smarts, but he's not the sharpest knife in the drawer. I can't see him having the imagination to make something like that up, plus the whole set-up seems to corroborate Hemmings' story, about Libby blackmailing him.'

I glance briefly at Davis. 'But why? Why would she want to kill her whole family?' she asks.

I shake my head. 'She told Phillips about abuse of some kind, abuse the family knew about but turned a blind eye to. And something about believing that her mother had tried to kill her when she was a child, a toddler, pushing her down some concrete steps...'

A thought occurs to me suddenly. Libby's head injury as a child... There seems to be, as far as we've uncovered, no tangible reason for Libby Drayton's behaviour and actions, for the frankly unscrupulous and deceitful person who appeared to lack empathy that she was. Could this have had something to do with it? Scientists and psychologists have proven that people who've suffered brain injuries sometimes experience behavioural changes, or developmental problems later in life. It's a thought anyway.

'Do you believe it, gov?' Davis looks at me. 'Do you think Evie is – was – capable of that? I mean, it's evident that she adored her daughter; there's nothing to suggest that there was any animosity there at all. Evie seems to be genuinely shocked to learn that her daughter wasn't quite the angelic little princess she had believed.'

My head feels crowded. For once, I'm not entirely sure what I believe. This is the thing about lies – often they're interspersed with the truth, a thin linear thread finely woven between strands of truth. The trick is how to unpick it all.

'I think Libby Drayton was a sociopath,' I say. 'I think she was a pathological liar who had no problem with blackmail, with lying and betraying people, even those closest to her.'

'Yes, but why lie and say she'd been abused? Why claim your own mother tried to kill you? It would make sense though, wouldn't it, to come up with a motive for her behaviour,' Mitchell says. 'A way to gain sympathy from people.'

'Yes,' I agree. 'I think Libby concocted these stories in a bid to manipulate people, and, like you say, Mitchell, garner sympathy from them. I don't believe her brother or Hemmings abused her or were abusing her. But there's something... I don't know. *Something just isn't right.* Somebody killed her. If it isn't any of our three suspects then we need to start looking in other places.' I feel a sense of defeat creep up alongside me, like somehow I'm back at square one again.

'Have we looked closely enough at Una Hemmings yet?' Davis suggests. 'She could've found out about her husband and Libby... maybe she knew what she was really like, knew it would destroy her husband's career and reputation if their secret came out. She strikes me as the type who wouldn't take it lying down – would want to protect her husband's reputation, a reputation she seems to trade off and one which has brought her a pretty decent lifestyle as well...'

I nod. 'You're right, Lucy, but yet again, the timings don't add up. Una Hemmings was sitting at the Draytons' dinner table at the time Libby's skull was being bashed in. Her phone records show that she didn't move from that location all evening and there are no records of her ever contacting Libby on her phone, on social media, nothing to suggest there was any kind of private relationship between them.'

I know what the team is thinking, that maybe – just maybe – we've been barking up the wrong tree all along and that this was simply a random stranger attack, that Libby Drayton just happened to be in the wrong place at the wrong time and that who she was – the trail of destruction she's left behind her – is simply circumstantial.

The weapon used to kill Libby, a rock, would also suggest that it may not have been a premeditated attack, that whoever killed her hadn't gone to the woods tooled up with a knife or gun, and that it was simply a spur-of-the-moment, opportunistic crime. Yet paradoxically, the more likely this scenario has begun to appear, the more I'm convinced that this isn't the case and that our killer is there, right in front of us, somehow hiding in plain sight. We're missing something vital, something pivotal that will turn this case on its axis, do a 360. The answer is there, in among the lies and deception, the thread that needs unpicking to unravel the truth.

I look at Davis. She seems tired and frustrated like myself.

Her phone rings and she picks it up with a sigh.

'Let's dig deeper into Tom Drayton's affairs, his business, his associates... oh, and the robbery at the pharmacy – the boy, Harry Mendes, a school friend of Libby's. I know her friends say there was no real connection between them, but it's definitely odd. Mendes had no record, wasn't known as a trouble-maker – by all accounts he was a decent, law-abiding young man. Did Libby convince him to do it? Did she somehow manipulate him into that spider's web of hers to break in and steal drugs for her?' I scratch my head absentmindedly. 'Obviously we can't ask him as the poor bugger is dead.' Mitchell had brought me the news soon after I'd asked her to look up his address. 'But let's talk to the mother – see if she can throw some light on any friendship between them?'

Davis hangs up the call.

'You and I, Lucy,' I say. 'Let's pay the Mendes another a visit.'

'No need, gov,' she says, her eyebrows raised. 'She's downstairs at the front desk now. And she's asked to talk to you.'

TWENTY-NINE

DAN

'Sorry to keep you waiting, Sara,' I say, pulling up an orange plastic chair. 'I'm Detective Riley – Dan Riley. You wanted to speak to me?'

I sense sadness hovering above her like a fog. I recognise it in people now, even those who're doing their best to conceal it. Some people, like Sara Mendes, seem to exude it, as if it's lingering on their skin like perfume. I suppose it's no real surprise given the fact that she's lost both her husband and her son within six months of each other to suicide – who wouldn't exude sadness after that? When Rachel, my first love, was taken from me before her time, a little piece of me went with her. I think that's how it works with death; you're never quite the same again when you lose someone you love; it alters you irrevocably.

'Thank you for taking the time to see me, Detective Riley,' she says softly. 'I appreciate you're very busy.'

'That's perfectly all right.' I smile. 'And actually, you've saved me a trip – I was planning on paying you a visit today.'

'Oh?' She sounds surprised but her body language contradicts this, almost like she was expecting me to say it.

'Yes. I'm sure you may already know, but I'm investigating the murder of Liberty – Libby – Drayton. She went to school with your son, with Harry. I'm sorry, by the way,' I add, which makes it sound like an afterthought, 'I'm really so sorry about Harry. I'm sure it's been a very difficult and traumatic time for you...' I mean it sincerely but even so, it still sounds like little more than token politeness. 'Sorry' just seems so inadequate.

'Thank you,' she says. 'And yes, it has.' But she doesn't elaborate. She clearly isn't here for platitudes and pity. So why *is* she here?

'Did Harry know Libby well?'

'Yes,' she says. 'They were at school together, at sixth form, St Saviour's. And they were in a relationship.'

'Oh!' Now, this is news to me. Everyone I've interviewed so far throughout this investigation has said that they weren't aware of any particular relationship, or even much of a friendship, between Libby and Harry Mendes. We've found no evidence, no phone records, nothing on social media to link them together. 'An intimate relationship, you mean, like boyfriend and girlfriend?'

She looks down at her lap. 'He was in love with her – deeply in love with her.'

'Is that what you came here to tell me today, Sara, about Libby and Harry being in a relationship?' My mind begins to accelerate.

'Partly. They kept it a secret, being together I mean. Or at least, she did – it was at Libby's behest that no one knew about them.'

'And why was that? Why didn't she want people to know?'

She smiles a little ruefully but doesn't respond.

'When did it start, this relationship?'

She exhales lightly, wraps her bright pink cardigan around her small frame, the vibrant colour of it in contrast to the sad grey vibes she's giving off.

'A few months ago. I can't be exact.'

'And he told you about them being together?'

'No,' she says. 'He never said a word to me about it. I heard them together in his room one night. I suspect she was creeping into the house at night once I was asleep.'

'So you never actually saw them together?'

She shakes her head. 'No, but it was her. I... I recognised her voice... I heard him use her name when I listened at the door once. I suspected that she was there at least a couple of times a week, possibly more. Sometimes I would be asleep, you see, or dealing with Emily... my daughter. She's twelve. She's all I've got left now...' Her voice trails off.

I nod, unsure what to make of what she's telling me and where it may be leading.

'Yes,' I say. 'It must've been difficult for your daughter too, losing her dad and brother in such quick succession.'

She nods but doesn't look up, and her sadness fills the room, settles upon everything in it like dust.

'You can't imagine,' she says quietly. And she's right. I can't.

'She adored her brother; God, she just loved Harry so much, and he was so... so good with her. She's... Emily's a special girl, you see, Detective Riley.' She looks up at me. 'She was born a little different, you know? They say she's on the autistic spectrum, but personally I think this is just a label, an umbrella term, something they can attribute her uniqueness to. Asperger's, autism, learning difficulties, whatever else they want to call it... but she's a very bright girl – she's not at all stupid.'

She says it as though she's had to explain this many times before.

'She just sees the world differently to most people; she's very sensitive to stimulation, to emotions. She can become easily overwhelmed and she suffers from insomnia, disturbed sleep patterns, somnambulism and—' She stops herself.

'And anyway, she and Harry had a very special and unique

bond. He seemed to understand her more than most, and could communicate with her even better than I can – she doesn't talk much, but when she does she can be very eloquent. So when she found him – Emily was the one who found his body, you see – well she... she just...'

I hear the emotion crack in her voice and rest my hand on hers. She's crying now, silent tears dripping onto the table.

'Do you have children, Detective?'

I nod. 'A little girl, coming on for two years old... and a stepson who's seven.'

She smiles wanly. 'Did you know, Detective, that a mother octopus never gets to meet her young? In a gloriously tragic act of self-sacrifice, she dies before they're even hatched, some say in a bid to allow her offspring to feed off her corpse, while others claim it's so that she won't cannibalise her babies. Either way, it's an act of love, to protect them.'

'No,' I say. 'I didn't know that. Don't get to watch too much TV in this job, I'm afraid.' I smile at her.

'What I mean is... our children... they're the most precious beings, aren't they, your heart living outside of your body. Their pain is your pain, isn't it? Their happiness too. You're only truly as happy as your unhappiest child – do you know what I mean by that?' She looks up at me with red watery eyes.

'Yes, Sara,' I say. 'I do.'

She wipes her nose with the back of her hand, meets my eyes. 'I'd do anything to protect my children, Detective Riley, *anything*. When Harry died... when he...' She screws her eyes tightly shut, the words too raw and painful to speak aloud.

'I was in so much pain... My boy, my beautiful boy... my firstborn child... It felt like my heart had caught fire inside of me and had burned right through my chest. I let him down; as his mother, I failed him. I didn't protect him enough; I should've protected him more. I should've protected him from himself, from...'

She doesn't finish the sentence, doesn't need to.

I pause for a moment, allow her to compose herself before I gently try and continue.

'It wasn't your fault, Sara,' I say. 'You mustn't blame yourself.' But of course I know that she can and clearly does. 'Did you tell Harry that you knew about this secret romance?'

I see the rise and fall of her chest as she inhales deeply.

'No.' She looks away, shakes her head. 'I didn't.'

'Why was that?'

She pauses for a moment, shifts in her seat.

'His father... well, you know what happened, I'm sure.'

She straightens up, takes another deep breath. 'Victor... my husband, he also took his own life, hung himself in the garage. Harry came home from school that afternoon and found him. He was close to his father... he looked up to him, you know, as a son should, I suppose. The trauma was devastating. He was inconsolable... It's not something a child should ever have to witness, is it, Detective Riley, their own father hanging from a light fitting in the garage?'

'No, of course not,' I say. 'It must've been awful... a dreadful shock to him.'

'To all of us, yes,' she says, wiping her eyes. She's struggling to hold herself together and it's difficult to witness, not to feel her emotions alongside her. 'But especially to Harry. He loved his father, Detective, even though he wasn't always the best... well, he wasn't perfect, you know?'

'Who is?' I smile slightly and resist the instinctive urge to take her hand in mine again.

'Libby Drayton was, by all accounts,' she says, 'according to my Harry anyway. I heard him professing his love to her; he was besotted with that girl. She seemed to come along just at the right time, although now I realise it was the opposite of that. He sank into depression after his father's death, suffered with dreadful insomnia, couldn't sleep because of the flashbacks, the nightmares. The doctors said he was suffering from PTSD and gave him medication. He was so, so... fragile...' Another tear escapes from the outer corner of one of her eyes and she quickly wipes it away. 'He was so vulnerable at that time, at the time he and Libby started... well, seeing each other.'

A trickle of unease forms like sweat on my brow. This isn't the first time the words 'vulnerable' and the name Libby Drayton have been used together in the same sentence.

'I didn't question him over it because... well, because he seemed so *happy*, you know? I saw such a change in him, in his demeanour, and in his state of mind. He was still grieving of course, but she... she seemed to bring him back to life somehow, lift him up out of the darkness he was in, the depression. I figured that maybe he just wanted something for himself, something that was just his to enjoy and experience, and that he would tell me about her, about them, when he was ready to. So I didn't pry, I didn't push... but now I wish I had.'

'Why's that, Sara?'

She wipes her nose with the back of her forefinger, composes herself.

'Because it was all a lie.'

'A lie?'

'Yes,' she says. 'Libby didn't love him. I don't think she even liked him very much, thought he was little more than a pathetic sad case, someone she could manipulate for her own gain.'

I don't take my eyes from her for a second.

'She was just the same as *him*...'

'Him? Who do you mean?'

'Her father,' she replies coolly. 'Tom Drayton.'

'You know Tom Drayton, on a personal level?' My antenna is twitching violently.

'Yes,' she replies. 'We had an affair, for about a year, on and off.'

I try not to look as surprised as I feel. Well, well, well. Tom

Drayton was cheating on Evie and... hang on, was that why he'd given Libby £3,000? Had she seen her father and Sara together at the Mendeses' and started blackmailing him *as well*?

'My marriage to Victor, it was – how shall I say – volatile,' she explains. 'Victor was suffering from depression himself, and he took a lot of his anger out on me...' Her eyes lower again and I realise how difficult this must be for her, how intrusive having to air her personal life to a stranger.

'He was abusive to you, your husband – physically abusive towards you?'

'Yes,' she states almost matter-of-fact, quickly adding, 'but only ever to me, never towards Harry or Emily – he loved his children, adored them. Never once raised a hand to them. It was only me he reserved all his anger and frustration for.'

'I'm sorry, Sara,' I say, suddenly wishing Davis were here now bringing her gentle touch with her.

'I still loved him,' she explains. 'That may sound ridiculous to you but... well, it's complex, all those conflicting emotions, loving someone who hurts you, wanting them to change, to stop, to get back to how you once were together, to happier times.'

I nod. I understand abuse, have seen more than my fair share of it in this job, sadly, and it's always the same, every single time: the victims, the women (and sometimes men) who I've interviewed, their stories, give or take the finer details, could all be one and the same. Abusers are the true liars of love.

'I know how difficult, how complicated it can be, Sara,' I say. 'And I'm not here to judge you.'

She gives the faintest smile of gratitude. 'I suppose that's how it started, with Tom and I. I went to see him at his clinic. I had a bad back, you see. He saw bruises on me, on my body and he asked me about them, how I got them... He was so...' She stops, thinks about what words to use. 'So kind, so easy to talk to. He wasn't pushy or intrusive, but I knew he knew how I'd got them – I could tell. Anyway, it was a gradual thing. I certainly wasn't looking for it; please believe me when I say that. I'd never been unfaithful to Victor throughout our entire marriage, not once – never even thought about it.'

I nod. I believe her.

'He said I needed long-term treatment for a slipped disc, very painful, so I saw him weekly and... I'm a private person, Detective Riley, but somehow I found myself opening up to him, about my difficulties at home... He always seemed to ask me the right questions; he struck just the right balance between showing concern without prying too much. He was attentive and listened to me, didn't judge me, didn't tell me to leave my husband – he just listened. Looking back, I realise he knew exactly the right things to say to me, how to pull me in. I didn't realise at the time that he was manipulating me; I didn't recognise it for what it was.'

She sucks in a breath. 'When he kissed me for the first time it felt natural.' Her head dips once more. 'It felt good at first to feel wanted and loved, to feel affection and kindness from someone, to feel desired and worthy of love.'

'What happened, Sara?' I say.

'I realised it was wrong,' she says. 'I was married, he was married, although he told me he wished he wasn't, not anymore anyway. He said he was falling in love with me, wanted to leave his wife... but I... I couldn't do it. I'm a Catholic, you see.'

She looks away. 'I tried to pull away from him, stopped going to see him at the clinic. It was for the best. But the more I seemed to pull away, the more... aggressively he pursued me, like a game, I suppose. I was very weak,' she says, racked with what appears to be self-loathing. 'I hardly had any fight left in me, I was so emotionally drained by everything – the abuse, Emily, the financial difficulties we were facing... and then... and then somehow Victor found out.

'I still don't know how. He would never tell me, although I suspect now that Tom might've told him, although he denies this. I was always very careful, you see, ashamed as I am to admit it, but I was careful to cover my tracks. There were no text messages that could be considered incriminating or anything like that, and most of our' – she shifts awkwardly in her seat again – 'our *relationship* was conducted either in his office, and once in a hotel room, when my husband was away on business.'

'How did Victor react when he discovered the affair?'

She shakes her head, her slim shoulders sagging. 'He went berserk. Understandably, I suppose. I would've felt the same, I'm sure. It was the worse beating he ever gave me. He was beside himself, crying, hysterical, angry, hurt... I probably deserved it,' she adds quietly.

'No,' I say, 'nobody deserves that, Sara, ever.'

She looks up. Her face is stained with tears and flushed red.

'The beating left me with some bad injuries – a cracked rib, a fractured hand, a black eye and bruising. I was in a terrible state, could barely walk or eat, and I couldn't leave the house for days. I lied and told Harry I'd been in a car accident. I don't think he believed me but he accepted my explanation and he took care of me. But a few days later, Victor was dead. He... he...' Her voice catches into a sob. 'He just couldn't cope.'

I shake my head. It's a sorry, sad and tragic tale.

'Even after Victor's death, Tom still wouldn't let up. He kept coming to the house wanting to see me, wanting to' – she swallows – 'wanting to carry on the affair. I mean, my husband, the father of my children had just taken his own life and Tom Drayton wanted to go to bed with me... He pretended to care, of course; he was very good at that, so convincing, but I'd started to see through him by then, and the guilt was overwhelming. I told him it was over. I told him many times, but he just wouldn't accept it, became almost obsessive, even a little frightening at times and then... when I discovered that she was stringing him along, that Libby had just been using Harry to get him to do her dirty work for her—'

'Dirty work?'

'Robbing the pharmacy. The only reason she'd ever become involved with my boy was to seduce him so that she could use him as her foot soldier and get him to steal drugs for her.'

'And you know this how?'

'I overheard them talking about it. I overheard everything. She brainwashed him. Harry was a gentle soul, a kind and honest boy, a good boy. He'd never have contemplated doing such a thing if she hadn't somehow managed to get under his skin like some kind of wicked, evil Svengali.'

Sara's tone has changed. Her voice sounds harder, tinged with anger, even hatred, and my sense of unease begins to grow inside my chest.

'The police raided our home. They found the drugs that he'd stolen for her underneath his bed – he was hardly a criminal mastermind. He was arrested and bailed, given a date to appear in court. He was beside himself; I was beside *myself*. My boy, my beautiful boy...'

Her voice disappears into a whisper. 'I heard her,' she says coldly. 'I heard that wicked, *wicked* girl... she was laughing at him, telling him he was useless, pathetic, how much of a spineless failure he was because he'd been caught. She confessed that she'd been using him all along and that she didn't love him and never had; it had all just been a lie to suck him into her poisonous web. She told him he was a loser just like his father and how he should follow in his footsteps... I never thought he actually would do it, go through with it, not my Harry, not my darling Harry. But... but he did. He took his own life, just like his father.'

She's sobbing now and I suck in a deep lungful of air, my head shaking from side to side.

Sara Mendes leans forward across the table towards me; her lips are trembling, tears splashing down the front of her blouse.

'That... that girl... that thing... whatever she was, she was twisted, Detective Riley, evil personified, the face of an angel disguising the devil within. She knew my boy was vulnerable and in a dark place mentally, and she calculatingly and deliberately lifted him up and then sent him crashing down again and he wasn't strong enough – he couldn't handle it, not so soon after his father's passing. She as good as handed him the rope he used to hang himself with, encouraged it, and that's why—'

She pauses and I can see her whole body is shaking, vibrating with emotion.

'Why what, Sara?' My guts are churning over violently inside my abdomen. My professional judgement tells me not to ask the question and that I should stop this conversation now, ask her to think about what I think she might be about to say, but it's too late.

'Why I killed her,' she says. 'Why I killed Libby Drayton.'

THIRTY

Jesus, could it be any colder tonight? She wraps her arms tightly around herself as she makes off down the path through the woods. She isn't relishing the idea of stripping off and changing her clothes in this weather but she'll be quick. She's become a dab hand at it now anyway, has had enough practice over the past few weeks.

She smiles smugly to herself, thinks about the impending evening ahead with Cody as she feels for the bag of drugs inside her rucksack, checking it's still there and intact. Jim Hemmings has come up trumps again, although she can tell he's getting seriously stressy about their little 'understanding', especially since she's upped the amount she needs from him each week – she wants to keep Cody sweet.

Poor old Uncle Jim, the silly old bastard. He'd looked ready to have a nervous breakdown when he'd seen her tonight at her parents' house. She could feel the anxiety coming off him like a foul odour. She thinks of his sad, craggy old face and how he could barely manage to look at her in front of his wife and her parents. Ha! What a joke of a man he was; what a pathetic joke they *all* were. Dr Hemmings and his dirty little secret, and her dad too, acting like the doting husband and father when he'd been off shagging Mendes' mother on the sly. She had to hand it to him though; Tom was quite the convincing actor. Evie was clearly oblivious. Oh well, the dumb bitch deserved it for being so stupid, so gullible. They all deserved it, lying and cheating and deceiving one another, masquerading as these oh-so-good and decent people when really they were anything but. At least *she* was being true to herself.

Suddenly, Harry Mendes' image flashes up inside her mind. She really doesn't want to think about him – it's annoying – but her subconscious keeps betraying her and she can't seem to help it. Harry's funeral had been a big affair; hundreds of people had descended upon St Saviour's church, packing it out, so much so that not everyone had been able to get inside. It was ironic really – he'd never been as popular in life as he seemed to be in death. It was as if the entire school had made an appearance, all the girls crying and wailing dramatically like they genuinely cared about him. They were all such liars, such fakes.

She'd crept into the church largely unnoticed, although Katie had spotted her and summarily blanked her, not even a nod or smile of acknowledgment. Admittedly that had stung a little. She'd sat through the eulogies, bored and not entirely concentrating, wondering when it would be deemed appropriate to leave. She didn't want to draw attention to herself, not on that occasion anyway.

The only reason she'd shown her face at all was so that it didn't look like she didn't care. She hadn't wanted to see Sara Mendes though, Harry's mother. She didn't want to witness all that grief and despair first-hand. But morbid curiosity had got the better of her, and her eyes had sought her out in among the congregation. Flanked by friends and family, Sara had almost collapsed at one point and had to be supported upright, forcing Libby to look away.

After the final hymn, she'd slipped away quietly, leaving a

small bunch of flowers behind and a card upon which she'd written the words: *'RIP Harry, you will be missed – The Draytons x'.* Bending down outside the church to lay the flowers, she'd been instinctively aware of someone watching her and, spooked, had spun round.

Emily, Harry's weird lump of a little sister, had been standing statue still behind her, just staring at her, her face an expressionless mask, like a ghost's. She had smiled and nodded at her but received no acknowledgment in return; it was as if she was looking straight through her. Bloody freak. It had made her feel uncomfortable and a touch annoyed, if she was honest. She hadn't *made* Harry top himself so why should she feel bad? People got dumped all the time and never reached for a fucking noose! It wasn't *her* fault – she didn't tie the rope around his bloody neck. He did that; he did that to himself.

Now, her phone rings suddenly and startles her, the ringtone amplified in the stillness of the icy cold night air, shattering her thoughts.

Brandon. What did that sack of shit want?

'Yes?' she answers the call abruptly.

'We need to talk.' The accentuated inflection in his voice immediately tells her he's been drinking.

'I'm busy.'

'I don't care, Libby. I'm coming to find you.'

'Fuck off, Brandon,' she says, hanging up. She has no desire to talk to him about anything, not after he'd made her beg for his help that time and had so clearly enjoyed it too. Well, he'll be the one squirming soon enough when the folks discover what she's left in his bedroom drawer, *when she makes sure they do.* She'll relish every second watching him trying to wriggle his way out of that one.

Libby imagines the scenario in her mind with a hint of malicious glee. The shock on her parents' faces, her mother's tears, her father's disbelief. She'll not accuse him outright of abusing her – that wouldn't be authentic enough. No, she'll be ambiguous; she'll simply gently allude to the idea with a coy look, a regretful drop of the head, a lone tear. Maybe she'll even try and stick up for him, deny it while allowing her body language to confirm that her parents' worst fears may actually hold some weight – oh yes, she knows *exactly* how to play it. Evie will believe her even if Tom doesn't, or doesn't want to. Evie would believe her if she told her the moon was made of ecstasy, she's that gullible. She feels sorry for her – almost.

Her buoyant mood returning, Libby's thoughts turn to Cody again. It's too early to tell if he's completely on board yet, but she senses she's making headway. He hadn't been totally horrified when she'd talked about killing someone, had he? She'd made out that she wasn't being serious of course, but she knew that subconsciously she'd planted a seed; one she knows will take time to germinate and ultimately harvest. But she can wait. The best things come to those who do and all of that...

She rubs her scar instinctively; it always burns in the cold weather, brings about one of her goddamn headaches. She approaches the tree stump – a makeshift seat – the spot a little over halfway where she usually changes her clothes, and swiftly looking up and down the path, she steps back into the woodland for cover as she undresses, placing her jeans and hoodie into her rucksack and slipping on a pair of tights, a little black minidress and boots. Shivering in the inclement elements, she hooks the rucksack onto the branch of a nearby tree, making sure to place the drugs into her Gucci bag and slinging it over her shoulder. Security at The Chapel won't bother searching her – she's a regular now. Besides, Cody has cut that dickhead of a manager in anyway. He lets him deal on the premises for a fifteen per cent stake; a deal she'd successfully negotiated herself, and one that kept them all happy – for now at least.

Suddenly, she feels a hand on her shoulder and swings round in fear, almost loses her footing on the icy path.

'What the— Jesus! You scared the fucking shit out of me!'

Jim Hemmings is behind her, his face lit up by the warm orange glow of the streetlamp.

'What the hell are you doing creeping up on me?'

She bends forward, clutches her chest until her breathing steadies itself. 'Wait... are you spying on me? Were you watching me get undressed?' She smirks at him in disgust.

'Libby, please,' he says, a little out of breath. 'We really need to talk.'

'Talk, ha! Why does everyone want to talk to me all of a sudden? What do you want to talk about?' She continues to walk along the path with him trotting a step behind her.

'Please, Libby, just wait, hear me out... this can't go on. I can't keep doing this... you've got to stop.'

She rolls her eyes, ignoring him.

'Look, when they do an audit, a stock check at the pharmacy, they'll realise the drugs are missing. There'll be an enquiry, Libby, an investigation and they'll find out it was me and it'll be over – my career will be over and there'll be no more drugs and no—'

'That's your problem,' she interjects, stopping and turning to face him. Jim Hemmings needs to fully understand who's pulling the strings here. All this whinging is beginning to piss her off. 'And if it becomes your problem then you'll have to find another way of getting the drugs for me, won't you? Unless of course you want me to go to the police, show them the video, show it to Una, to my parents, accidentally leak it on social media... better to be a thief than a pervert, don't you think? Thieves are acceptable in the prison system but paedos and pervs... well, that's a different story.'

He's hyperventilating and she can see his hands are shaking.

'I'll be struck off, Libby, and then there'll be no access to anything. No more drugs for you. I don't know why you want them in the first place – you've always hated drugs, always been against them.'

'I am.' She shrugs. 'They're not even for me.'

'What? So... so who *are* they for?' His voice is high-pitched, and she hears the desperation in it.

'Never you mind.' She rolls her eyes again, can't be bothered to explain.

'Please, Libby, I'm begging you.' He has his hands outstretched towards her now. 'You got what you wanted... now put an end to all this craziness please! People will be hurt, lives will be destroyed, the lives of people you love – your parents, Libby, think of them if no one else, what it will do to them if they were to find out.'

His face looks distorted in the low light, like a grotesque mask. She really does despise him for being so weak, so spineless.

'Find out what?' she says sweetly. 'That my old uncle Jim has been grooming me sexually, that he threatened to kill me if I told anyone about what he's been making me do?'

He's shaking his head, placing his hands on top of it. If he had more hair she's pretty sure he'd be tearing it out.

'This is insanity! Why are you doing this to me? Why, Libby, *why*?'

His whiny voice is starting to seriously grate.

'You have everything you could want, a beautiful home and a family, your whole life ahead of you – you're talented and beautiful... you don't need to do this. I've done what you asked me to, I got you the drugs – one time you said, *one time* – but it's been three times now and I can't... I just can't do it anymore, Libby. Please, you don't have to do this. It was a mistake... .what happened that day, it was wrong and I'm sorry. I should never have... I shouldn't have done it. It's my fault, I'm to blame, I accept that, but please, *please* don't do this...'

He tries to stop her from walking away from him, places his

hand on her shoulder. Instinctively, she swings round and lashes out at him, scratching his face. He jumps back in alarm, his hand shooting up to the wound.

'Don't touch me, you creep. You're pathetic, do you know that?' she hisses at him. 'A sad, old, balding, hopeless, pathetic creep of a man. You did what you did because you *wanted* to. And now you'll do what I want you to do as a result of it. You put yourself in this position. No one else but you.'

He's burying his head in his hands. She thinks he might be crying. He's so *weak*.

'You came to the surgery deliberately that day with an agenda, a plan... You knew exactly what you were doing, you evil little bitch!' He's trying to sound angry, but it's ameliorated by his sense of hopelessness, she can tell.

She starts to laugh, throws her head back a little.

'Well, if that's so then you should've thought about that before you bundled me into the back seat of your shitty car, shouldn't you? *You* knew exactly what you were doing then, didn't you, Uncle Jim? I didn't have to give you any instructions, did I?'

She snorts derisively, placing a hand on her hip. 'This is the trouble with people – they just don't think things through well enough, and then they start booing like babies when it all doesn't quite go their way, throw themselves a pity party for one, act like a victim. But actions have consequences, Jim. And here they are.'

She fans her arms out theatrically and looks him up and down disdainfully. Despite him being twice her size, she's not even frightened of him, he's that pathetic.

'That afternoon in your car was singularly the worst three minutes of my life!' She laughs some more. 'Face it, you're finished, *Dr* Hemmings, whichever way you look at it.'

He stops then and she turns round to look at him, still

clutching his face where she's scratched him, despair and hopelessness practically glowing from him like a neon sign.

'Go back to the dinner party,' she says dismissively. 'Go and drool over my mother who probably secretly thinks you're as sad as I do,' she adds, leaving him standing there, a broken, hunched figure in the darkness.

Fuck Jim Hemmings, springing up on her out of nowhere like that and making demands of her, she thinks as she stalks off along the path, aided by a flush of adrenalin. Once she's got what she wants from Cody, she might think about letting him off the hook – at least until she ever needs him to do her another favour down the line, that is. But for now he'll have to play ball until she says otherwise.

These men, they were all so pathetic, governed by that thing hanging between their legs all the time. Women were the ones who always seemed to get the bad rep when it came to being easily manipulated and led, but men were just as easy pickings if you knew what you were you looking for. The trick was finding someone's Achilles' heel, something she seemed to have an innate talent for. In Hemmings' case it had been her mother, or the memory of them back when they'd been at university together. All she'd really needed to do was trigger this memory, transport him back to a time when he'd been younger, better-looking, happy, hopeful... It hadn't been too difficult. She'd seen pictures of her mother from that time and it was true, she was the spitting image of Evie as she was back then, and she'd worn that perfume, that hideous perfume that her mother used to wear, sickly sweet, cloying, the one that brought on her headaches and gave her flashbacks to the accident when her mother had tried to—

Just then, she senses footsteps behind her, hears the crunching and snapping of frozen twigs. *Jim?* Jesus, she'll scream, she'll threaten to call the police, tell them he's harassing her and tell them why.

'What part of fuck off don't you understand?' she says, going to turn round, but she doesn't quite make it before she feels the pain in the back of her head, sharp like she's been struck with an axe.

The force of the blow sends her falling forward, her face meeting the icy ground before she has time to put her hands out in defence, to break her fall. She screams out in agony and shock, a high-pitched, painful ringing sound in her ears... but the second blow quickly follows before she has time to recover and she groans with the impact.

Disorientated, she attempts to pull herself up from the frozen ground onto her knees with her hands, but she's incapacitated; the messages from her brain to her limbs feel distorted and jumbled, unable to reach them.

Desperately trying to remain conscious, she tells herself not to close her eyes, not to let the darkness close in on her, to try and fight. *Get up, Libby! Get up!* But the pain... the pain is paralysing, and her head feels weighed down, like a ball of lead.

Groaning, she feels the sensation of being rolled onto her back and the smell hits her nostrils, that familiar metallic smell, the one that haunts her dreams. It's running into her mouth, onto her lips... *blood, her own blood.*

'Ohhhh, ohhhhh, Goddddd...' She tries to focus on the blurry form standing over her, the smudged outline of a human being like a watercolour left out in the rain.

She's slipping in and out of consciousness now, mumbling and moaning, unable to scream, to cry out.

Squinting through the pain, her vision fleetingly comes back into focus.

'*You?*' she says as the next blow comes and meets her dead between the eyes.

THIRTY-ONE

EVIE

She feels almost humbled by her own humanity as she sits opposite Dan Riley and tries to take in what he's telling her. She listens, critiquing her own reactions, like she's on the outside of herself looking in. So Sara Mendes has confessed to killing her daughter. She's not even sure how she feels about this; the shock has numbed her completely and, on top of everything else she's recently learned, she wonders if she'll ever come out of such a state or if she'll stay this way, forever emotionally paralysed.

'Libby coerced Harry Mendes into stealing drugs for her from the pharmacy and when he messed up... well, she told him that she'd been using him, that their relationship had never meant anything to her. That's when she started blackmailing Jim Hemmings.'

Evie wants to smack the detective's face and tell him he's lying, that he's a dirty fucking rotten filthy liar and that her daughter, her beautiful, kind, sweet Libby would never ever contemplate doing any of these terrible things. That's what she *wants* to say, what she wants to be the truth. But her heart knows it isn't, no matter how much her head or instincts or anything else attempts to convince her otherwise. Her daughter had behaved monstrously and cruelly; Libby had hurt people, damaged them and betrayed them. Who had she been, this stranger she'd produced from her body? She feels responsible by default, faulty and defective somehow, like she has unwillingly, unknowingly, been complicit in it all. '*It's the parents I blame. They must've gone wrong somewhere along the lines.*'

'You should've told me, Evie,' he said, gently chastising her. 'The affair with Tom, it gave Sara a motive. That and what Libby had said, what she'd done to Harry, what she'd made him do – and what he went on to do as a result.'

Sara had lied to her about Libby and Harry not knowing each other well, right to her face. But as Dan explains it all to her, it all somehow makes horrible, diabolical sense. It was an eye for an eye. Libby had coerced Harry into robbing the pharmacy. She'd simply used him then discarded him. And Sara had been seduced by Tom, who'd preyed upon her at her most vulnerable.

She wants to be angry, she wants to shout and scream until the wallpaper peels from the walls in protest. How could Sara Mendes have sat opposite her in her sitting room so calmly, looked her in the eyes knowing what she'd done to her daughter? How could she have lied so brazenly, so blatantly without any reaction whatsoever? She was sure she'd felt that woman's sadness, her anguish and pain. It had felt so real, so genuine. It didn't make sense; none of it made any sense.

'Why now?' She looks at the detective. 'Why has Sara Mendes confessed now?'

'I don't know, Evie,' he says. 'Maybe it was seeing you, maybe the guilt just got too much for her to bear, maybe she knew we were going to link it all together somehow and she knew that time was running out.'

'But there was nothing to link her with Libby's death,' she says, still unable to take it all in. 'Her DNA wasn't found at the scene, was it? Why didn't she dispose of the phone? Why burn her own clothes yet keep a vital piece of evidence like that?' Evie is surprised by her own clarity of mind to even ask such questions.

Dan sighs gently. 'The answer is I really don't know, Evie. Sara says it was spur of the moment, unplanned. She'd gone for a walk that evening and came across Libby on the path and... and she just flipped, saw red. All the pain and grief and rage she was feeling, it all culminated in that terrible moment.'

'Oh God.' Evie buries her head in her hands. 'Did she tell you if Libby said anything? What her last words were...'

'It would've been very quick, Evie,' he says softly. 'Sara says she came up behind her and—' He stops himself. 'She wouldn't have known very much about it, would've been incapacitated, unconscious very quickly. She wouldn't have suffered.'

But Evie doesn't believe him. Libby would've felt *something*. Pain, fear and terror would've been the last things she'd experienced.

She starts to cry but no tears come. She's cried herself dry these past few days, enough tears to fill a reservoir. She knows she'll have to tell Tom about Sara being charged, but she doesn't want to speak to him, doesn't want to hear that faux sincerity in his voice, pleading with her to let him come home, to pretend that none of it ever happened and 'start over'.

The doorbell rings.

'Shall I get it?' Dan is already up out of the chair. She doesn't have the strength to lift herself.

'There's press everywhere out there!' Brandon follows the detective through to the kitchen and immediately clocks her expression. 'Has something happened? Well, something *else*, I mean?'

Clearly Tom hasn't told him that she's kicked him out, probably couldn't face telling him why, the coward. Somehow, though, seeing Brandon's familiar face undoes her and she rushes to him, puts her arms around him.

'Jesus!' He takes a step back.

She never hugs him and suddenly now she regrets it, regrets there ever being any animosity between them, animosity she realises she is largely to blame for.

'Are you OK, Evie?' He blinks at her, stunned and confused. 'What's going on? Where's Dad? I've been trying to call him since I went back to mum's but he won't pick up... I was getting worried.'

She opens her mouth to speak but Dan Riley diplomatically interjects. 'Perhaps I can have a word with you, Brandon, in private.'

Brandon nods, looking a little shocked as he follows Dan from the room.

A few moments later, Dan returns to the room with Brandon in tow. He looks sheepish, shocked and pale in the face.

'I'm sorry, Evie,' Brandon says, sitting next to her at the table and embracing her. 'I'm just so... so sorry.'

She looks at him through sore, dry eyes. Libby had treated him appallingly too, planting her underwear in his bedroom drawer, trying to make it look like... Oh God, it was just all so abhorrent, so twisted. She hates herself for ever having believed it.

'Why did she hate me so much, Brandon?' she says, feeling the strength in his hands as he holds her own. He looks so much like his father, so handsome like Tom that it breaks her heart. 'Why did she have so much hatred inside of her?'

He's shaking his head, crying the tears that she no longer can. 'I don't know, Evie... I just don't know.'

Dan takes a seat at the table. 'I need to ask you something, Evie.' He addresses her apologetically, the way everyone seems to address her now. 'The accident that happened on holiday, when Libby was a child, when she fell down some steps and fractured her skull...'

'What about it?' Evie asks. 'What has that got to do with anything?'

He pauses, casts her a sorrowful look. 'Cody Phillips, the man Libby was getting Jim to steal drugs for... something he told us that Libby had said to him...'

'What? What did she say?'

'That she remembered the incident... that she had flash-backs from it.'

'But she was only four years old,' she says. 'The doctors said she'd never remember it, that it was a blessing she was so young and would forget.'

He nods, draws breath. It's clear he doesn't want to say what he's about to.

'Well, Cody Phillips says she talked to him about it, told him that... that she believed *you* had pushed her.'

'What?' Evie blinks at him, stunned. 'I... I pushed her? Deliberately? She told him that?'

'So he says, Evie.' The detective's voice is calm and soft – there's no accusation in his inflection.

'No... no, that's simply not true! She was just a baby! She was my daughter! I would never... I could never have harmed a hair on her head!'

Shockwaves ripple through her followed by a terrible sense of injustice. She can't take any more. She'll surely combust, explode into flames. 'Oh God... Oh dear God...'

'It's just another one of her lies,' Brandon says, comforting her. 'A lie to gain sympathy, to manipulate people. That's what she did, Evie, lie and manipulate.'

'I think Brandon's right,' Dan says. 'Sadly.'

'Do you think that's why she hated me so much, that she believed I'd tried to kill her as a child? Kill my own daughter, my own baby?'

Dan's head lowers. He doesn't answer her. Had her

daughter died secretly believing her own mother had tried to murder her?

Nausea rises up through her diaphragm, causing her heartbeat to accelerate. The thought was too unbearable to entertain.

'Did you notice a change in her, in Libby, after that accident? A difference in her behaviour, in her personality?'

Evie can barely think straight; she can barely think at all.

'I... no... I don't think so, I... She suffered from headaches as a result of it, terrible headaches on and off throughout her life and there were the fits but they seemed to resolve themselves in time. The doctors prescribed her medication but she was never good at taking it – she hated drugs of any kind. I was always hard pushed to even get a paracetamol down her.' She snorts gently at the irony.

'It's just that sometimes head trauma can affect behaviour... it can trigger certain chemicals in the brain, alter moods, personality...'

'And you think that's what happened with Libby. That the accident, the injuries she suffered could have done something to her, made her... made her the way she was?'

Dan opens his palms. 'It's possible.'

'Well, it would explain it, wouldn't it, how she'd become so... so... twisted, so... *immoral*.' She latches on to this idea, clutches it tightly. She doesn't want to believe that it was nature that had made her daughter the way she'd become, a defect in her genetic make-up, defects that perhaps she was responsible for, her and Tom.

'What happens now?' She glances at Dan. 'With Sara, I mean? Will there be a trial? Will she go to prison?'

'Yes,' he says, gently placing his hand on top of hers across the table. 'She will.'

Evie nods, thinks of Sara Mendes, and of everything she shares in common with her daughter's killer. Both are women who have lost so much – mothers, husbands and children. She thinks of the girl then, Harry's little sister Emily, recalls the image of her from the other evening when she'd been at her house. Sara had told her about her daughter's learning difficulties, her sleep-walking and about her condition. She'd felt such empathy for her and had seen how much Sara loved her daughter, how protective she was of her and how she was all she had left to live for. She wants to feel hatred towards the woman who's taken her only child's life so brutally and who'd been having an affair with her husband. She should feel hatred towards her, shouldn't she? She should feel glad that Sara Mendes will be locked up behind bars for what she's done. So why doesn't she? It's neither hatred nor even anger as such that she feels, but sadness and pity, just a deep sadness that consumes every fibre of her shattered soul.

Dan stands to leave. 'I have to go now, Evie. I'll be in touch,' he says in that soft, soothing voice of his that she's grown so familiar with these past few days. 'As soon as I have anything else to tell you, I promise I'll be in touch.'

She nods, remembers something. 'The charm,' she says, 'the mother-and-daughter charm that's missing from Libby's bracelet. Did you manage to find it?'

He looks down at his feet momentarily. 'Not yet,' he says. 'I'm sorry. If – when – I do, I'll bring it straight to you, OK?'

'Thank you,' she says, her voice hoarse with emotion. 'She didn't deserve to die, did she, Detective Riley? Even after all those terrible things she did and all the people she hurt... she didn't deserve to pay for it with her life, did she?'

He turns back towards her. 'No, Evie,' he says sadly. 'No, she didn't.'

THIRTY-TWO

DAN

I sense the jubilation coming from the incident room before I've even entered it, open the door to the raucous chants of 'For he's a jolly good fellow...' and the sounds of corks popping. It's difficult not to break into a huge grin as I clock the elated expressions on the faces of my hardworking colleagues beaming back at me, their tiredness overridden by the desire to rejoice in the fruits of their labour. Yet I don't feel much like celebrating; I don't feel much like it at all.

'A full and frank confession, eh, boss?' Davis hurries towards me with two glasses of champagne – well, I say champagne, it's probably cheap plonk from the local corner shop, but it has bubbles in it at least.

'I don't know how you do it.' She chinks my glass with hers, adding, 'Well, actually I *do* know... because you're brilliant, gov.'

'Are you drunk already, Davis?' I smile at her.

She giggles. 'I've always been a cheap date.'

'Well, I'll drink to that.'

I swallow a mouthful of fake champagne. It tastes sweet like lemonade. Hell, knowing the budget at the Met it probably *is* lemonade.

'Archer's doing naked cartwheels in there,' Davis continues, rolling her eyes backward in the direction of my boss's office.

'Now there's an image I'd rather not have, thank you, Lucy.'

'No doubt on the phone to her stylist as we speak, booking in a last-minute wash and blow before she goes in front of the cameras.'

'Yeah, for which hair?' Harding quips, collapsing into laughter. It's clear they've all started earlier without me – much earlier.

'So CPS came good then, gov,' Mitchell says triumphantly. She looks a little tired around the eyes. We've been on the Drayton case for nearly a week straight and I can count the number of hours sleep I've had on one hand. 'Gave the go-ahead to charge her as soon as we located the phone.'

'Which was exactly where she said it was,' Baylis adds.

'Done deal!' Harding perches on the edge of the desk, raises his glass. 'Now maybe I can go home and see the other half – if they still remember what I look like, that is.'

'Or maybe they're trying to forget what you look like, Harding,' Mitchell quips, and everyone joins in laughing – everyone except me.

'Yes, well, good work, everyone,' I say, although the words somehow stick at the back of my throat as I say them. 'You've done yourselves – and me – very proud.'

'So come on, boss, fill us in then!' Baylis nods enthusiastically. 'She was doing the dirty with Tom Drayton wasn't she, Mendes? Is that why she killed her, to get back at Drayton? Did he jilt her?'

I take another swig of... well, whatever it is, and try to dislodge the knots that have formed inside my lower intestines.

'Turns out Libby and Harry Mendes were secret lovers,' I say, 'only Sara found out, overheard them together at the house.'

'Why the secret?' Mitchell asks. 'Both over the age of consent, school friends, families lived close by each other...'

'Because she was using him,' I explain. 'She needed someone to rob the pharmacy for her, get her the drugs she wanted to give to Cody Phillips to sell. The same Cody Phillips she was also, I suspect, hoping to manipulate into killing her entire family.'

'Jesus.' Harding's mouth forms an 'O' shape. 'Was there anyone she *wasn't* manipulating?'

'Or blackmailing,' I add. 'Even her own father, it turns out. She saw him and Sara together at the Mendeses' house one evening...'

'Which would account for the mystery three grand from his bank account to hers!' Mitchell says. 'Of course!'

'Brandon, Jim Hemmings, Harry Mendes, Cody Phillips and even her own father... just pawns in Libby Drayton's elaborate games, I'm afraid. She manipulated them all.'

'You think she was serious about killing her whole family so that she could inherit?'

I shrug. 'It's possible. I'm just glad we'll never get to find out. I'm no psychologist, of course, but I'd say it was highly likely that Libby Drayton was a borderline narcissistic sociopath, maybe even a psychopath, although we'll never know for sure now.' I sigh. 'Sara's story is that she heard Libby confessing to Harry that she'd been stringing him along and that it had all been fake, a lie, and that she didn't love him at all... anyway, he was dead two days later.'

'And she blamed Libby. Sara Mendes blamed Libby for Harry's suicide and that's what made her flip and kill her?' Mitchell says.

'That's about the size of it, yes.'

'Blimey,' Harding says. 'Talk about a dish best served cold.'

'I think it's what pushed her over the edge,' I say. 'It would push most of us, to be fair. Losing her husband and then her son... within weeks of each other. Add to that the affair with Drayton, an affair Sara believes Tom told her husband about and that was a contributing factor in his suicide, and you've got some decent grounds for clear motive. She described what Libby was wearing, how she'd hit her from behind, rolled her over and... well... we know the rest. Only our killer could've known these details – as you know they were never released publicly.'

'All that rage...' Mitchell says, her voice trailing off. 'What she did to that girl's face... all that hatred.'

'Well, I think it's fair to say that Libby Drayton certainly made a few enemies in her young life,' Davis says. 'Not that anyone deserves to die such a horrendous death.'

I nod but I'm not entirely present, can't fully concentrate or join in with the team's euphoria. I keep thinking about Sara Mendes' confession, keep running it over and over inside my head. I can't deny that it all adds up. Sara has motive, she knew details about the crime scene that only the killer could possibly have known, plus the attack itself, 'frenzied', was as she'd described it.

'Once I started I just couldn't stop,' she'd told me. 'All the pain, all the rage and grief and anger just came out of me in this manic, frenzied way and I couldn't stop it... just kept on hitting and hitting her. It was as if I'd been taken over, like it wasn't really me, like I was someone else, someone possessed.'

She told me that afterwards, once she'd realised what she'd done and the red mist had lifted, she'd slipped into a state of blind panic and had taken Libby's phone and fled home, where she'd then hidden it in her garden shed, inside one of her husband's old toolboxes. Then she'd taken a shower before burning her bloodstained clothes in the open fire in her living room. Sara said she'd been wearing a white padded coat that evening and forensics had found fibres that matched that description in the hearth. Although we found nothing that puts Sara at the scene of the crime and there were no witnesses, her confession, the phone and the forensics are enough to put her in the dock.

So why don't I feel elated? Why don't I feel a sense of closure like I usually do whenever I crack a case? Maybe I'm just exhausted. Maybe...

I start shuffling up the papers on my desk as the team continues to celebrate and try not to think about Sara Mendes, a most unlikely killer.

'You OK, gov?' Davis's voice filters through my thoughts, breaking them. 'Do you fancy another glass?' She waggles her champagne flute – possibly the only authentic thing about the whole affair – in my direction.

I shake my head; wrinkle my nose.

'Can't say I blame you... tastes like dishwater with bubbles. Anyway, some of us are heading off to the White Hart to continue the celebrations – you coming? I know I'm going to...'

'Maybe,' I say, touching her arm. 'I'm not really in the mood, to tell you the truth, Lucy.'

She looks at me with a hint of concern. 'Been a difficult one this, hasn't it, gov? Complicated. Then again, what isn't?'

I smile at her. 'Very little sadly, Lucy,' I say, and she smiles.

'Well, maybe we'll see you down there, if you change your mind?'

I spy Parker in my peripheral vision; he's standing on his own and looks pretty much how I feel right now – distracted. I turn to him and raise my glass.

'Boss.' He returns the gesture.

'You did well on this case, Parker,' I make a point of saying. 'You were great with the family, a real support. Keep it up and you'll be going places.'

He nods. 'Thank you, sir... sorry, boss.'

I smile. 'You not joining the others down the pub? Don't fancy celebrating the fact that we've got our man, or in this case woman?'

He shakes his head, comes over to my desk. I can tell by his reticence that there's something on his mind. I stay quiet for this very reason.

'Sara Mendes...' he says after a moment's silence.

'What about her, Parker? Is something troubling you?'

The question is undoubtedly for both of us because something *is* troubling me about her confession and yet I don't know what it is.

He shakes his head. 'It's all sewn up.' He shrugs. 'We've got everything we need. Killer's confession and insider knowledge of the crime scene and forensics to back up her claims. She believed Libby was responsible for Harry's suicide – or partly anyway, and the affair with Tom had caused her husband to do the same. She saw her that night and just flipped out. Diminished responsibility...'

He pauses and I wait for it.

'And yet...'

Bingo! I *knew* there was a 'yet' coming.

'And yet, well, what was Sara Mendes even doing down the woods that night?'

'She said she was going for a walk,' I say, 'that she couldn't concentrate, felt stressed and agitated so she thought some air might do her good.'

Parker nods. I can almost hear his brain working overtime. 'Cold night for a walk in the woods in the dark, wasn't it?'

'It was simply chance that she saw Libby on the pathway that night, or so she said, just ill-fated chance,' I tell him. 'She saw her, the red mist came down, and all that anger and rage and hatred and grief she felt over Harry, over her husband and Tom, just erupted in that moment.'

'One thing that surprises me is that she left her daughter, Emily, at home alone. She doesn't seem the type to do that, not with the girl having special needs and all of that. Seems odd.'

He's right; it does seem out of character, but then again, we don't know so much about Sara Mendes' character, only what she's shown us – what she's allowed us to see.

'Plenty of people leave their kids home alone sadly, Parker, it's not uncommon. And anyway, Mendes wasn't in her right mind at the time, wasn't thinking rationally.'

He nods slowly. 'No, I guess not.'

There's a pause.

'Well, goodnight, boss, and thanks for everything,' he says before turning to leave.

Once alone in the incident room, I sit down at my desk and enjoy the silence. I say silence, but my brain is ticking loudly, processing everything over and over again like a scanner. Maybe it's because I feel like this case solved itself and that I didn't play much of a part in that. Sara Mendes wasn't on my radar; perhaps she should've been sooner and that's why I don't get that sense of accomplishment that I usually do when I have my killer safely locked up in a cell. I suppose I would've got there eventually, found out about the affair, about Libby and Harry and begun to dig deeper, but in this case I didn't have to. The killer came to me before I got to them.

I imagine Sara down in the cells now, a broken, grieving, wretched figure, a shadow of the woman she had once been before she'd lost her husband and son, before the Mendeses' lives collided with the Draytons' and created all of this mess.

It comes to me then, the thing that's been niggling at my brain. Parker had picked up on similar thoughts to my own – of Sara leaving her young daughter Emily alone that night. She'd been extremely protective of that girl, highly attentive and caring, that much had been patently obvious. What also struck me as odd was the conversation she'd overheard between her son and Libby Drayton. Why hadn't she spoken to Harry about what she'd heard? She was clearly concerned for his well-being, his state of mind, so why hadn't she told him that she'd overheard the terrible things Libby had said and intervened? It doesn't make sense. Something just isn't sitting right.

I'm about to leave when Archer walks through the door.

'Dan!' She smiles, surprise registering on her face. 'Why aren't you with the others, celebrating? They've all gone to the White Hart. I was planning on joining them. You'll come, won't you?'

I shake my head. 'Thanks, ma'am, but I really must get home to the wife and kids...'

'Oh, come on! One pint isn't going to make much difference, is it?' she says, cajoling me. 'Let me buy you a drink, for goodness' sake! You've certainly earned it.'

That's just it though; I don't feel like I have at all.

'You and the team have worked like dogs on this case for nearly a week straight – and now we have our culprit safe behind bars... what's not to celebrate?'

'Nothing, ma'am,' I say, when what I really want to say is 'everything'. 'It's just that...'

Her smile begins to fade a touch. 'It's just that what, Dan?'

I shake my head. 'Nothing.'

'So you'll join us? C'mon, I'm buying. Half a pint, is it?' She laughs and it suits her, softens her a little.

'What's going to happen to the girl?' my nagging conscience forces me to ask. 'To Emily, Sara Mendes' daughter.' The poor child has lost her entire family – her father, brother and now her mother.

'She's staying with Mendes' sister,' Archer says casually. 'No doubt the courts will decide what's best for her in the long run.'

I nod sagely. What's best for Emily Mendes is to be with her doting mother, but I know that won't be the case now, not for a long time at least.

Archer hovers in the doorway of my office, looking at me with her steely grey eyes.

'I'll be over in a bit,' I say, placating her. 'Just a couple of loose ends to tie up here first.'

'As you wish, Riley,' she says, turning to leave. 'I'll make sure that half pint is waiting for you.'

The Mendeses' front door is sealed off by police tape and it takes a fair amount of physical effort to break through it. I have to boot the door in, which takes considerably more effort and makes much more of a din than I hoped it would. I don't want to alert anyone to my presence. I know I shouldn't be here, that it's officially a secured crime scene, but I'll worry about that as and when – or if – I need to. I'm looking for something, but I don't yet know what that something is, which I realise makes no sense whatsoever. I just need to find the thing that I don't know I'm looking for.

It's still and dark inside the house. I smell the chemicals left behind by the forensics team, clock some of their paraphernalia where they've dusted and scraped, searching for tiny particles of the truth. There's that word again – *truth*. Something that can't be compromised, that exists only of itself, an oasis surrounded by a desert of ambiguity. My intuition tells me that it's here, somewhere in this house.

Instinctively I take the stairs, two at a time, spurred on by a force within me that can't be described. When I was a boy, my father used to play a game with me called Hot and Cold. He'd hide an object, a pencil, a lighter, something small in a room and then I would look for it. If I got close to the object, he would shout out, 'Warmer! Warmer! Boiling hot!' And if I went in the wrong direction, 'Cold. Colder. Freezing!' He said I was naturally very intuitive when playing the Hot and Cold game, something I hope to capitalise on in this moment.

I enter Sara Mendes' bedroom – a neat, feminine room with floral wallpaper and matching bed sheets. I start to open a few drawers, rifle around inside. Clothes, underwear, bedding... nothing of interest. *Cold*.

I look inside her wardrobe, scrape the clothes that are hanging inside along the rail. I check the pockets of her jackets and coats; open the few shoe boxes... *Colder*.

I check her dressing table, look inside her jewellery box and finger the small earrings and necklaces... *Freezing*.

I check underneath the bed – there's nothing there save for some carpet fluff. I pull up the mattress and put my hands inside her pillowcases. Nothing. *Cold*.

Growing despondent, I break the seal of tape outside Harry's old bedroom, search among the remnants of a boy who had his whole life to look forward to before he took it. It reminds me again of the power and hold Libby Drayton appeared to have over people, and to my shame, I fleetingly think how it is perhaps a good thing that she's no longer here to continue her reign of destruction.

When Harry's room gives up nothing of significance, I go into Emily's room, still unsure of what it is I'm actually looking for. It's a pretty room, the sort I imagine my Pip to have one day when she's Emily's age. Pink velvet drapes hang almost sorrow-fully from the window, the pristine unicorn bedspread covered in soft toys. Only the boy-band posters on the wall suggest that transition from child to teenager; everything else could belong to a five-year-old. *Cold*.

I do a mandatory search of her drawers, empty them out, her nightdress and small underwear scattering onto the carpet, my sense of frustration – or something else – growing inside me. I check the bed, underneath and inside the covers... I hear my father's voice inside my head: 'Warmer, Danny Boy... warmer...'

I open the wardrobe, rifle through the small garments hanging up: nothing. But my dad's voice is growing louder in my mind.

I pick up a pair of shoes, small with a buckle and a bow on

the front. I think they're called Mary Janes, though I've no idea how I know this. With my instincts screaming like sirens in my head, I put my fingers inside one and... I feel something, something underneath the sole of the left shoe, a hard lump. BOILING HOT!

Frantically, I peel back the sole and... I take it carefully between my fingers, dropping the shoe to the floor as I stare down at it with shaking hands.

'Oh, Sara,' I say, overcome with such a deep sense of sadness that it forces me to sit down on the edge of the bed. '*Oh, Sara.*'

THIRTY-THREE

DAN

Sara Mendes looks like a small, scared child as I enter the cell, the weight of the door clicking loudly behind me. Her pale face shows her exhaustion and the fear that she's trying – and failing – to conceal from me.

'How are you doing, Sara?' I ask her, taking a seat on the edge of the plastic mattress, a mattress covered in the anguish of a thousand men and women who've preceded her. 'Is there anything you need?'

It's a ridiculous question really, I suppose. I'm sure there's plenty that Sara Mendes needs, her own bed for one thing and to be with her daughter for another.

'I'm fine.' Her voice is a whisper, like she barely has the strength left to speak. 'Thank you.'

I smile; nod. I can tell she's wondering why I'm here, why I've come to see her. The interviews have all been completed, over fifteen hours of them in total. She'd given a detailed confession, had cooperated fully with the investigation and expressed her deep remorse and regret.

It was clear from her confession that Sara Mendes was a woman so entrenched in the grief over her husband's – and particularly her beloved son's – death. It was this terrible agonising grief that had driven her to do what she'd done, affected her mental well-being and her ability to think rationally. She has no criminal record, no history of any violent behaviour whatsoever. In fact, the opposite could be said – she was, is, a gentle, placid woman in nature, demure and softly spoken. The judge will take all of this into consideration, I'm sure, though she's still looking at a long stretch behind the door.

'How's Emily?' she asks me. 'Have you seen her?'

I nod. I've been round to her sister's house. Emily's auntie has been awarded temporary custody of her daughter, something Sara had cried tears of joy about when she'd heard.

'At least I know she'll be safe with my sister, that she'll look after her. Emily needs a lot of care and attention, you see; she isn't like other children, other girls her own age – her mental age is somewhere around seven years old. She gets scared when I'm not there. I know she'll be scared now, wondering where I am, but at least my sister is with her and she hasn't been lost in the care system, because that's what I was most afraid of... that she'd be placed with a family who wouldn't understand her, wouldn't understand her needs.'

'She's a bit confused,' Sara's sister, Mandy told me during my visit to the house. 'She thinks her mum has gone shopping and that she'll be back to read her a story before bedtime. She doesn't really understand. She doesn't understand much at all. It's all so tragic,' she sighed. 'Losing her father, and her brother and now her mother too...'

I nod, watching Emily from across the room. I go over to her, crouch down on my knees.

'Hey, Emily,' I say, smiling at her. 'My name is Dan, Dan Riley, and I'm a friend of your mother's.'

She stares up at me, her face an expressionless blank.

'She doesn't talk much,' Mandy explains. 'She's always been quiet but ever since... well, particularly after Harry passed, she's been practically mute. I think it's the drugs too. She's like a zombie most of the time, out of it.'

I pull my wallet out of my pocket and flip it open.

'This is my daughter, Juno,' I say, showing her the photograph, one that was taken when Pip was around fourteen months old. She's sitting in her high chair, laughing – it was one of those lucky- moment-type photographs that don't come about often. 'I call her Pip,' I say.

She stares at the picture for a few seconds but says nothing. Mandy hovers over us. I need to get rid of her, to speak to Emily alone for a few moments.

'I hope you don't mind me asking, but could I get a drink of water? My throat feels terribly dry.' I smile up at her.

'Gosh, of course!' Mandy says, as though apologising for not thinking to offer. 'Would you prefer tea perhaps, or a coffee?'

'Ah, now tea would be wonderful.' I thank her as she leaves the room.

Once Mandy is safely out of earshot, I turn to Emily. 'Listen, I wanted to talk to you about something if that's OK Emily? Is that OK?'

She continues to stare out of the window, clutching a doll by the hair.

'Your mum told me that sometimes you get up and walk about in your sleep, is that right?'

She pauses, nods slowly.

'And that sometimes you even walk out of the house and go off somewhere, on a little adventure. Do you know what I'm talking about, Emily?'

She silently nods again.

'Do you remember anything about these times when you're asleep – you know, like remembering a dream perhaps? When you wake up, do you remember that you went for a walk, what you did, who you saw...'

She turns round then and faces me. She's a beautiful child, dark brown soulful eyes like her mother's and long silky hair. To look at her, you would think she was just your average young girl, a girl on the precipice of her teens.

'Sometimes,' she says. It's the first time I've heard her speak.

I smile. 'And do you remember, recently, from one of your sleepy walks, if you saw this girl?' I pull out another photograph from my inside pocket of Libby Drayton, show it to her.

Her face clouds over instantly and she turns away, starts hitting her doll's head against the window ledge, smashing it down onto the wood over and over again. I can see she's becoming distressed, agitated. I place the photo back inside my pocket.

'Do you know the girl in the photograph, Emily?'

She doesn't answer me, continues abusing her dolly.

'Do you know her name?'

'She hurt Harry,' she says, and I nod, remembering that it was this little girl who'd found her beloved brother hanging from a rope, the first person to witness his lifeless body, and I have to stop myself from reaching out and touching her in case it spooks her even more.

'I know,' I say, 'I know.'

I pull something from my pocket and hold it in my open palm, show it to her. 'Did you take this from her, Emily? That night on your sleepy walk. Did you take it from her?'

She smacks the doll hard against the ledge once more, causing its plastic head to become detached from the body. We both stare down at the decapitated doll at her feet on the carpet and then she looks up at me.

'Dolly's dead,' she says.

* * *

'I went to see her yesterday,' I say to Sara. 'She's a little confused, not sure where her mum has gone, but she's OK. She will be OK.'

'They wanted to take her away from me when she was younger, you know, put her in an institution,' she says. 'Assisted living, they call it, but it's an institution really – everybody knows that.' She sniffs back tears. 'I wouldn't hear of it. Victor thought it would be for the best, but the best for whom? Not for Emily – she needed to be with me, with her family, not hidden away out of sight with strangers looking after her, standing in as her parents...' Her voice trails off. 'Just because she isn't... isn't the same as other girls her age, just because she's different. Different is still frowned upon in today's society, isn't it, Detective? We mock and berate what we don't understand.'

I pause for what feels like an age.

'I know what you did, Sara,' I eventually say, my tone gentle. 'And I know why you did it.'

I think I see a tiny flicker of fear dance across her eyes. She doesn't blink.

'Yes, well, I just hope that one day Evie Drayton will forgive me,' she says. 'That she can find it in her heart to grant me the forgiveness that I can't grant myself.'

'I think what you've done, what you did, is the ultimate act of love, Sara.'

I take her hand in my own. It's shaking. I think mine is too.

'Perhaps I would even do the same thing in your shoes.'

I sense her unease travel through my fingertips.

'We searched the house. Everything was where you said we'd find it: the clothes you burned in the fireplace, the phone in the old toolbox in the garage – it was all there. But she forgot to tell you about it, didn't she? Or maybe she chose not to.'

I see her visibly swallow.

'I'm sorry.' She laughs a little nervously. 'I'm not following you, Detective Riley.'

I smile resignedly. 'Yes, you are, Sara,' I say as I pull it from my pocket and place it on the mattress in front of her.

She stares down at it, doesn't take her eyes from it.

'The charm from Libby's bracelet, the one she was wearing that night when she was killed, the mother-and-daughter charm. She took it, didn't she, a souvenir perhaps. Evie had noticed it was missing though, had thought that maybe it had been mislaid by forensics. I found it, in Emily's bedroom, hidden in a pair of her shoes underneath the sole. You didn't know about it, did you? She didn't tell you...'

'I... I...' Sara tries to speak, but panic has rendered her speechless. 'No... no, I put it there. It was me.'

'She came across her that night during one of her sleep-walks, didn't she? She saw the girl who she felt had taken her brother away and she beat her to death with a rock. Maybe she wasn't even aware of it at the time, didn't know what she was doing; maybe she only realised when she came round from her dream state and just panicked... And she came home, didn't she, covered in blood – in Libby's blood – and you told her it was all a bad dream, a nightmare... and you burned her clothes, and after placing your own DNA on the phone, you hid it some-where. You didn't destroy it because it could be used as evidence of your own guilt – if it came to it, you could guide us to that phone, and the remains of the fire and take responsibility for it.'

She starts to cry then. 'No. No,' she says. 'You're wrong.'

But it sounds heartbreakingly disingenuous and we both know it.

She stares at me, wide-eyed with fear.

'Emily's not a violent girl, Detective. She wouldn't do such a thing – she's just a little girl. It was all just a dream...'

Tears are streaking her pale face, and she turns away from me, lest I see the truth in her eyes.

'I've always told her,' she says, 'that once you tell someone about your bad dream it goes away, and that you never have to remember it ever again. I told her that it was all over now and that she didn't need to be scared.'

She pauses, sighs resignedly. 'I can withstand a life of incarceration knowing that she's safe, with my sister, the next best thing to me. She's the only good thing I have left in my life that hasn't been taken from me.'

I swallow back the granite lump that's wedged at the back of my throat, obstructing my windpipe.

'She's on stronger medication now, tablets that render her a zombie, practically. She's no threat to anyone; she poses no danger. Please...'

She hands the small silver heart charm back to me and I look down at the inscription upon it with a heart so heavy it feels like I may topple forward from the weight of it: 'mother and daughter'.

THIRTY-FOUR

Her heart is racing inside her chest as she sits on the small banquette inside the quaint old pub and waits for him. It's a beautiful pub, its sixteenth-century charm somehow giving her a strange modicum of comfort. This place – so Joyce, the landlady, has proudly informed her – has seen the horrors of two world wars, and even a fire that had almost completely destroyed it, and yet still it somehow remains standing, a stoic refusal to be beaten, rising up from the ashes to survive another day.

Nursing a sticky gin and tonic, she takes a tentative sip and lets the alcohol warm her insides. Spring is on its way now; the daffodils have come, yellow beacons of hope sprouting upwards from the earth, making the world a little brighter – it's the small pleasures in life that she holds on to now.

Her heart stands still inside her chest as she sees the door open and he walks through it, immediately struck by his change in appearance. He looks older and thinner, as though something in him has been intrinsically lost forever. She supposes she's probably the same.

He smiles as he sees her, but it's not the smile she remembers him having. It's different somehow; they're all different now.

'Jim.'

She can tell he wants to embrace her but is fearful of rejection. Part of her wants him to, perhaps out of shared history, or perhaps just simply from the need to be held.

'You look well,' he lies, or perhaps not. She supposes she has made more of an effort today than she has in a while, even wearing a slick of lipstick and a squirt of her favourite perfume – one she remembered he'd always liked. Perhaps she's not lost forever after all.

'Thank you – thank you, Evie, for agreeing to see me,' he says, his once familiar voice now resembling a stranger's.

She supposes that's what they are to each other now; perhaps that's all anyone ever really is anyway – just strangers that you know.

'I know it can't have been easy to say yes and I'm grateful.'

Jim has spent the last three months in Belmarsh prison. The judge was lenient given his impeccable previous good character and the deep remorse he'd shown in court. He hadn't wanted to send someone of Jim's character behind bars, someone so altruistic – an upstanding member of the community, a GP who'd never made a real mistake in his life, until her daughter had come along. And the truth was, Evie hadn't really wanted that for him either, despite everything. She knows that to hate Jim Hemmings would be like her swallowing poison and expecting him to die instead.

'I got you a gin and tonic,' she says, pushing it towards him. 'I thought you could probably do with it.'

This small gesture of kindness appears to undo him and he starts to cry, his face crumpling as he tries to hide it with his hands.

'Oh God, Evie...'

'How have you been?' she asks him. 'Although I suppose that's a silly question after where you've been.'

He gulps back a mouthful of his drink and wipes his eyes, composing himself. His tears were no good to her now. They changed nothing.

'I've been where I deserved to be,' he says.

She looks down at the table briefly.

'I haven't come here for your pity. I don't deserve it and I'm not asking for it.'

'Then why are you here?' She's really not sure why either of them is, to be honest. Perhaps it was the hope for some kind of closure for them both, a chance to say goodbye and step away from the ruins of their respective lives.

'I... I don't know... I...' he stammers, and she imagines that all the words he's mentally prepared for this occasion have abandoned him, as pre-rehearsed words are wont to do. 'It's selfish of me, to want to see you... I...'

'I heard that Una's had a breakdown,' she says. 'And that she's in a psychiatric unit.'

Evie isn't sure how she feels about this: primarily sadness, she supposes. After all, none of this was Una's fault, was it?

Jim's eyes drop down to the table. 'I went to see her,' he says quietly, 'at the hospital. I don't think she can ever forgive me. And maybe that's for the best anyway... which reminds me...' He pauses. 'She asked me to give you this.' He takes an envelope from his inside jacket pocket, hands it to her.

'A letter...?' Evie stares at the familiar handwriting on the front for a moment.

'Aren't you going to open it?'

'Later,' she says, slipping it into her handbag. 'And if it's any consolation, Tom and I are getting a divorce,' she tells him, quickly adding, 'It's what I want; it's my decision.'

Jim nods silently. He doesn't look surprised, but then again she hadn't expected him to be.

'I'm sorry, Evie.' He removes his glasses, wipes the rims of his eyes again. 'All of it... all of this... our lives... all our lives ruined.'

Evie sighs heavily. 'I sometimes think that perhaps if he'd never had the affair with Sara Mendes in the first place then none of it would ever have happened.'

But even as she says this she isn't entirely convinced of it. She'd always thought life was a series of 'what ifs' that you could trace back right throughout your life. But she knows now that really life is simply a series of 'what *is*'.

'Anyway, I'm happy here now with my little Welsh cottage. It's a beautiful place, peaceful and remote.' The remote part is what had sold it to her. People scare her now. She's better off alone.

The trial had been harrowing enough, the press interest and sensationalism unbearable, just as she'd anticipated. People had come to know her face – she had become something of an unwilling celebrity – and they either pitied or scorned her. She wasn't sure which was worse. The idea of becoming anonymous again was too appealing. Brandon has promised to come and visit her soon, and the cottage has a lovely spare room should he choose to stay. She hopes that he will; she would like the opportunity to atone for some of her own mistakes.

There had been no elation, no celebration when Sara Mendes had been found guilty of Libby's manslaughter on the grounds of diminished responsibility. The judge had taken into consideration her mental state following the deaths of her husband and son and the pressure of caring for a child with disabilities as well as having lived through battered wife syndrome. He'd recognised that she'd made a haphazard attempt at trying to conceal her crime, a crime he described as 'violent and frenzied' but applauded her for admitting her guilt and for the deep remorse she'd shown for her actions.

Had it been justice for Libby? Evie didn't think so, not

really, but inside she'd felt torn, had felt guilty for feeling that Libby had partly been the architect of her own demise, a demise that somehow seemed almost inevitable now. Sara had received just twelve years. She would be out in six, when she would no doubt be reunited with her daughter again, an option she herself would never be granted. And the shame she feels that perhaps it's just as well is something she keeps a secret inside of her, something she struggles to reconcile within herself. Something she'll take to her own grave.

'It sounds good,' Jim says. 'A new start, if that's possible, for any of us.'

She smiles at him slightly. What was the alternative?

'You, above everyone, deserve to find some kind of happiness, make some kind of life for yourself where you can be happy.'

Happiness. It's an inside job, isn't it? Or so everyone says anyway. Perhaps they really are right after all and it does begin and end only with the self and that everything, everyone in between is either a positive or a negative simply passing through.

Their eyes lock together silently for a moment, a lifetime of unspoken words passing between them. She finishes her gin and tonic, places the glass back down onto the table.

'I should go now,' Jim says, and she nods. After today, she knows she will never see Jim Hemmings again and that all those invisible threads that have bound them all together for all these years will be severed forever. She sees from the way he's looking at her that he knows it too.

'Promise me you'll read Una's letter,' he says. 'It's important.'

She manages a thin smile as he stands.

'I hope you'll forgive me one day, Evie,' he says. 'That you can find it in your heart to forgive me, for everything.'

. . .

Left alone in the pub, Evie orders another gin and tonic and takes Una's letter from her handbag, opens it.

My dearest friend, Evie,

I've lost count of the times I've begun to write this letter, only to screw it up and throw it in the bin. I could have filled ten wastepaper baskets, maybe more over the years. I would start off skirting around the things I want to say. I would use memories we shared and colourful anecdotes about when we were young and the endless joy of our youth, how we laughed and loved, how we dreamed of our collective glorious futures in which we would both forever feature. I would write about your pregnancy – and about my lack of one – and your perfect marriage and family, how I admired you, envied you, how I wished I could be you.

Now, however, I realise these were all just excuses, happy distractions to divert you – and myself – away from the truth.

And so here it is:

It was me who was holding Libby's hand that day in Tenerife, the day she fell down the steps and fractured her skull. I remember at the time, in all the confusion, that you thought you'd been holding on to her but it wasn't you. It was never you. I let go of her hand. I pushed her.

Evie gasps aloud, causing Joyce to look over at her and mouth the words, 'Are you OK?'

It was never ever my intention to hurt her, not seriously. My intention that day was to be the hero, the saviour. Perhaps in some way I was trying to make you look bad, like you hadn't been watching her properly and she'd fallen over and grazed her knee and there I was, Auntie Una to the rescue, and wasn't I just marvellous? Wouldn't I just make such a better, more attentive mother? But it went wrong. I tried to reach out and grab her but I was too late. She fell.

I live with the sound of her hitting the ground and the screams of the people below, of your screams, of my own. They have rightly haunted and tormented me ever since. Maybe they'll be the last thing I ever hear.

For all these years I've allowed you to believe that you were responsible for what happened that day. I watched you punish yourself. I witnessed your guilt, even comforted you in it.

I lied to myself so convincingly that it became visceral; the lie became my truth in the end.

I was – am – a coward. I didn't want to live with the guilt of what I'd done; I knew it would be the end of our friendship without question. Libby was the daughter I never had, never could have, and I was scared to lose you both. I couldn't expect anyone to understand why I did it; I didn't understand it myself.

What I did that day was selfish and cruel and unforgiveable, but my intention was never to cause serious harm. If you can ever believe only one thing, I hope it will be that.

I know of course that no apology could ever fill the chasm of the years of regret and pain my actions caused that day. I do not ask your forgiveness; nor will I ever expect it.

My motivation for writing this letter is not to try and expunge the guilt I feel and have made you feel too, but to try to free you of yours so you no longer have to carry a burden that was never yours in the first place.

I have no right to tell you that I have always loved you, Evie, and I will miss you forever,

Una x

Evie looks down at the page, reading the same lines over and over again with a shaking hand. It's only as the ink begins to spread that she realises she's crying.

The love, the lies, the jealousy and the deceit, the hidden truths and secret yearnings, the complex, tightly woven intricacies of all of their lives linking together to create one huge tapestry of tragedy in which they've all been blighted, unwillingly, unknowingly and otherwise.

Has Una's confession brought her relief, knowing that she hadn't been holding her daughter's hand that day? Perhaps. But what difference did it make now anyway? What difference did anything make? Libby had still died believing it was her mother who'd pushed her... Libby was still never coming back.

Anger and sadness wrestle for first place inside her. How could Una have done such a stupid, terrible thing? How could she have let her believe all these years that she'd been responsible? Had the head injury Libby had sustained as a result turned her into a sociopath, impaired her ability to feel empathy and remorse, or had she simply been born the way she was? Was Una's jealousy to blame for all of this?

Questions begin to circulate endlessly inside her mind but they'll never be answered now. And perhaps it's best they remain that way for the answers change nothing. Time cannot be reversed. Time is the only thing ever truly lost.

She finishes her gin and tonic, places the glass back down onto the table.

'I'll see you tomorrow, Joyce.' She smiles as she makes her way towards the door, throwing the letter into the open fireplace before she walks through and closes the door behind her.

THIRTY-FIVE

DAN

My father died suddenly of a heart attack on a Sunday – his favourite day of the week. 'Ah, Sunday, Danny Boy, the day of roast dinners and rest!'

He'd always enjoyed a nip of brandy every Sunday since the day Mum died. 'She wouldn't have approved,' he used to say, swigging it back surreptitiously as though she was looking on. 'It's the only good thing about her no longer being around!'

The shock of it left me heartbroken and reeling, has left me reeling still. The last time I'd seen him was at mine and Fiona's wedding when he'd seemed his usual larger-than-life self, a picture of health. I simply couldn't believe it – not my dad, my pops.

He'd always been a big, strapping man, my father, tall and broad in stature. In his youth – 'before you were even a twinkle in my eye' – he'd had designs on becoming a professional boxer, so he told me on my wedding day.

'I was good too,' he'd said modestly, 'bloody good, in fact. Right Hook Riley they used to call me. Floored a fair few with one punch I tell you – boom! Out for the count!'

I'd laughed.

'Right Hook Riley, eh! You could've been a contender!'

And I'd smiled, wondered what else I'd never known about him. I realised, in those blissfully unknowing last times I got to spend with him, that he'd been a man with hopes and dreams too once, one with private ambitions, things he would've liked to have achieved and places he wished he'd visited but never did, and I saw a glimpse of the man he was before he ever became 'Dad'.

Losing a parent is a terrible thing, it takes away part of your own identity, a piece of security that you never even realised you took for granted. We think our parents will live forever – I still believed this even after my mum passed. I told myself that I still had Dad – my big, strapping, eternally there father. He would never die, would he? The idea that I'll never see my father alive again, will never hear his unfiltered repertoire booming down the phone at me seems incomprehensible. I'll even miss those awful pregnant pauses, the silences he always refused to fill.

My dad had been my one constant since the day I was born. He wasn't a sentimental man, nor a tactile one; he didn't read me bedtime stories as a child or kiss it better when I fell and hurt my knee – that was my mother's job. He was from a generation of men who never cried, and for whom a clip round the ear was a term of endearment. But he taught me how to be strong and kind, how to be fair. He taught me integrity, a strong work ethic, values – all the things that have stood me in good stead throughout my life so far. He taught me how to be a man. I'm going to miss him more than any words can ever do justice.

Just after the Drayton case, I'd spoken to him on the phone, unknowingly for the last time.

'What's on your mind, son?' he'd asked me. 'Something's troubling you, I can tell.'

I'd smiled. Nothing ever got past him, not really.

I'd sighed. 'The case I was working on, the murder of the

young woman, Libby Drayton, the girl in the woods...' I'd thought of Evie Drayton then. Felt that I'd let her down somehow. That I hadn't got the justice for her that she deserved. The world needs more people like Evie Drayton in it.

I think back to that night, the night of the dinner party, that bitterly cold fateful evening that Libby went missing, a night that saw Evie's life as she knew it unravel, only to expose one underneath she didn't recognise as her own, that she had no idea existed.

He'd listened silently as I made my confession – how I believed that it had really been Emily who'd been truly responsible for Libby Drayton's death and that her mother had, in a heartbreaking act of self-sacrifice, claimed responsibility in a bid to spare her daughter.

'I knew it was the girl,' I'd said. 'And Sara knew that I knew it too.'

I recalled the look on Sara Mendes' face when I'd shown her the charm I'd found from Libby's bracelet – one of sheer fear and panic, and, paradoxically the look on Evie Drayton's when I'd returned it to her, how her eyes had lit up and she'd begun to cry as she thanked me profusely for finding 'the last thing I have left of my daughter'.

'Where did you find it, Dan?' she'd said, smiling as she replaced it onto the bracelet.

I'd opened my mouth to speak but she'd interrupted me. 'It doesn't matter anyway. All that matters is that it was found, and that it's back here with me, where it belongs.'

Looking back, I suspect now that Evie, an intelligent woman, had her own suspicions too.

Both women's faces haunt me for different reasons, in different ways. Of course I'd thought about voicing what I suspected, had grappled with myself internally. I knew I had a professional obligation to, a moral one even, and yet... I didn't.

In their respective and different ways, both Evie Drayton

and Sara Mendes were innocents in all of this complex case. Both women had suffered so much, lost so much. What good would it have done if I'd pushed forward what my intuition was telling me? Emily would've been taken away and Sara left with nobody to live for. Besides, I knew I could never *prove* my suspicions – there wasn't enough evidence to put her at the scene of the crime, and the charm I found in her shoe was circumstantial, certainly not enough on its own. I suspect that Archer would've laughed me out of her office if I'd voiced what I suspected, chiding me and my 'infamous intuition' as she closed the door behind me.

'I don't know that I did the right thing, Dad,' I'd confessed to him.

'Sometimes,' he'd said, 'doing what we think is the right thing can be the hardest thing of all. Family, Danny Boy, family is everything. Having children, it changes you, these small people you'd do anything for, who you'd die and lie for to protect. But you never know what you'll get in life, son, who those people, those little people, will turn out to be and go on to become. It's a lottery, son. Don't reproach yourself, for anything.'

There had been one of his infamous long pauses before he'd added, 'You're a good man, Daniel Riley, and I'm proud of you, son – the man you are, the man you've become.'

I wonder now if my father had somehow instinctively known that his own death was imminent because he'd added something profound before he'd hung up. 'Life is a circle, son. We're born, we live and then we die to make way for the next generation. It's the way it is, the way it should be...'

Those were his last ever words to me.

Juno was restless on the drive back to London. It was a hot day and the air con – typically – had packed up. By the time we reached the motorway, we were all melting and irritable.

'Pip want potty! Pip want potty! Mummy! Dadda! Need pot pots! *Neeeed* pot pots!'

'We'll have to stop at the next service station,' Fiona said, flustered, using one of Juno's baby wipes to remove the beads of perspiration from her face. 'She'll never shut up otherwise... and actually I really need to go myself.'

I rolled my eyes with a touch of frustration. Small children and travel – especially in twenty-eight degrees with no air con – do not good bedfellows make.

'Jesus, Fi...' I sighed. 'We only left twenty minutes ago... why couldn't she, why couldn't *you* have gone before we left?'

She shot me a sharp sideways glance. 'I did,' she replied, 'but I need to go again.'

'Jesus, you're worse than she is,' I snap a little; it's the heat.

'It's not my fault,' Fiona quickly retorted.

'Pip go poo poo... need poo poo!' Juno was continuing to wail in the back as Leo tried to distract her – unsuccessfully I should add though I gave him full credit for effort – with his iPad.

'No? Well, whose fault is it then?'

'Yours actually!'

'*Mine?*' Having buried my father just twenty-four hours before, and in this bloody stifling air-conless heat, I'm really in no mood for a set-to.

'And how do you work *that* one out?'

'Well, I wouldn't keep needing to pee if I wasn't in this condition,' she replied.

'In this condition? In what condit—' And the penny suddenly dropped. 'You're not...?'

I could see the smallest flutter of concern on her face as I took my eyes off the road for a second to look at her. She was nodding.

'Yes, Dan, I'm pregnant,' she said, looking in the rear-view mirror at Juno behind us, who was still loudly announcing her growing need to defecate.

And in that moment a strange sensation came over me, like something had lifted, any doubts I had, any fear or guilt I felt dissipating as I heard my father's last words to me. 'It's the circle of life, son. We're born, we live and then we die to make way for the next generation. It's the way it is, the way it should be.'

I placed my hand on Fiona's knee. It felt slippery with sweat, and I squeezed it, her look of concern fading into a tentative smile as I turned to her.

'Here we go again,' I said.

A LETTER FROM ANNA-LOU

I want to say a huge thank you for choosing to read *The Night of the Party*. If you enjoyed it, and want to keep up to date with all my latest releases, just sign up at the following link. Your email address will never be shared and you can unsubscribe at any time.

www.bookouture.com/anna-lou-weatherley

If you enjoyed *The Night of the Party*, I would be so grateful if you could spare the time to write a review. I'd love to hear what you think – it makes such a difference in helping new readers to discover one of my books for the first time.

I love hearing from my readers – you can get in touch on my Facebook page, through Twitter, Goodreads or my website.

Anna-Lou

facebook.com/annalouweatherleyauthor

twitter.com/annaloulondon

ACKNOWLEDGEMENTS

'Thanks' is such a glib word, an overused word, a bland, everyday word that doesn't hold the weight I would like it to. Sometimes it just doesn't cover it. But sometimes it's all we have.

So, with all the weight in the world, I thank Claire Bord, my editor. Claire has been with me throughout my journey. She has been there from the start, and luck and fate, and the stars, I feel, has maintained that. As well as being a superb, clever and brilliant editor, you're just such a lovely person, and I cannot say, especially now, how this is worth its weight in today's world. Your support, your advice, your time, your knowledge, your patience, your dedication, your professionalism – all of it has simply played a huge part in my career, more than you can ever realise. This book would definitely not be the one that it is without your expertise and guidance. The trust I have in you as my editor is as unwavering as my respect for you. I love the way we work together and I'm very grateful for it. 'Thanks.'

Here are some names: literally everyone at Bookouture – just such an amazing team and incredibly supportive talented authors – I'm so lucky and proud to be part of it (from the very beginning). Kelly Hancock, Kitty, Lola, Kim Nash, Noelle, Sue Traveller, Maria from the Spar, the people at the Spa in Beckenham, Sue Watson, Clare Boyd, Susie Lynes, Casey Kelleher... so many people I admire for all different reasons, but one and the same is that they're good, lovely and supportive people; kind, loving, sweet, caring, genuine human beings. The world needs more people like them in it.

There are not enough words to describe the love I have for my family: my mummy, Jennifer Ann Weatherley; my sister, Lisa Jane Powell; my brother, Marc; and of course, my children, my darling Louie and my baby Felix (he will hate me for saying that, but he is and always will be my baby).

Love honestly doesn't cover it. But without them I am nothing, I am nobody, their love defines me, and I love the fact that it does. I don't know how I could or would ever want to live without any of them. My mummy especially is an inspiration and just such a good person – she, my sister and brother are the people I trust the most. I just love you all so very much. And I'm sorry. You all know why.

I'd also like to thank my agent, the inimitable Mr Darley Anderson – the best in the business. I'm so grateful for the time and support you've given me, the knowledge and the belief, the expertise, wisdom, and the kindness. Many years ago, you said something about the bigger picture that resonated with me and it never left me. You were right. Thank you for still having faith in me. I'm extremely, supremely proud to have you as my agent. You are, after all, a literal and literary legend. x

I'm dedicating this book to my eldest son, Louie. He's a teenager and, thankfully, nothing like Libby. I am so proud of the person he's become after facing adversity. I'm proud of the man he's becoming and how he's learned and is learning from his mistakes, like we all do. I want him to know how much I love him (how much I love my sons, how much I love you all), and that as his mum, how proud I am that he's matured into the wonderful young man he is and the older one he will go on to be.

I love you, Lou.

This is for you. I'll put thirty on if it does well.

Made in the USA
Columbia, SC
18 February 2022

56451283R00178